STONE COLD

STONE COLD

DWARVISH DIRTY DOZEN™ SERIES BOOK FOUR

AARON D. SCHNEIDER
MICHAEL ANDERLE

DON'T MISS OUR NEW RELEASES

Join the LMBPN email list to be notified of new releases and special promotions (which happen often) by following this link:

http://lmbpn.com/email/

This book is a work of fiction. All of the characters, organizations, and events portrayed in this novel are either products of the author's imagination or are used fictitiously. Sometimes both.

Copyright © 2023 LMBPN Publishing
Cover Art by Jake @ J Caleb Design
http://jcalebdesign.com / jcalebdesign@gmail.com
Cover copyright © LMBPN Publishing
A Michael Anderle Production

LMBPN Publishing supports the right to free expression and the value of copyright. The purpose of copyright is to encourage writers and artists to produce the creative works that enrich our culture.

The distribution of this book without permission is a theft of the author's intellectual property. If you would like permission to use material from the book (other than for review purposes), please contact support@lmbpn.com. Thank you for your support of the author's rights.

LMBPN Publishing
PMB 196, 2540 South Maryland Pkwy
Las Vegas, NV 89109

Version 1.00, June 2023
ebook ISBN: 979-8-88878-264-4
Paperback ISBN: 979-8-88878-265-1

THE STONE COLD TEAM

Thanks to our JIT Team:

Zacc Pelter
Dorothy Lloyd
John Ashmore
Paul Westman
Peter Manis
Jan Hunnicutt

If we've missed anyone, please let us know!

Editor
SkyFyre Editing Team

DEDICATIONS

This book is dedicated to my brother who for all the ups and downs has remained a stalwart friend and ally. Ever ready to challenge, but never failing to support he sees me as I often wish I could see myself, and most days I would consider it a life well lived to be the man he believes me to be. Thank you, little brother. This one's for you.

— Aaron

To Family, Friends and
Those Who Love
to Read.
May We All Enjoy Grace
to Live the Life We Are
Called.

— Michael

ACKNOWLEDGMENTS

I'd like to acknowledge once more, and probably in perpetuity, my family for being so ready and willing to go down this road with me. Without all of you I'm not sure I could have made it this far, nor that it would have been worth it even if I did. This book, as with all my endeavors, is in no small part yours as well as mine.

If you see me comin', better step aside
A lotta men didn't, an' a lotta men died
One fist of iron, the other of steel
If the right one don't get you
Then the left one will.

— *16 Tons*, Tennessee Ernie Ford

Looms but the Horror of the shade,
And yet the menace of the years
Finds, and shall find, me unafraid.

—William Ernest Henley

He clasps the crag with crooked hands;
Close to the sun in lonely lands,
Ring'd with the azure world, he stands.
The wrinkled sea beneath him crawls;
He watches from his mountain walls,
And like a thunderbolt he falls.

—*The Eagle*, Alfred, Lord Tennyson

SOUTHERN YSGAND VALE MAP

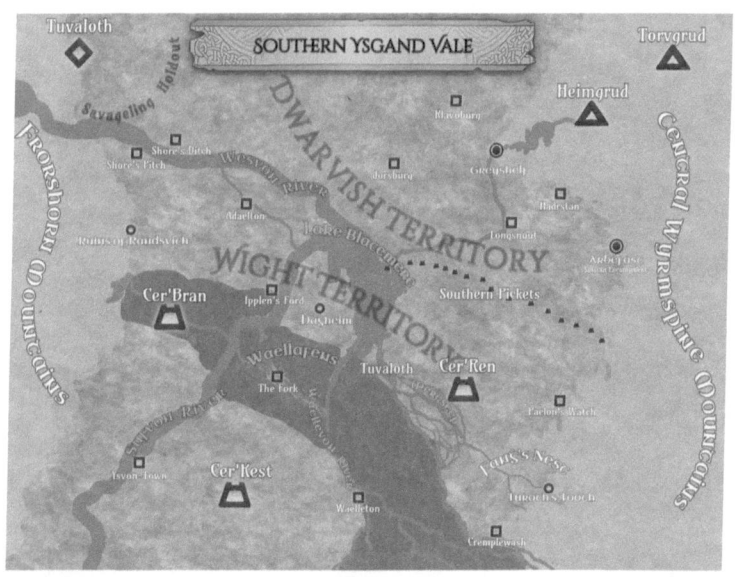

LEXICON

Military Ranks
—Enlisted—
Dwan - The base rank of the Holt'Dwan and also a term that generally refers to a dwarf serving as a soldier
Fordwan - A line officer, typically promoted from veteran dwan
Ascedwan - A dwarf soldier who has developed a useful skill (cooking, herbology, engineering, musical instrument, etc.), marking them out for additional pay/responsibility
—Commissioned Officer—
Dogordwan - field officer of a cavalry detachment
Frothdwan - commander of a cavalry squadron
Schildwan - quartermaster of a division
Tweldwan - commander of a division
Stendwan - commander of an established garrison, a castellan
—Command Staff—
Kuadwan - command staff, responsible for logistical matters
Lardwan - command staff, responsible for communication and intelligence
Vindwan - command staff, responsible for tactical direction

Ondwan - command staff, supreme commander of the Holt'Dwan

—Informal Positions—

Cubldwan - An unofficial position, represents when a soldier is selected to work under a superior officer, usually either a Tweldwan or one of the command staff

Military Terminology

Adyrclaf - a class of theropod typically used as a mount by the svartalf

Blotferow - a class of trained and bred pigs, suitable for use in battle

Cwellocs - a short-hafted dwarvish polearm intended for use in heavy armor

Duabuw - standard issue crossbow of the dwarven army

Holt'Dwan - A dwarven army, typically composed of between eight and twelve divisions

Magsax - standard issue sword of the dwarven army

Worcsvine - a class of trained and bred pigs, suitable for draft work

Slurs

Badger - Derived from drawing comparisons between the animal and dwarves

Clacker/Creaker/Rattler/Shuffler – a slur for the ambulatory undead who serve in the wight army given for the sounds they make

Grem - Derived from drawing comparisons between mythical gremlins and goblins

Longshanks - Can be used for any people group taller than dwarves but typically used for humans

Midges - An elvish slur regarding humans due to their much shorter life spans, though it can be applied to the like of goblins, halflings, and orcs

Myrkling - Derived from the dwarvish word for dark/dangerous forest (myrkvaul) and denotes an elf of svartalf or dark elf lineage

Savageling - a slur for the wosealf or wild elves of the Ysgand Vale

Wheezer - a slur for a wight after the sound of the undead voices

Miscellaneous

Cyniburg - the current ruling dynasty of the Dwarvish Empire

Dwarrisc - the dwarvish language

Svartalf - the dark elves of the Arawuvasc Principalities, a vassal state of the Dwarvish Empire

Wosealf - the wild elves of the Ysgand Vale, thought to be the original occupants of the Vale

PROLOGUE

They crept along the unforgiving cliff face. Overhead, the moon refused to shine.

Digits groping like the antennae of some blind cave insect, they tested every handhold as they moved. None fancied a quick trip to the ground below. There was a fifty- or sixty-foot drop onto a hard stone slope, and if that didn't kill a wretch outright, the roll down the jagged, shale-toothed mountainside would take care of it.

Their limbs were burning with exertion, and sweat beaded the ends of their long noses. They were closer to their goal than any point of retreat. Each knew that, feeling it in the strain trembling like a sustained note of warning in their backs, shoulders, and hands. They were going to reach the top, or they were going to die.

"Almost there," hissed their leader in a sibilant lie through snarling teeth. They were making progress, but there was nothing "almost" about the next twenty feet, especially since the pitch of the stone flexed outward. For the last ten feet, they'd be hanging by whatever their fingers and toes could grip as they dangled nearly horizontal to the earth. Even though they were remarkable climbers, he'd lose half of the group if they went that way.

Their only hope was that, with their grapnels, he and Jask could reach the timber supports that lay just beyond the daunting shelf. He'd hauled the iron-pronged tool and its weighty spool of rope up and across the cliff face, cursing it even as he handled it as delicately as a babe. He couldn't have it clanking and grinding against the stone, nor could he afford to let it fall.

To keep from being fatally affected by someone else's failure to maintain their grip, they'd dispersed while going up the cliff. If they had to wait long for him to secure the grapnel, grips would give way, and even well-honed reflexes and a life of climbing in the Wyrmspine wouldn't save them.

This had to work.

He braced to make the throw, ignoring the burning prickle in his bandaged forearm as he adjusted his grip.

"Steady, Traz," the leader muttered as he willed his toes and fingers to bite deeper into the stone. "You've got all the time in the world."

They did not. Every second counted. The climb had taken longer than they expected, and they were still outside, not in position within the fortress. If the clouds cleared or, worse, if the occupiers of the fortress applied their fire mirrors to sweep the valley floor in front of the lower gate, a withering torrent of enemy missiles would do considerable damage. Thinking about that would only cloud Traz's judgment, making his grip unsteady and his throw weak.

"No hurry," he told himself. "No rush."

Out of the side of one eye, he caught a flash of movement as Jask hurled his grapnel at the stout timbers. That was followed by a rattle of iron points on timber, a jarring jangle that set Traz's teeth on edge. He wanted to curse Jask, but he knew it would more likely be he who got them all killed. The first sound could be shrugged off by a tired sentry. The second would draw them to investigate.

His shoulders trembled again; he had no choice. He spun the grapnel and let it fly.

Again, the rattle, and again, the grapnel bit and held. That was no small thing since, despite Jask's good fortune, it was a gamble whether a grapnel would find purchase.

"A good sign," he mouthed as he tugged on the rope before ascending. From the stark world of stone and open expanses, he climbed into a crowded environment of wooden beams and stout bolts. This jungle was familiar to him, being like the arboreal expanse where he and his kin snatched, scuttled, and sprang from branch to branch, neither foot nor hand deigning to touch the ground. As he hung suspended, a wave of homesickness washed over him.

He would have liked to stay there. To live among the trees and forget about badger holes and the designs of the Dead Ones. He'd rather...

The planks creaked.

Terror seized him, and he willed himself to hold still. The enemy must be right above them. Raising his chin while fearing the movement might betray him, he looked up.

The boards were closely fitted and would originally have provided no space to see. Time and wear and the ongoing siege had forestalled maintenance, allowing seams to open. Through the narrow gaps, Traz could make out the inky sky. Head tilting this way and that, he caught the shape of a sentry standing just over them, looking out from the battlement.

He wanted to wait until the sentinel moved on, but then he felt the tug of another climber on the rope. His position was about to get crowded, and while none of them were heavy, half the team dangling from an iron hook forged by a village blacksmith from old horseshoes was a recipe for disaster.

The leader looked for Jask to see if he was aware of the

danger, but rock and crisscrossing beams were all he could see. "No choice," he mouthed, lips peeling back from his jagged teeth as he finished his transition from rope to support beams. The movement was silent, and the sentry didn't stir.

The others would be coming, and he had to handle this before they arrived. He looked at the timber jungle and found the answer. Vagaries in the mountain's face had necessitated a gap between wood and stone that was wide enough for him to creep through, barely a stride behind where the sentry stood.

His grimace twisted into a smile as he crept toward his target, the aches in his fingers and toes forgotten. He strained to keep watch for signs that the sentry had heard him, but so far, nothing.

Traz's smile widened as he drew himself up on the platform. Only a step from him was the sentry, helm glinting in the faint light the heavens furnished. The badger had a shield in one mailed paw, and the other lay on the rail.

Traz's feet scuffed on the boards and he froze, but the squat figure didn't move or seem to notice. The leader of the climbers caught the faintest sound of the others coming up under the platform and winced, but the watcher maintained his vigil. Traz had heard that the mountain-dwelling folk were dense and inattentive, and this one certainly exhibited that ineptitude.

He couldn't waste time hoping that would continue or that one of his subordinates wouldn't do something even the deaf dwarf would notice.

The sentry's armor presented a challenge, but Traz had a long knife, and the knotted beard plait dangling from the hilt proved that was not an insurmountable problem. Muscles coiling as he drew the dagger, the leader prepared to pounce, one wide, strong hand splaying and flexing in preparation. He had to be quick, but he'd gotten good at knowing where to deliver the stroke as he pulled an unsuspecting head to one side. Traz drew a final breath.

"That's enough o' that."

The gruff words tore through the stillness like a cleaver, and

Traz twisted to find the source of the voice. Thus, the shield only slapped the side of his face instead of squashing it. The leader of the infiltrators rolled bum over brains to one side, only prevented from plunging over the edge by fetching up against rails that cruelly bit into his back.

Traz lay there, trying to draw breath into his lungs as the sentry stooped to pick up the knife he had dropped.

"What were you going to do with this?" the sentinel mused in a gravelly voice as he stood over the infiltration's leader, fiery beard glinting. "You weren't planning on something naughty now, were you?"

"From the looks of things, he isn't alone," came the deep basso voice that had foiled Traz's pounce. "We've got grems in the woodwork."

The red-bearded badger, eyes burning, held up the long knife so the beard plait swung before his eyes. "You've already been naughty, eh, grem?"

Traz's world came back together, and his heart hammered. Behind the looming dwarf, the sentinel, a wall of flesh in dwarvish iron, stumped to the gap Traz had emerged from. With a quickness that belied his bulk, the badger plunged an armored paw into the darkness, and a trembling squeak of dismay made Traz's heart sink.

A second later, another goblin was roughly dragged through the gap. Traz saw Kloon's bloodshot eyes. The young goblin ineffectually clawed and bit at the mail-shod limb that was hauling him onto the boards, the pair of stilettos on his belt forgotten in his panic.

"What did I tell you?" the stout dwarf grumbled, shaking his head and clucking his tongue. With a fluidity born of long practice, the dwarf plunged one of their broad-bladed swords into Kloon's chest. The young goblin didn't even have time to scream before his body went limp.

"Well, that's that." The wide dwarf grunted and pitched

Kloon's body over the rail. "There's got to be a better way of doin' this."

The wide brute bent over the gap, whose edge was only a few feet from the grapnel line the other members of his team would ascend.

Traz tried to surge to his feet. His progress was checked by a heavy boot to the chest. "Hold on," the dwarf intoned as he squatted next to Traz. "We've still got to deal with this." Traz fought to catch his breath as he looked at his blade and its trophy beard.

"How'd you get this, eh?" the red-bearded dwarf asked, batting the plait so it swung back and forth. "Did you kill the dwarf this belonged to, or did you just scavenge the dead for the best one?"

The goblin heard the grunts of the other dwarf, still bent over the gap like a pig rooting for fungus. He might have laughed at the image, but then he heard the sharp twang of metal snapping.

"Got it!" the wide dwarf exclaimed as he straightened, red-faced but grinning. Screams from below the platform quickly plunged out of hearing. Traz wanted to mourn his team since several were distant relations and he'd served with all of them for several seasons, but their deaths didn't distract his focus from the decorated blade inching toward his face.

"It's got a good edge for grem work," the dwarf growled as the blade's cold touch brushed Traz's face. "Didn't have to saw to get this braid, did you? Just one quick slice, and you had just what you wanted."

The goblin squirmed against the rail, not just from the icy touch of the knife but from fear that the badger might see the actual story of how he'd gotten the braid. If the dwarf had any idea, Traz would envy his dead comrades. He sank back, hoping he could find a way out of this situation.

Something moved farther down the platform, and Traz remembered that not all of his team had fallen to their deaths.

Jask's team! Traz hadn't heard them. Hope surged in the goblin's chest, and his eyes darted to the dwarf lest he reveal the other goblins' presence.

He had to fix both dwarves' attention on him to give Jask and his team a chance.

A smile stretched the goblin's thin lips, revealing sharp teeth.

"Died nasty, he did," Traz teased in broken Dwarrisc as he ran a finger along the plait. "Took a long, long time."

He braced himself for the resulting fury, which might see the dwarf try to choke the life out of him. The other dwarf might cheer his comrade on, or maybe he would draw his compatriot off their prisoner. Either way, they would focus on Traz, so Jask and his team could fall on the burly pair unimpeded. The dwarves were large and well-armored, but with three goblins attacking each and the element of surprise, the result was a foregone conclusion.

However, the fiery-haired dwarf did not bellow and surge forward. With icy calm, he met the goblin's gaze squarely, his eyes snakelike in their flat evaluation. "Tell me about it," he growled. "Tell me what you did to him."

Traz's eyes widened. He hadn't planned for that response. As though trying to make up for his comrade's disappointing performance, the other dwarf waddled forward, looking concerned.

"Remember our orders, Waelon," the broad dwarf called, reaching out but not quite touching his fellow's shoulder. "We need some of them alive."

The one named Waelon shrugged and inched closer to Traz. "Come on," he pressed in a cajoling tone as he waggled the knife to set the plait swinging. "You're proud of your work. I can see that. Tell me about how you took this fine trophy."

Traz willed himself not to cry out for Jask to attack. If they were to have a chance, he couldn't spoil things. He felt the danger in the dwarf's calmness, but he'd hold out a little longer. Surely Jask's team was nearly in position.

"No tell," Traz replied, hating how scared he sounded but unable to keep the tremble out of his voice. "Know it bad for badger."

The red-bearded dwarf nodded. He appeared to consider that a reasonable point. Through it all, his eyes never left Traz, who felt as though he were under pressure. He was certain he would rupture.

"You must've had some time on your hands," Waelon rumbled, his face coming closer until he was nose-to-nose with the goblin. "Much more time than we can afford for your friends."

Taz's face twisted, and his stomach sank. "Wha—"

Dwarvish crossbows whanged and bolts zipped toward Jask's team, followed by the thumps of bodies hitting the planks. Traz vaguely wondered why there were not more screams and cries of pain, but he realized a stout dwarvish bolt fired from a few paces would deal tremendous damage.

Tearing his gaze away from Waelon's, the goblin saw bloodied bolts embedded in the rail and his dead comrades and then a stone path beyond the wooden platform. On it stood a score of dwarves with their crossbows at the ready, while half again that number was priming their weapons in case another shot was necessary.

"Y-you knew?" Traz wheezed, his eyes drawn back to the fiery-whiskered dwarf.

"Aye," Waelon growled. "Did your wheezer think he was going to put one over on us? Send a few grems scuttling up here and catch us sleeping, one hand on our danglers?"

The goblin ran a drying tongue over his thin lips and looked at his dead team members again.

"Oh, don't feel bad for them." The dwarf's teeth flashed in his beard. "You'll be envying them soon."

Traz gulped and tried to square his narrow shoulders, but which earned a pitying look from the wide dwarf behind Waelon.

"All right," the stout dwarf called. "Quit playing with the wretch and get him on his feet. The ondwan will want to see him."

A smile that made Traz's heart stutter spread across the red-bearded dwarf's face. "Fair enough," he purred as he let the edge of the long knife rest on the goblin's throat. "On your feet, killer. You've got a meeting with royalty."

Given the disapproving look of the wide dwarf behind Waelon, Traz wasn't certain what the joke was, but he found his voice. "I got nothing to say to badgers," he snarled, and the blade at his throat drove him back a step. "Even king ones."

Waelon gave a sympathetic nod that was more disconcerting than a snarling visage. He was still nodding as the edge of the weapon moved up, forcing Traz onto his tiptoes as the rail pressed into his back. His heart hammered when the night wind stirred his lank hair.

"Nothing to say," Waelon muttered, mulling the words over as the goblin leaned over the rail. "Well, if you've got nothing to say, there's no point in inviting you in for a bite to eat and a spot of tea, is there? Might as well send you on your way with the rest of your friends."

The dwarf's eyes gave a pointed look to the dark drop beyond the rail.

"They made it down before you," Waelon observed with a pensive frown, "but I'm pretty sure they're waiting for you if you want to catch up."

The knife pressed in and Traz teetered, certain he was about to fall. His climb-worn fingers gouged the wood, but that wouldn't be enough to keep him from tumbling over the edge if Waelon gave him the slightest push.

The goblin leader's life was measured in heartbeats. He could not escape the muscular armor-clad dwarf. A push—no, a twitch

—and Traz would go over the edge. His single thin lifeline was his cooperation.

A loose tongue might mean he was treated relatively well. The badgers were notorious brutes but were also pragmatic. There was nothing they wouldn't do to win, but they wouldn't waste effort torturing a willing informant. That option was better than death.

Traz's lips peeled back, and his dry mouth fought to form the assenting words, but his tongue seemed trapped behind his teeth.

His thoughts returned to those split open on the cold, hard earth below and the bloody bodies nearby. He wanted to surrender—knew he should—but something within him refused, holding his mouth hostage even as it forced words through his lips.

"I got nothing to say to badgers," he repeated, his eyes tearing up, though he didn't know why.

The dwarf's eyes met the goblin's, and Traz waited to be pitched into the open air. However, seconds passed, and the only thing that went over the edge was Traz's knife after the dwarf yanked the beard plait off the handle with a flick of the wrist.

"You are the bravest grem I've ever met," Waelon growled, not without respect. "I'm not sure that's a good thing for you. Courage has a cost, and before long, you're going to wish I'd pitched you over the rail."

Traz barely kept a scream at bay as the merciless fingers clamped on his bandaged forearm. As fresh blood stained the wrappings, the dwarf dragged him back onto the platform and slammed him down on the boards. As he lay face to face with Jask's bolt-filled corpse, the goblin leader almost wished the dwarf had tossed him over.

The badgers didn't waste effort on things that weren't in their way, but they were ruthless and savage about overcoming obstacles.

He'd just planted himself firmly in their way.

CHAPTER ONE

"What do you mean you don't have time? We're in the middle of a siege. You have nothing *but* time."

A biting counter to the statement flew up Torbjorn's throat, but he throttled the barbed words before they reached his tongue. If the months holed up in Greyshelf had taught him anything, it was that his betrothed was never wrong, especially in matters where she didn't know what she was talking about.

Ghedau might have been a talented ascedwan, perhaps the best, though Torbjorn doubted that, but she'd never commanded much. She *had* learned to yell loud enough to get a nearby dwan to help her carry away the wounded or for a porter to fetch bandages, but that wasn't the same as leading troops on the field, much less coordinating forces and supplies during a battle. Let alone directing an entire army occupying a massive fortress under siege.

Explaining that he didn't have enough hours in the day to attend to everything required of him was a pointless exercise.

Ghedau had declared it so, and the dwarfess, true to the nature that Torbjorn assumed was inherent to all members of her sex, was confident about her declaration and would not be dissuaded.

Insistence was out of the question. His best hope lay in evasion.

"I'm supposed to have new prisoners coming in," he replied in a manner he hoped sounded offhand, as though he'd just thought of it. "You know that I like to be present for the initial interrogation."

From the other room, he heard a disgusted snort. He could imagine Ghedau's face as she added the necessary adjustments to her adornments. Shaper knew she'd made that sound often enough over the past several months for him to know the expression.

"What do you have a lardwan for if not handling the interrogation of prisoners?"

She's not wrong, Torbjorn admitted with a sigh.

Chewing his lip, he frowned at the crackling hearth in front of his chair. Typically the cold wasn't troublesome, but he'd been walking the battlements and platforms earlier, and the chill had found its way into his bones. Having a fire in the sitting room between the suite of rooms he and Ghedau shared allowed him to chase away the cold without turning his room into a sweltering den of fur and woven draperies.

I'm not sure what Glastuc did to make it so, the ondwan mused, *but I can't light my pipe without it warming up enough to make me sweat and itch.*

Torbjorn imagined it had to do with the furnishings, or runework, or some alchemical treatment, but he hadn't had the time or the energy to have the place stripped. Not that he'd been able to spend much time there anyway. Usually, if he got any sleep, it was stolen on a barrack's cot or a gatehouse bunk between rushing from one vital meeting to the next.

"You know I like to see them firsthand," he continued, certain this line of retreat was failing him but unable to come up with anything better. "Reports don't catch all the little things. The nuances that let you know if you've caught one worth keeping."

There was a throaty laugh and the soft rustle of fabric from the other room. "Are you sure it isn't because you like to see them all tied up and helpless?"

The purr in the dwarfess' throat told Torbjorn that was flirtatious banter, but he felt unequal to the task of responding. He managed an absent grunt while kneading at a patch of soreness above his knee with his enchanted wooden hand.

I don't suppose she'll give it a rest, he reflected. *I don't blame her. She's got more than a good time riding on getting me two-backing.*

His eyes shifted to the door to his room, which on the rare occasions on which he slept in the ondwan's apartments, he kept locked tightly to ward off nocturnal visits. He'd learned to take that precaution early on.

There was another rustle from the other room, and then Torbjorn felt as much as saw Ghedau fill the doorway. "If you want to tie somebody up," she murmured, "you could try me. I don't think I'd mind."

Torbjorn told himself to keep staring at the fire. He would lose himself in its dancing flames. However, something tugged at his gaze. The dwarfess lounged against the doorframe, her impressive bust thrust forward and her hands running down her sides to dance over the flares of her wide hips.

Torbjorn was drawn toward the sight. His eyes lingered on every curve, and hunger was present everywhere except in his belly. He flexed his arms, eager to crush her to him. His thick fingers clenched, ready to remove impediments, and his mouth watered at the thought of tasting…poison. Toxin. Venom. Death.

Like icy water quenching forge-fresh iron came the memory of what Ghedau, the dwarfess who should have been his wife by now, had done. It brought the smell of the dying command staff soiling themselves, the gurgling wheezes of old warriors trying to breathe through swelling throats, and the sight of the young attendants' eyes rolling in terror as their bodies betrayed them.

Torbjorn tore his gaze away with a growl and stood sharply, sending his chair back a handful of inches. He stalked toward the fireplace to seize the poker. He needed to grip and squeeze something. He almost reached for the magsax on his belt, but he wasn't that far gone. Not yet.

With the stout poker in his hands, he felt an overwhelming desire to give it a few practice swings.

Teeth grinding, he settled for thrusting it into the crackling logs. The hard point bit with a satisfying crunch. He dug into the wood until he felt the heat of the flames lapping his knuckles, a dull glow forming.

Seeming oblivious to the danger, Ghedau approached his shoulder. "Why ram your iron into wood when I'm right he—"

"Shut up," the dwarf commander snarled with a vehemence that did not require volume to drive his former betrothed back, hands raised in a warding gesture. Her terrified eyes danced between his face and the hissing point of the poker. He wasn't sure when he'd turned to her, poker in front of him, but Torbjorn silently advanced toward her.

"Torbjorn!" the dwarfess squawked, backing up and bumping into the doorframe against which she'd so recently leaned. "Torbjorn! Please!"

He wasn't sure if it was the fear in her eyes, the shrill cry, or the smell of the glowing poker in his hand, but Torbjorn came to himself so fast that it hurt. He was nauseated by a roiling disgust that surged when he looked at Ghedau and again when he closed his eyes and considered what was inside him.

The dwarfess' voice intruded on his reflections. It trembled, yet every word was clear as though she were incanting a spell whose mispronunciation would be disastrous.

"You don't need to go to the dinner," she murmured. "I'll go.

It's the least I can do since you've been working so hard. It's all right. It's just a few of the tweldwan and—"

"Stop, please."

The words sounded wretched even to his ears, but when Torbjorn opened his eyes, he saw his former betrothed standing rigid. The fear hadn't left her eyes despite her composed offer, and it made him want to crumple to the floor.

He became aware of the poker handle biting into his hand. With leaden limbs, he trudged over to the hearth and placed the poker back in its stand with a dull clank. The glow of the fire's kiss had faded from its tip, though Torbjorn imagined it was still dangerous to the touch.

Ghedau's voice intruded on his thoughts. "I think you are right. A dinner will send the wrong impression to the officers. Make them lax."

"No," Torbjorn muttered and put a hand on the mantle. The warmth of the stone radiated through his weary bones. "Have your dinner, but I won't be there. I have duties to attend to with the prisoners."

Torbjorn could feel the struggle within the dwarfess as surely as the stone under his palm. "You are confused." He sighed. "Now you're scared to ask. I'm sorry. I shouldn't have acted that way."

The gown rustled. "I am just trying to make you happy." The words were almost pleading, but the tone was accusatory.

"For good or ill, we're trapped in this lie together, Ghedau." Torbjorn removed his hand from the stone to face her stare. "Whatever your intentions and my failings, and whatever either of us feels about it, this position, this situation, and this relationship are a cage."

To her credit, the dwarfess took his words on the chin, refusing to look away.

"It would be bad enough if it was just you and me," the dwarf commander continued, "but the entire Sufstan Holt'Dwan is here with us, bound up and tossed in. Until relief comes from Heimgrud, and I'm not sure it ever will, the lives of over two thousand dwarves rest on us maintaining this ruse that I'm the Chosen of the Shaper and you were gifted by him to bring about my miraculous recovery."

Her jaw worked, and the muscles in her throat clenched, but she held his gaze.

"We have to keep going," Torbjorn intoned, the words a judgment. "That doesn't mean this is any less of a lie or we are any less guilty. One day, we'll have to pay for it, and I expect it will end with us on Grimmoth's stone."

Ghedau paled at his prediction, and her mouth became a grim line. "We'll see," she managed between clenched teeth.

Torbjorn's laugh rasped like a file over stone. "Did you imagine this was going to end with a crown, a throne, and you sitting on Mount Smarthdun, surrounded by royal whelps?"

The dwarfess didn't answer except to raise her chin, daring him to do his worst.

"There's no happy ending for us, Ghedau," Torbjorn promised. "This ends with us both accepting the judgment due. Maybe not today or tomorrow, maybe not for years, but you have made us both unfit to take the throne. Therefore, I'll see that we don't, no matter what I have to do."

Ghedau's eyes flashed with a dangerous light Torbjorn had seen before, but as always, it vanished in one sweep of her long eyelashes. A heartbeat later, she looked away, her gaze roaming the floor.

Torbjorn heaved another sigh, and a hollow numbness stole over him. He also got a desire to vomit when his eyes wandered toward the poker.

"Go to dinner with the tweldwans and make my excuses." He mopped at his face with a hand, not able to look at her. "I'm going to see about the prisoners. Maybe for once, we'll get good news out of all this."

For a second, they stood regarding each other, and Torbjorn's gaze pierced time. She was young and shy. He was young and a fool. Their eyes had danced over each other, an innocent perusal of the future. The promise of things to come, things good and true. They'd exchanged those trailing looks, and then their eyes met, and both were happy with what they'd seen. Staring a little longer, they'd hoped for even more to be happy about. It had been so pure.

The vision was gone in an instant, and he saw her and she saw him as they were now and forever.

Swallowing bile and blinking back tears, Torbjorn left without another word.

CHAPTER TWO

"Why is there only one?"

Klaus, reinstated to lardwan, frowned from his desk at the two dwarves herding their prisoner forward.

"Why do you think?" Waelon rumbled as the sole remaining goblin infiltrator shuffled forward, shackles clinking. The red-haired dwarf still had the plait of beard dangling from one fist, looking for all the world like he'd gotten into a brawl and tugged out his rival's plait and not thought to return it.

The lardwan eyed the braid, then looked from Waelon to Gromic and then back. "Does that belong to someone you know?" he asked, pointing at the plait. "Are you keeping it for them while they're out?"

The jest was met with icy silence by Waelon and a laugh so weak from Gromic that it was insulting.

"Traz here was carrying this as a trophy," Waelon replied flatly, glaring at the back of the goblin's head. "I thought it was worth keeping to put its owner to rest."

Klaus fought back the blush of embarrassment that rose at the explanation, and when he spoke, his voice was thinner.

"I see. Very good, Fordwan. Carry on."

"Move it, grem," Waelon spat, driving the goblin toward an iron lattice in which a door hung open in cold welcome. The goblin's limbs were weighed down by the shackles, but the progress made after the shove was slower than the burden justified. Waelon gave a warning growl, but it only drew a wet snarl from the goblin. The former ranger's meaty paw smacked the goblin's head, and the prisoner staggered the last few steps into the cage set into the wall.

No sooner was the goblin inside the enclosure than he whirled and thrust his manacled hands toward Waelon's face.

"Take off," the goblin hissed, rattling the irons.

Waelon was drawing back to slap him again when Klaus spoke. "Please remove the prisoner's restraints, Waelon."

The former ranger looked over his shoulder at the lardwan, who gazed at him impassively. A retort crackled in the air between them. The goblin felt it and shrank back, fearing a tempest. Waelon's dark eyes met Klaus' cold blue eyes and found an icy regard he couldn't melt despite his glare. Gromic almost stepped between the two and made a self-deprecating remark, but he thought better of it. These two needed to deal with their differences on their own.

The silence stretched, and Traz shifted from foot to foot, chains jingling.

"Very good, *sir*," Waelon growled between his teeth. He tucked the plait into his belt, freeing both his hands for the task. Turning so quickly that the goblin flinched, the dwarf seized the manacles in one hand and produced a key from his belt pouch.

Waelon's glare turned on the goblin. He nearly bored a hole through the creature as he undid the manacles. Traz understood the implicit threat as his hands came free. The defeated infiltration leader could try something, but the grim dwarf was watching, and his response would be brutally final.

Discretion triumphed, and the goblin backed up until his stooped back met the cold stone wall. With a low, resigned hiss,

Traz sank to the floor. The door shut with a click, and the former ranger gave the recoiling goblin a final lingering look.

"That will be all, Fordwan," Klaus declared with an appreciative nod. He turned back to the reports on the table before him. "You may both go."

"Eh, beggin' your pardon, Lardwan," Gromic began. The stout dwarf hesitated, drew a breath, and looked about.

Waelon squared his shoulders and crossed his arms. "Commander's supposed to be down here soon." His chin rose to show his defiance.

Klaus lifted a sheet of parchment with a report of the movements spotted on the valley floor over the last week. The only sign of the lardwan's irritation was the trembling of the cured hide, which set the cramped script to dancing.

"Yes, I am expecting the ondwan to come down for the interrogation." A hard edge came into Klaus' tone. "I wasn't told to keep you here until he arrives. You are supposed to return to your posts."

Gromic, knowing Waelon's response would be less than gracious, stepped forward, elbowing the former ranger as he did so. He chuckled, the beads of sweat on his forehead congealing into a glistening sheen. "I think Fordwan Waelon means to say, 'We'd be happy to wait until you're done with the prisoner and then escort him down to the holding cells.' No trouble at all, sir."

Klaus nodded and smiled to acknowledge the stout dwarf's attempt at courtesy.

"I appreciate the offer, Fordwan Gromic," the lardwan replied. "When an escort is needed, I'll call for a pair of dwan to haul our guest downstairs. There's no shortage of them hanging about, and I'm sure those manning the outer defenses will benefit from your expertise as a veteran fordwan."

Gromic bobbed his head at the complimentary dismissal, but Waelon produced a phlegmy snort. Klaus pitched the parchment on the table and rocked back, either incensed or trying to avoid the incoming glob of spittle.

No sputum emerged, but the look the former ranger gave the lardwan was scornful.

"Do you have something to say, *Fordwan?*" Klaus asked, emphasizing Waelon's rank.

"Why have us waste time watching frost spread on bones, eh?" the red-haired dwarf shot back, his voice rough.

"I understand that standing sentry is not anyone's idea of a good time," Klaus began, adopting a disarming tone. "The nature of war is such that we all have to spend a good bit of time doing things we don't want to do. Believe me, if you had to read as many reports a day as I do, you might think staring into the valley is relaxing by comparison. Some of our fellow officers are making me cross-eyed with their scrawls."

As though to emphasize the point, Klaus rubbed his eyes with his thumb and forefinger while the other hand flapped at the pile of reports. "Not the glory we signed up for, but this is how wars are not just fought but won."

The lardwan looked at the two dwan, his gaze softening when he saw Gromic nodding accommodatingly.

Waelon's eyes seemed intent on setting him ablaze. "Wars are won when the enemy is broken," the former ranger growled. "You aren't liable to get that if you wait for the enemy to beat his skull out on your walls instead of taking the fight to 'em."

Klaus opened his mouth to reply sharply, but he shut his jaw with a muted click and slumped. "Gnawing that bone, are we?" The senior officer sighed as he met Waelon's glare with a bemused stare. "Tell me, Fordwan, have you forgotten how chain of command worked in your time in the shabr'dwan, or did you never understand?"

Waelon's heavy arms crossed over his chest as his chin thrust forward. "Just one ranger patrol. One, and either the lad or the blade-ears. No great loss either way if we don't make it, and the valley open to us if we succeed."

The lardwan of the Sufstan Holt'Dwan had wearied of this argument a month ago, and now it was comical. Well, comical was not the right word, but Waelon's outrage as he stood there scowling struck Klaus as absurd. A laugh formed in his throat and grew until it shook his shoulders. "No," he managed. "Still no."

Waelon sucked a breath between his teeth and took a step toward the parchment-piled desk. "It could work!"

Klaus couldn't bring himself to stop laughing. "Or it could not. It doesn't matter. Orders are orders!"

The former ranger advanced to slam a fist on the desk. "You laugh as we rot in here while every day, another dwan joins their clan!" Waelon roared, face flushed. "All coins to be spent, taxes to be paid, so you can keep sitting on your arse and shuffling reports!"

Gromic put his hand on the big dwarf's shoulder to draw him away. "All right, that's more than enough. Waelon, come on."

"You're a coward!" the former ranger bellowed. "You just want more bodies to keep between you and the enemy! That's it, isn't it?"

Klaus shot to his feet quickly enough to send his chair scooting across the floor. The desk was still between them but the lardwan's eyes locked on Waelon's and refused to flinch before the fiery accusation therein. "You want to talk about coins, eh? Want to talk about being cowards, huh?" The senior officer leaned over the parchments until he was nose-to-nose with his accuser. "Let me let you in on a secret that you should have learned when you became a fordwan. You must have been too thick or too cowardly to understand."

The red-bearded dwarf strained against Gromic's grip, gaze fixed on the dwarf in front of him.

"We're *all* coins to be spent," Klaus declared, giving another bark of laughter. "From the freshest dwan to Torbjorn and everyone between. We give our lives to serve the Holt'Dwan, which serves the Cyniburgs, who serve the Empire, which serves the dwarvish race. That's what being dwan means. What it's always meant!"

"What do you think I'm trying to do?" Waelon hissed back. His struggles ceased, but his glare sharpened. "Why do you think I came up with the plan?"

Klaus' lip curled beneath his mustache. "You can't lie to me as readily as you lie to yourself, Fordwan. Your plan is meant to serve your interests and needs, not the Holt'Dwan's."

Waelon seized the desk, sinews flexing as he flipped it out of the way. "It's *my* life I'm putting on the line, you son of a bitch!"

Amidst the storm of parchments descending around him, Klaus' glare did not falter or relent. "If you valued your life, that might mean something."

Half a dozen curses and recriminations formed within the former ranger, but none became an actual reply. In the end, the big dwarf was silent for a heartbeat before his voice, low and dangerous, sawed through the air. "What is that supposed to mean?"

"It means you're confusing fatalism with courage and martyrdom with service," the lardwan snapped. "If you're floundering for a way to kill yourself, you can always pitch yourself off the parapets you're guarding. I'm not obliged to give you a patrol's worth of rangers to keep you company on the way down."

Waelon gritted his teeth, but the bald accusation hit home with more force than anyone had a right to expect. The fire in the big dwarf's eyes no longer threatened to leap out and consume the lardwan and his reports.

"I'm not suicidal," the former ranger insisted, chin dropping defensively until his beard splayed across his chest. "I'm just trying to do what needs to be done."

Klaus wasn't ready to give up the initiative he'd seized and leaned dangerously close to the dwarf. "It's not up to you to decide what needs to be done. It's not up to me either, nor up to any dwarf in this Shaper-forsaken stronghold. That burden falls squarely on Ondwan Torbjorn of Clan Cyniburg. The problem is that for years, you've had access to him to serve and advise, but it is not the place of a fordwan to the commander of the entire Holt'Dwan."

Waelon didn't need to say anything to confirm that Klaus' words had found their mark again. The furrowing of the red brows over the dark eyes and the slouch spoke of an uncertainty foreign to the former ranger.

"Things have changed," the senior officer pointed out, retreating a quarter-step, "and they're liable to change again when reinforcements from Heimgrud arrive. At any time, we can only do our duty. That is what makes us dwan."

"A dwan serves," Gromic recited at Waelon's shoulder. "We know that. We've known it for longer than we was more than a twitch in our dads' britches."

Waelon blinked, then his shoulders sank. "A dwan serves. A dwan serves."

"A dwan serves," Lardwan Klaus agreed, then cast a quick look around him. "I know how the fordwan can do so currently."

"Very good, sir," Gromic replied, jerking his head at the door. "Waelon and I'll just head off to our posts."

"Just a minute," Klaus warned, looking up sharply from the mess strewn across the floor. "The two of you can tidy things up while I have an introductory chat with our new guest."

Both fordwans frowned, and their eyes drifted to the floor. It would only take a moment on their hands and knees to collect the reports after they righted the desk.

"The reports were organized by date," the lardwan continued, nudging a piece of treated hide with his boot. "If you can't read them, and I won't blame you if that is the case, you can create a separate stack for the illegible offerings. Make it smaller than others, please."

Like any good officer, Lardwan Klaus turned on his heel and made for the goblin's cell.

"You had to flip the damn desk, didn't ye," Gromic grumbled as he ambled forward. A few sheets slid free of his initial grab, and the stout dwarf managed to squeeze in a few curses between huffs.

"Seemed like the right thing at the time," Waelon muttered as he sank beside his comrade. "Besides, it's not like you couldn't afford to spend a little time bent over, getting reacquainted with your toes."

Klaus ignored the profanity-laden response. The bantering continued, the desk was righted, and the collection and sorting began. Despite his efforts, he couldn't help smiling as he stepped to the cage and rapped on the door as though he were inviting a friend to a picnic.

The lardwan grinned, showing all his teeth.

"Hello there."

CHAPTER THREE

"Look, I'm sure you have questions, so how about we help each other out, eh?" Klaus began in a confident impression of a dwarvish functionary going about his business. He'd interrogated a fair number of subjects while serving in the Holt'Dwan, but goblins were always a troublesome group. Their expressions and body language and motivations and values were difficult to interpret.

Traz looked from the two dwarves scooping up parchments to Klaus, bulbous eyes narrowed as his thin lips curled. The lardwan had no idea if the creature was scared, suspicious, angry, or hungry. The dwarf stifled a sigh and the urge to look around for Torbjorn. He'd expected his friend to join him, but he had delayed long enough.

"I can imagine what you are thinking," the senior officer began, then shook his head. "On second thought, I'm sure that's not true. Regardless, we've got to find a way to get along, so let's assume you're wondering if that little conversation we just had helps your chances of escaping your current predicament or guarantees an ignominious end.

"I'm here to assure you that it has no bearing on any outcome, but I'll leave that to you to figure out. I'm just going to explain a few things if that's all right with you."

Trav studied the dwarf before him, his suspicion evident in the tilt of his head as he nodded.

"Good, and let me just say that I appreciate that you speak Dwarrisc," Klaus continued. He retrieved a chair from the wall and set it in front of the cell. It was stoutly built and proportioned so any race could use it, if not comfortably. Versatile furniture was not uncommon in the Vale, but this chair was noteworthy for the patches of raw wood where chains had rasped the frame and the dark splotches that suggested a brutal history.

"Believe me when I say I don't think either of us would appreciate having to rely on my mastery of your people's language for this interview," the dwarf called over his shoulder as he dragged over a small end table with one hand while carrying a jug and some cups. The table was of similar construction to the chair but had none of the chair's menacing aesthetic. Klaus situated the table, then set down the jug and cups. The cups required some fiddling before the dwarf was satisfied.

He finally turned to the goblin. "I'm an advocate for clear communication and expectations." He put a hand on the back of the chair and gripped the handle of the jug. "What you're looking at could be interpreted as the two ways your time can be spent here with us."

The goblin was still watching him.

"We have questions, and you need to answer them honestly," Klaus continued, his tone matter-of-fact and his voice steady. This was just business, not personal. No malice.

"There may be some you do not know the answer to," the dwarf acknowledged. "I encourage you to be clear and convincing when that happens. If not, it will slow down the process, as will refusing to answer."

Klaus leaned on the back, then let go and pointed at the jug.

"Just as resistance has its consequences, cooperation has its rewards."

He raised the jug and poured some of its contents into one of the cups. The lardwan noted the goblin's attention as the white liquid flowed into the cup. Klaus knew goblins and their ilk had an unusual fondness for dairy products, but none was more universally loved than the creamy tears that come from a cow's udder. There hadn't been much milk in the last shipment of supplies, but it filled a jug. That was all he needed to set things in motion, even if he subsequently promised the goblin a river of the stuff.

"I'm not sure of its provenance," Klaus admitted as he hoisted the cup and made a show of inspecting the contents. "It *looks* good."

With that, he took a long draught from the cup, letting some of the milk spill out of the corners of his mouth. The translucent white beads rolled down his mustache braids and vanished into the depths of his beard. The lardwan smacked his lips appreciatively.

Klaus hated milk. He'd rather drink water from a scummy cave puddle than the filmy effluence from some beast's teat, but as he'd told Waelon, he wasn't here to do what he liked.

Clamping down on his gag reflex, he held the cup out to the goblin with a smile. "Would you like a drink?"

The goblin's lips twitched, but he tracked the cup with a raptor's focus. The first stage of the battle was already going against the infiltration leader. Klaus prayed this would go quickly. There were still many reports to go through. He noticed that Waelon and Gromic had departed. Torbjorn was nowhere to be seen.

The goblin nodded and crawled forward. "Yes." Traz hissed and slid one long arm between the bars. "Give me."

Klaus thrust the cup forward but stopped just out of the blunt-clawed hand's reach.

"Why did you come here?" the lardwan asked like the question had just occurred to him.

The goblin grunted in irritation as he strained forward, and he managed to scrape the cup with one digit. The violence of the attempt knocked the cup to one side, and milk spilled on the stone floor.

"Careful," the dwarf warned, forcing himself to keep a congenial tone. "Wouldn't want to waste it."

"Give and I tell," Traz growled, arm still outstretched. "Too thirsty to talk."

"We're talking right now," Klaus countered as he withdrew the cup, teasing. "I'll remind you one more time. Cooperation, then gifts. Not the other way around. Otherwise, we'll have to resort to the other method." Klaus' gaze swung to the scarred and blood-stained chair. "I know which one I'd prefer."

Traz's eyes had widened at the sight of the spilled milk. They narrowed as they swung toward the chair and back to Klaus before settling on the cup. "Came here to kill badgers," the goblin growled. "Sneak in and cut throats."

The lardwan, stifling a wince at the slur he'd never become as accustomed to, frowned but held out the cup.

"Well, I didn't suppose you were coming in to tie knots in all our beards," Klaus replied. "You don't strike me as the sort to go on a suicide mission. You must have known that with so few, you'd be caught and killed before you could kill more than a handful of us."

Traz let the cup hang before him for two heartbeats before he snared the vessel. The lardwan let the cup go without protest and studied the goblin as he greedily slurped the milk.

"Wheezers say they attack," the goblin continued when he broke away to peer into the cup, concerned that he might have missed some. "As distraction."

Klaus' arms crossed, and his frown deepened. It didn't add up. "If the attack on the cliff gate was a distraction, it was a poor one," he mused, watching the goblin to see the effect of his words. "Even those at the gate could see it was a half-hearted affair, and they chased them off with bolts and curses. Wasn't the sort of thing that would draw attention away from the upper parapets."

Traz shrugged, and after stretching his tongue out to lap the up-ended cup, he held the drinking vessel out. "Wheezers say and we do. More."

Klaus took the cup, careful to avoid the part the goblin had licked, and filled it again.

"Your masters aren't fools," Klaus observed, pouring slowly. "Even if the attack on the gate was fierce enough to keep attention from the upper parapets, how many could you have killed? A dozen, maybe two if I am generous, but then you and your forces would face a fortress with very light arms and no way out. You're a fine climber, but even you can't imagine you could have just scampered back down without catching a bolt."

Traz shrugged, and Klaus stopped pouring. The goblin hissed, then his head bobbed, and he ran his tongue over his teeth before he spoke. "Not climbing back down," the goblin snarled. "Another way out. Secret way."

Klaus forced his hand to stay steady when he rested his fingers on the cup. The lardwan reminded himself that this could all be lies, fantasies fabricated to get more milk. An alarm chimed in the back of his mind. He had to play this carefully.

"Are you certain you want to take this route?" Klaus warned, looking at the chair. "Speaking of secret passages without proof seems like lying. If you are, I'll end this friendly interaction." He raised the cup to his nose as though sampling its bouquet, forcing his gorge back as he did so.

"I'd hate for you to miss out on sharing this with me for the sake of a few lies."

Traz's hands clenched on the bars and he threw his weight against them, but the stout dwarven iron didn't so much as quiver.

"No lies," the goblin snarled. "There is tunnel! Tunnel stupid badgers not find."

Klaus' heart rate quickened, but before he could ask the next question, the ondwan spoke. "The Sufstan took possession of this fortress nearly a century ago and searched out its secrets. You're lying."

Klaus didn't bother to turn, just smiled when he heard Torbjorn trudge into the chamber. His old friend knew how to make an entrance.

"No lies!" Traz whined, recoiling. "Wheezers tell me is tunnel."

Torbjorn stood just behind Klaus. The lardwan could feel his glare lancing over his shoulder to impale the goblin. "Then your masters lied to you, and you're only a puppet," Torbjorn rumbled as he reached for the jug of milk with a scarred hand. "I'm not about to waste another drop on lies or any more of my time tolerating you fouling my air."

His fingers tightened on the jug, and Traz threw himself at the bars and stretched out both hands. "No, not lies," the goblin squealed. "Proof! Wheezer give map."

Torbjorn's eyes shifted to Klaus, and the lardwan answered over his shoulder as if he'd felt the look. "Waelon searched him and found no map."

The ondwan nodded, and his gaze returned to the goblin. He tipped the jug, and drops of milk hit the stone floor. Klaus tried not to think about making sure the stuff was cleaned off before it soured and made his office uninhabitable.

"More lies," Torbjorn chided, his face a stone mask.

"No, no, no," Traz sobbed, trading his dignity for the precious liquid that was dribbling on the floor before his eyes. "See map."

The blunt claws tore away the bandage on his forearm. "Map," Traz hissed, jabbing a finger at the bloody blotch on the knotted muscle of his forearm. "Wheezer put map in me."

Both dwarves set their vessels on the table and moved to the goblin in the cage.

"I'm not certain what I'm looking at," Klaus admitted as he squinted at the rough lines stitching Traz's arm.

"That's not a map." Torbjorn scowled at the wound. "It's just some scratches. Do you take us for fools?"

Klaus was inclined to agree, but the sharpness in Torbjorn's tone, combined with the anger radiating off the dwarf, had the lardwan wondering if Torbjorn wasn't taking his role too seriously. One look at the goblin's face showed that the creature was desperate to meet their demands, though whether to avoid the consequences or get another cup of milk, he wasn't certain.

"Wait, wait, wait," the goblin squawked as it used the balled-up bandages to mop the crusted blood off the puckered flesh. "Little time. Only need little time."

Torbjorn grunted to show how little he thought of that idea. "You've got time." He chuckled. "You've got until a pair of dwan show up to pitch your arse off the parapets."

Torbjorn turned to give the shout that would summon the dwan, and the goblin shrieked, *"NO! WAIT!* Magic working. Just need time."

Klaus squinted at the lines, but they were still impossible to decipher.

"Magic, eh?" Torbjorn snarled, his demeanor turning tempestuous. "You think I'll put up with sorcery in my fortress, do you?"

Torbjorn turned on his heel and stalked toward a hook set into the wall from which keys dangled on a brass ring. "I'll pitch your wretched hide over myself!"

Traz continued to plead as he returned to cowering at the back of the cell. Scrubbing with the bandage had broken the scab, but the goblin didn't seem to notice as he alternated between staring at the ondwan in terror and pleading with the lardwan.

"Perhaps we're being a bit hasty," Klaus began, shifting his footing to suggest he might intercept Torbjorn's advance without making any move to do so. "I mean, what would it hurt to give him a few more moments?"

"You're such a soft touch." Torbjorn scoffed and brushed past the lardwan to fit a key into the cage door. "I've got a fortress to defend, and I've no time to waste. Neither do you. I'm getting rid of this waste of flesh."

The door swung open, and Torbjorn's frame filled the frame, his shadow stretching like the specter of death toward the shrinking goblin. "Are you going to face the end with honor, or do I have to drag you out like a whining cur?"

Torbjorn's tone sparked concern in Klaus. He'd fought, bled, and killed with the ondwan since they were young, and he'd learned to read him. This was not Torbjorn playing his part in the interrogation. A deeper and darker fury was driving him, and if it did not release him soon, the ondwan was going to haul the goblin to the parapet by the scruff of his neck.

If they went that far, could Torbjorn stop?

"*SEE? LOOK! SEE!*"

The cry was both exultant and pitiful in its urgency.

Klaus moved to his ondwan's shoulder to get a look at the source of the declaration, but Torbjorn remained in place, gripping the frame of the door. The lardwan saw faint shivers in the dwarf's shoulders and fingers, testimony that the dwarf commander was struggling to master himself.

"Come here and prove it," Torbjorn ground out.

The goblin slunk forward with the marked arm held out.

"See?" Traz insisted. "Magic working now."

The dwarves' eyes were accustomed to the gloom of subterranean life, so even with their shadows blotting out much of the light, they could see that the lines of the formerly tangled tattoo had rearranged themselves. The ensorcelled lines formed a blueprint in the goblin's flesh. It took Klaus a moment to orient himself, but then he saw the upper floors of Greyshelf.

A curse invoking his ancestors and culminating with the dread Grimmoth escaped Torbjorn's lips as he grasped the implications.

Behind the looming bas-relief in the assembly hall was a narrow passage that wound through the living rock of the Wyrmspine Mountains. Even if their entire force had been composed of keen-eyed rangers, they might have gone a lifetime without knowing about this tunnel. If the wights knew there was a hidden passage, they certainly knew where it exited.

"They weren't a knife in the back," Klaus muttered, his stomach churning as he followed that train of thought and met his ondwan's grim eyes.

"They're a key in a door," Torbjorn finished, turning back to the goblin. "That's it, isn't it? You kill the sentries and scuttle over to let the wights in."

Traz's head bobbed, and a sob escaped from his throat.

"If they were willing to risk him coming up this way, it must mean they can't open it from their side," the lardwan muttered, his mind racing through the options and potential outcomes.

"How do you open the passage?" Torbjorn demanded.

The goblin cringed, but Torbjorn seized him by the throat and hauled him forward until they were nose to nose.

"How?" the commander growled, a frigid edge in his voice.

"Carving, black eye," Trav rasped through his constricted throat. "Black-eye prince all I know!"

Torbjorn released the goblin, who sank onto his haunches, arms dangling at his sides.

"They must have forces waiting for the goblins to unleash them." Klaus mused. "Given that this much time has elapsed, they probably realize they've been found out."

"They have to know it has gone balls over brains, or whatever passes for it with the wheezers," the ondwan snarled, crackling with dangerous energy.

"They might bugger off," Klaus offered unconvincingly. "Or they might try to force their way in. They might think losing the element of surprise is better than waiting until we collapse the passage or prepare a proper welcome."

Torbjorn stalked back to the table and snatched the jug of milk, then went back to the cell door.

"That means we've got no time to waste," the commander observed. He thrust the jug into Traz's chest hard enough to drive the goblin back a few steps. "Enjoy your reward, my little friend, and wish us luck. I doubt the wheezers will look kindly on your cooperation with our investigation."

Trav staggered back against the wall, clutching the sloshing jug to his chest as the cell door slammed and was locked. Thick tears seeped from his protruding eyes as the goblin sank to the floor, mewling and muttering to himself in his language.

Neither dwarf paid any attention as they headed out of the room. "I'll send word to every dwan we can spare," Klaus promised as he fell in behind Torbjorn. "If we can make sure they don't make it more than a step out of the passage, they'll just be target practice."

"Maybe," Torbjorn murmured. His path deviated from Klaus' as he made for the passage that would take him to the assembly hall. "I'm not satisfied with plugging the crack. Have the Sablestone Guard assemble immediately, along with my shabr'dwan."

Klaus paused, but Torbjorn went down the passage. "Waelon and Gromic are on watch, and—"

"I didn't ask!" Torbjorn bellowed without bothering to look over his shoulder. "Your ondwan gave you a command. Do it!"

CHAPTER FOUR

"That hurts!"

Haeda started and took a step back as the dwarf she was tending jerked. "If you'd been a little slower, you'd be dead, and I wouldn't have to listen to you bellyachin'," she shot back.

Glaring, she pushed the dwarf back onto the pallet so she could return to scouring the javelin wound. She *had* let her mind wander as she worked, which her less-than-adept hands could not afford. She had been far too rough when she cleaned the slice on the dwarf's jawline and neck, but she'd been thinking about her child.

NO! her mind roared at her. *Not ours.* Never *ours.*

The dwarfess blinked and shook her head to dispel the cloudy thoughts.

"Remember, that scratch is on *me*," the dwarf grumbled as he settled down and waited for Haeda to return to her work.

"Considering who I'm working on, that isn't in your favor," Haeda groused in return. "Now shut up and hold still, grem-face."

The dwarf scowled but obeyed as Haeda dipped a cloth in the herb-enhanced water in the bowl beside her. Tomza had shown her how to prepare the concoction, a useful mixture that cleaned wounds as well as promoted healing, but Haeda knew she'd done a poor job. Her herbs weren't ground fine enough, and the bowl smelled too strong, suggesting that the water hadn't been hot enough.

You were moonin' over that long-shanks babe then too, she thought as she cleaned the wound. *Ever since she headed across the Heimlagu, you've been the next thing to useless. Just admit it.*

Haeda choked back a snarl as she wiped the wound, scraping off crusted blood. That elicited a grunt of protest from the dwan. Her eyes darted to meet his glare and answered it with a scowl that dared him to complain.

The wounded dwan decided that lodging another objection was pointless, so with a long-suffering sigh, he fixed his eyes on the ceiling in sullen silence.

Haeda felt a twinge of regret but couldn't get it from her chest to her tongue. Instead, she set to work as tenderly as she did when ministering to her beloved swine.

Careful, she warned herself. *You'll trade one ache for another, thinkin' like that.*

Her efforts continued as she mulled the internal warning. *Maybe, but it's different. My lasses died bloody, but they died serving. Died doing what they were meant for. The little one? Well, she might be scared.*

Haeda realized her vision had blurred and her view of the wound was compromised. Soon she'd hardly be able to tell if she was cleaning the dwan's grimy neck or his soggy britches, not that either would be the worse for her efforts. Still, she wasn't keen on giving the young dwarf ideas, so she turned to one side to wring out the rag and swipe at her eyes.

Keep it together, she scolded. *Those dewdrops aren't helping.*

"Haeda."

The former driver's head snapped up and she started, dropping the rag into the bowl with a splash and a curse. Standing in the doorway was Tomza, the dwarfess' new senior officer.

Though Haeda had also earned the rank of ascedwan and was a veteran, most of her time in service had been spent in the shabr'dwan, and her specialized training was in worcsvines.

Given that the siege didn't provide much need for draft beasts, Haeda had been reassigned after Torbjorn took command. The commander had explained that he meant no dishonor by placing her under Tomza. The lass knew healing as well as most of their senior battle-barbers, and she would treat Haeda no differently for her background, so it seemed best to place her under Tomza's command.

At the time, it had been a sensible move. Torbjorn had held her in place with his deep, knowing gaze. Since then, though, the relationship had been tense at times.

That tension crackled in the air as the former driver dabbed at the healer's brew that had sloshed on her at the interruption.

"Damn it, lass!" she hissed, glaring at her sodden clothes. "He'll be ready for your wicked little needles when I'm done and not before."

Tomza bristled, but as was becoming common, the younger dwarfess swallowed her authoritative rebuke and pressed on to the matter at hand. It was now happening so quickly that Haeda would have missed it if she wasn't looking at her. That stirred more regret that refused to go anywhere near Haeda's clenched jaws and rigid tongue.

"Is he stable?" Tomza asked in a flat, mechanical voice.

"More than stable," the dwan replied from the pallet before rising with a quick twist to keep Haeda from snaring him. "I'm so good we don't need to even bother with your needles. You've got more serious cases than me."

The declaration was followed by a nervous chuckle, and the young dwarf's gaze darted between the two females.

"Wound still needs packing to keep it from oozing," Haeda observed, "but he'll live."

"Good," the officer replied in a tone that suggested nothing of the sort. "We've got to go."

"Go?" Haeda asked, looking up with a frown. "Go where?"

The dwan on the pallet heaved a sigh of relief. "I'm just glad you won't have to spend any more time on little ol'—"

"Shut up and hold this in place," Haeda interrupted as she put the dressing in the dwan's hand, then pressed the hand against his wound.

"Don't know, but word came down that the ondwan's calling for us," Tomza replied as she slid back through the doorway. "Wants us in the assembly hall now."

At the mention of Torbjorn's personal summons, Haeda was on her feet so fast that the dwan on the pallet lurched away in surprise.

"Bad Badgers back together again," the driver chortled, clapping in excitement. "Music to my ears."

"'Bad Badgers?'" the wounded dwarf echoed.

"Shut it and keep the pressure on," Haeda warned as she followed Tomza out of the room. "Otherwise, I'll come back and stitch you up myself."

"Any idea what this is about?"

Gromic had to shout over the din in the assembly hall. The vaulted stone ceiling and the tiled floor amplified the echo of every tramping foot and rattling harness as scores of dwarves came in and shuffled about the chamber. Though each shabr'dwan was technically assigned to a cohort, the personal summons from their ondwan gave them permission to gather near the back of the hall in whatever groups they chose.

"Not sure," Ober admitted as he looked around the hall. He nodded toward the bas-relief on the far wall. "If they're gathered us, it must be serious."

The Sablestone Guard was preparing for a sortie. It was strange to see the elite unit donning their peculiar armor. Without the Sablestone plate and baelgeld framing, it was clear that for all their intimidating reputation, they were just dwarves. True, many of them had frames to match Gromic and Waelon, but they were flesh and blood creatures.

After the armor was on and their grim, leering helms were in place, each became more. They were no flesh and blood but stone and metal. Their tread signaled doom, and their presence promised brutal devastation to all who dared stand in their path. They were an avalanche made flesh, the fury of the mountains in mortal form.

Every moment, another dwarf joined the ranks of the Titans as the attendants finished armoring them.

"It's like we're getting ready for a real fight," Waelon growled, an eager edge in his gravelly voice. "Though why we're up here rather than down at the gate makes bugger-all sense to me."

"Maybe the wheezers are coming for the Lake Gate?" Tomza asked, though one might wonder if she'd asked the question out of actual curiosity. Her eyes were fixed on the middle distance, and her voice was cold as the grim expressions on the Sablestone helms.

"Can't be," Gromic muttered, his eyes tracking the movement of Sablestones with a critical eye. "You'd have to march through the mountains for a few days, scattering whatever force you had just to get to the shores of Heimlagu. The Sounders would pelt you full of holes as you moved toward the gate, and that's not even considering that you couldn't bring proper siege equipment over unless it was in many small pieces."

Haeda nodded, suppressing a shudder. "That's if you're lucky," the former driver intoned darkly. "If the Sounders aren't about, you'll have the Sumplings to contend with. I'd rather catch a bolt than see one of those things again."

Gromic spared a moment from his observations to give the

dwarfess a grim nod. "Aye, true enough. Wheezers are cold, but they ain't stupid. They're not goin' to waste their forces on an attempt at the Lake Gate."

"Then why are we here?" Ober asked, scratching his chin as he looked at the bas-relief. The imposing stone sculpture was worn, but the climactic battle between warriors and a sprawling entity was still discernable.

"You're here to help me flush some rats from the wall," a familiar driving voice stated.

The sight of Torbjorn of Clan Cyniburg would have been enough to cheer the hearts of his dwans, but seeing him resplendent in his Sablestone war harness, rune-engraved *cwellocs* in hand, brought an odd kind of rapture. He was like one of the dwarvish lords of old, striding forward with a strong arm to scatter his enemies like potsherds under a hammer.

They all stood in silence, admiring this resplendent reincarnation of their commander.

Except for Gromic, who sniffed before rushing to his commander. Torbjorn was now his ondwan but would forever be his tweldwan. Eyes streaming, the stout dwarf fell to one knee before the leader he'd worn the Sablestone armor for all those years ago.

"My tweldwan," Gromic croaked, head bowed as words struggled to escape his tightening throat. "Good to see you, sir."

Torbjorn loomed over Gromic, but he bent and took his faithful fordwan by the shoulder. "Get up, Gromic," he growled, blinking rapidly as he spoke. "I've got work for a good dwan, but you don't have much time to prepare." His alchemical and baelgeld-infused armor easily drew the massive dwarf to his feet.

"Prepare?" Gromic asked, broad brow crinkling. "Tweldwan, I'm ready when you are. Just tell me where I need to be."

Torbjorn managed to laugh as he looked at his friend. "Where I need you is by my side." He gestured at the Sablestone contingent, who had almost finished arming. Off to one side, a pair of young dwans in the tabards of Sablestone cubldwan stood beside an untouched suit of armor.

Gromic gaped, then fresh tears rose to his eyes. He tried to go to his knee once more. Luckily, Torbjorn squeezed the stout dwarf's shoulder, and they locked eyes.

"Get over there," he growled. "Or I'll leave you behind."

With a spryness that surprised even Torbjorn, Gromic sprinted toward the waiting armorers.

"Hard to believe they had armor to fit that lump sitting around." Waelon huffed, arms crossed. "You sure you didn't set the ol' tub o' guts up for rude awakening when they can't cram his arse into that can?"

Haeda tried to set Waelon ablaze with her eyes, and Ober shook his head in disgust.

Their commander's shoulders shook. "It's the suit he wore when we first served together." Torbjorn chuckled. "As you might imagine, they couldn't find a dwarf it would fit, and no one wanted to transport it back to Torvgrud for recycling. The damn thing is heavy."

The Bad Badgers stared at their commander, then Waelon finally gave a rare hoot of laughter.

"It has sat in the Black Armory waiting for him all these years!" The former ranger guffawed. "Just because he was too fat for his armor to fit anyone else? Bwahaha, the Shaper does love a fool!"

The laugh was infectious. All the shabr'dwans started laughing, even Haeda, knowing that Gromic would have laughed loudest if he hadn't been otherwise occupied.

Klaus emerged from the throng of dwarves, and the company's laughter faded. The lardwan had donned field armor for the first time in a good while. As he came up, he pinched and tugged at the straps and belt as though someone had loosed rodents beneath his harness.

"Speaking of someone too fat to put on their armor," Waelon groused under his breath.

"I'll admit it's a bit tighter than when I was a spry young dwan," Klaus acknowledged with a nod. "To be fair, compared to brutes like you and Torbjorn, I was just a slip of a thing in those days."

"Don't worry, you're gorgeous," Torbjorn remarked with a smirk. He cocked a warning eyebrow at Waelon. "What's the state of things?"

Klaus left off fiddling with his belt and glanced around the room, muttering. When he swung back to the ondwan, his lips puckered in an irritated line beneath bunching brows.

"Two tweldwan still haven't assembled," the lardwan growled. "Neither has Dogordwan Yorm of Clan Merihn."

"Maybe the squealer thought the call to arms didn't apply to him if he couldn't bring his pet," Waelon observed. "Wouldn't be the first time the pig-pumpers let good dwans fight for them."

Torbjorn's scowl suggested he didn't disagree, but he only shrugged.

"I'll deal with them later," he rumbled, then nodded at his lardwan. "We're moving now. See these three situated in the flanking cohort, and then see Waelon outside."

Waelon straightened, hands falling to his belt and fingers dancing over his axe. "Outside?"

Klaus nodded, grinning at the former ranger's expression as he motioned for the others to follow him.

"Yes, Fordwan," the lardwan called over his shoulder. "Looks like you're getting that patrol after all."

CHAPTER FIVE

"Just like old times."

Torbjorn smirked at the declaration from his trusted fordwan as he stomped into line. However, he wasn't sure that Gromic was being honest.

Clad in Sablestone, they'd weathered more than their fair share of engagements against a variety of foes. Men, elves, goblins, and even other dwarves, along with various coalitions and other bizarre adversaries through the long campaign across the Vale and before. They'd fought orcish mercenary reavers near the Fork, chasing and being chased by the flesh-hungry brutes over the boggy ground. Then that one time, fighting riders from the Norling Steppes on the fallow field outside Ysvon-Town, turning massive creatures into pincushions while trying to avoid being stomped into the loamy earth.

Yes, there had been many battles, many wounds, and even, Torbjorn admitted, many victories. This time was different. "Fordwan Gromic," Torbjorn instructed, taking the helmet off the hook on his belt. "Please have the guards assemble in front of the bas-relief."

The stout dwarf, encased in Sablestone armor and just

donning his helmet, nodded and marched toward the assembly of elite guards as though it had only been yesterday when he'd been in command of their unit.

"All right, lads," he began. His usually jolly tone had a menacing timbre from within the engraved helm. "I want an advancement column formed sharpish, and I'll plant my boot in the danglers of any layabout that dares to drag about. We've got the ondwan with us today, and you're not about to disgrace the Guard with laxity!"

Torbjorn wasn't sure if it was a testament to Gromic or the Sablestone Guard that nothing resembling laxity was on display as the heavily armored dwarves fell into line. Only a few months ago, the ones commanding them had been brought in as prisoners and traitors. That seemed irrelevant to the veteran soldiers, though it might have just been their grim-faced helms.

"If I've got to face a tunnel full of monsters," Torbjorn muttered as he clomped over to the bas-relief. "I'd rather face it with them at my back."

Looking at the carvings, the ondwan was concerned that their erosion was worse than expected. Some of the graven warriors were little more than pitted silhouettes, while in other places, they were a testament to the sculptor's skill. Some pieces were gone, though whether by violent hands or just the vandalism of time, he couldn't know.

In his efforts to find the black-eyed prince, Torbjorn got frustrated as face after face among the warriors revealed a blank marble stare. Eyes inlaid with brass were rheumy with verdigris, but any dwarf worthy of the name knew that even in their prime, they would not have been black.

None of them had black eyes! Had the goblin lied to them? Had the wights lied to the goblin? To what end?

Torbjorn heard the creak of his grip tightening on the hilt of his *cwellocs* before he felt the quivering tension in his gauntleted fist.

I'm sure this will inspire confidence when I reveal I gathered everyone here on the word of some milk-slurping, snake-tongued, son of a—

The dwarf commander's internal rant stilled as his roving gaze swept up in a final desperate plea for an answer and examined the visage of the writhing many-limbed horror. To say it was a face was like saying that the sun had a face. Its undulating tendrils coalesced at a central point no less unsettling for it being worked in stone instead of flesh.

Near the heart of the coiling mass, not in the center but just above it, barbed pseudopods created a hollow that Torbjorn realized was a socket due to the angle from which he saw it. Within that socket, something dark, hard, and reflective gave off the slightest gleam.

"Black-eyed prince," the ondwan muttered. The stone rippled and the eye protruded, summoned to its task. Given what the dwarves had recently learned of the valley and those who had once dwelt within, that shouldn't have unsettled him, but Torbjorn's mouth was dry and his tongue bitter at the subtle sorcery that suffused the very stones.

"The blind giants and their masters," he growled, thinking that dramatic epithets would help him shake off the dire mood as he hefted his polearm. The eye was too high for him to reach, even with the height his armor granted him, so he raised the weapon and tapped the eye with its blunt hexagonal hammer. The eye answered it by weeping inky tears whose stain vanished from the stone after they strayed a hand's breadth from the source.

Within the rock, stone shifted with groans that offended his dwarven ears. He knew masonry and the machinery of his race, and this was alien, a debased fusion of engineering and sorcery. His Sablestone armor barely flirted with such a marriage.

"Degenerates," he muttered, donning his helm as he joined the guard. The headgear shrank his vision to a portal suited to the passage opening before them as stone shrank and furled like a curtain swept aside by drawstrings.

Torbjorn stepped to the head of the column, waving aside a protest by Gromic. The ritual was warm and familiar. Torbjorn held his poleaxe in both hands and nodded at Gromic, who hoisted a tower shield and a magsax before bellowing, "Light up!"

Behind them, the guard tasked with holding the stout illumination pole sparked it to life. The wan blue light of the alchemical lantern probed the darkness before them.

"Guard advance!"

The Sablestone Guard advanced into the passage two abreast, the thunks of their boots creating a cacophony as they moved into the passage. Torbjorn smiled again. Subtlety and surprise were not tactical assets attributed to the Sablestone Guard.

"Good to be marching alongside you again, Ondwan," Gromic rumbled, the words echoing with the sinister tone unique to the helmets of the Guard.

"Likewise, Gromic," Torbjorn replied as they followed the passage into the mountain. "Let's just hope the others feel the same and follow through when things get interesting."

Gromic grunted, then cast a quick look over his shoulder. "Good so far, sir." He turned a critical eye on the lantern bearer behind them. "Hoist that lantern like a proper dwan! Damn it, dwarf, not like that! It'll clip the passage's ceiling. What's the matter, lad? You never done this before?"

"He might not have," Torbjorn growled as his gaze swept the tunnel before them. "Glastuc seemed keener on keeping them close than having them do their jobs."

The ondwan fought the urge to see if the column was staying in good order. He had to trust them to do their jobs and Gromic to do his. Their regular fordwan had been assigned with a few of the Guard to hold a crucial access point in the lower fortress. It was their responsibility to hold that chokepoint should the enemy win the day and press into Greyshelf.

It was not glorious, but it was honorable, and whatever the dwarf officer had thought, he'd known better than to argue with Torbjorn Kinslayer, the Bloody Ondwan and Chosen of the Shaper.

They marched on, and Torbjorn's stomach knotted. His eyes strained to the extent of the pale blue light, picking out every detail of the empty passage and searching for any sign of the enemy.

Where are they? Surely they didn't intend that Traz and his lot would use the tunnel as only an escape?

The sides of the passage fell away, but the light on the floor stretched on. "A cavern," Gromic pointed out with a nod and a pump of his shield at the yawning threshold. "Should we slow down and send a scout?"

Torbjorn almost shuddered at the idea of halting their march to have one of the lighter, quicker dwan teams do that. His shabr'dwans were next in line in the support cohort under the command of Tweldwan Kroiferd, a contemporary who'd had a fair relationship with Torbjorn before his disgrace and had not insulted or abused him or his dwans since. It was a shame that was the best praise he could offer, but there it was.

"No," Torbjorn barked, snapping to attention when he realized they were only a dozen strides from the portal. "If something is waiting for us out there, I want to hit it at speed and then form a bulwark across the entrance."

"Speed and then bulwark, yes, sir." Gromic nodded and then thundered, "Lads, double-time, and then a bulwark after we clear the tunnel."

The Guard responded with an efficiency that made Torbjorn grin. He'd forgotten how good it felt to wear the armor and feel the master craftsmanship working in time and purpose with his body. The last half-dozen strides became two bounds as the baelgeld runes flared and hissed.

Gromic and Torbjorn erupted into the cavern, creating

spiderweb cracks in the stone floor, with two dozen Sablestone dwarves after them. Seamlessly, they formed a rough box before the cavern entrance, weapons facing the walls of darkness that loomed outside the lantern's light.

They held for a heartbeat, breaths rasping through the masks of their helms, muscles burning. One heartbeat became two, then half a dozen. Then the impetus of the moment deflated as the footsteps of the runners from the next cohort were heard in the tunnel.

"Word?" came the call from the passage they'd just left.

"Maybe they ran away when they heard us coming?" Gromic offered. The comfort of his explanation was ruined by the helmet's acoustics and then the echo in the chamber. Torbjorn realized it had to be a sizable chamber to produce that, and its seeming emptiness made the embarrassment of the moment all the more consuming.

"Word?" the runner called again.

Torbjorn knew once he called the all-clear, it would prompt the question of what he wanted to do next: advance, reinforce, or, gallingly, withdraw. He was operating on the goodwill of the Holt'Dwan more than any ondwan ought to, and he was not sure which action would test that will—pursuing this fruitless march or admitting he'd rushed into this without proper forethought.

Before he could make up his mind, there was a rustling click, which might not have been heard were it not for the echo in the cavern. The sound was soft but distinct, and as one, the dwarves swung their gazes toward its origin in the darkness beyond the lantern light. Gauntlets creaked as knuckles popped around weapons.

Two cold stars emerged from the darkness, then two more, then scores.

A young dwarf gasped at the tunnel mouth, and the sound reverberated across the chamber.

The runner had crept closer to raise his question a final time but now stood dumbstruck. Torbjorn looked over his shoulder at the novice dwan's face, ephemeral and fragile in the blue light.

"Engage!" the ondwan shouted, happy to see the runner shocked to attention by the barked report. "Reinforce!"

The first leathery creaks and rattles chorused from the clackers as they shuffled forward and raised their weapons, but Torbjorn could still hear the fleeing footsteps of the young dwarf. *Hurry*, he willed as he raised his polearm to the ready.

"Come on, then," Gromic bellowed, beating his shield with his sword. "You lot already forget why you're here?"

As though summoned by the taunt, the skeletal foes advanced, corroded weapons clutched in bony hands.

CHAPTER SIX

"What are we doing out here?"

The question came from a ranger with her scalp shaved except for a thin line down the middle of her skull. That hair had been woven into a skinny braid that hung down the back of her neck and rocked like a furry caterpillar trying to stay attached to her head as she swept her gaze around. The sight made Waelon want to seize it and use his keen axe blade to finish the shearing.

"Looking for signs of the enemy," Waelon grumped, though he told himself that he should be in a better mood.

He had his ranger patrol and was leading them along the thin lip of stone that wound from under the Window, a part of Greyshelf near the top of the mountain. Descending from the small ancient gate of iron and stone had been an exciting experience. They had to dangle from ropes while swaying in the winds, then scuttle down more ropes to the narrow ridge that wound through the craggy, snow-seamed terrain and made its inexorable way to Heimlagu.

"We're always supposed to be doing that," the dwarfess shot back, keen eyes never ceasing their search. "We're Rangers, after all. Or most of us are."

Waelon sniffed, then spat at the insult but didn't otherwise respond. He checked the wind, then eyed their path, noting places to which patches of ice clung. With a frown and a low grunt, he continued his steady tramp.

"Hey," the ranger called, scuttling nimbly over rock and ice. The other rangers in the patrol negotiated the patches gingerly. "You never answered my question."

"I did," Waelon growled without looking behind. "You just didn't like the answer."

His eyes roved over the clefts and folds in the stone, marking points that might be promising. They had to get a better view of those and other possible points. *Might as well be a needle in a stack of needles.*

His foot hit a patch of ice as he considered that, and either Wyrd or poor luck chose that moment to remind him of his precarious position. Waelon's boot skidded over the slick surface, and his weight shifted without his permission. His heart seized, and it occurred to him that this would be an unfortunate way to go out. From this height, he'd have a very long time to look up or down and consider his poor fortune as the others threw him pitying, or perhaps satisfied, glances.

"Steady!" Waelon felt a hard hand clutch his bandoleer and swung around, the arc controlled by the guiding hand. Icy stone bit his cheek, and red rolled down it and congealed in the cold.

"Watch where you step," the female ranger warned, though it didn't sound cruel or scornful.

Waelon's burning eyes met hers, and he couldn't seem to force the word down before it passed his lips. "Thanks."

The other ranger produced a winsome, gap-toothed smile. "Don't worry about it." She winked. "Better yet, do. Then tell me what we are doing, eh?"

Waelon found it hard not to return the smile but started moving again, more cautious this time as he advanced.

"Torbj...I mean, the ondwan," he began, testing each step

before he committed his weight, "sent us out to look for enemy forces positioned in the crags. If we can spot movement, all the better, but if not, we look for smoke."

Waelon picked his way across the ridge and spied a switchback to a better position to overlook the territory.

"Smoke?" the dwarfess pressed, following Waelon close enough that he could smell the cabbage and bacon she had eaten a few hours before. Waelon was suddenly hungry.

"What's your name, lass?" the big dwarf asked as they paused to let the rest of the Rangers catch up.

"Clahdi," she replied as though surprised he didn't know. "Clahdi of Clan Davish."

Waelon frowned upon hearing his clan name come from the dwarfess' mouth but decided that it wasn't germane to their current concerns. "Clahdi of Clan Davish," he muttered, squaring his shoulders. "Do you always ask this many questions while on patrol?"

Waelon did another sweep of the mountainside—nothing had changed—then clambered up the switchback.

"I do." Clahdi sprang after her elder clanmate. "At least I do when the lads and I are called out—by the lardwan himself, mind you—to follow a disgraced former mad lad on a skurby hunt at the top of a mountain."

Waelon had accelerated to stay ahead of the goat-footed ranger, and he was winded as he stepped atop the new vantage point. The dwarfess alighted on the rocky shelf with insulting ease.

"Former?" he wheezed, trying and failing to hide his breathlessness. "Skurby hunt?"

Clahdi gave him a wry look, then waved at the rangers on their way up. She shielded her eyes and scanned the snow-covered mountainside. "Well, as anyone would tell you," she sighed, sending out a plume of white breath that the wind ripped away with vengeful insistence, "there's not so much as wayward grem wandering about to threaten us or Greyshelf. So, what are we out here for?"

Waelon straightened and swept the area, confirming Clahdi's assessment that no enemies were in sight. Then he checked for smoke again. When no plumes greeted his eyes, he gave an irritated grunt and stomped over to a thin drift of snow. After scooping up a handful that he compacted in his fist, he applied the frosty compress to his face to numb his lacerated cheek and wash the crusted blood off.

The other rangers started arriving, looking about with seasoned eyes before ducking against the wind. Hoods were pulled low and cloaks tightened as they set a watch on the rocky vantage point. Some shared terse words, but most just seemed content to wait for further orders.

Waelon turned from perusing the assembly to find Clahdi still watching him.

"We still skurby-hunting then, Fordwan?" she asked, his rank spoken with an edge. Among the rangers, they seldom used ranks since, out in the wild, leadership was about initiative, skill, and cunning, not a title bestowed from on high. When a ranger mentioned rank to another ranger, it was not a good sign.

Waelon didn't think Clahdi intended to provoke or challenge him, but she *was* letting him know that she and the others would need more than vague directions before they started looking to their interests. It was this sort of institutional independence that had attracted him to the rangers when he was a dust-eared dwan, fresh to life in the Holt'Dwan. Honor and confidence without pretense and the other gilding that was so often part of dwarven life.

Unfortunately, many of those aspects had been attractive to his brother not long after, but Raelon had not been temperamentally suited to the freedom. That had resulted in his sibling headed for the Deeping, which had forced Waelon to forsake everything, liberate his brother, and try to flee into the wilds.

They might have gotten away with it if Raelon hadn't insisted on setting that fire as revenge for his mistreatment. His brother's cackles amidst the flames had foreshadowed how his life would end years later in Ipplen's Ford.

Waelon lurched back a step, shaking his head free of the grip of the memories that had come pouring out. With a snarl, he pitched the bloody slush from his hand and spat on the stone before him.

He felt Clahdi's eyes on him, and he fought his initial instinct to surrender to a dark anger and bully and threaten to stave off her questions. He needed her and her compatriots to help him watch for Torbjorn's signal. This was important.

"We're looking for signs of the enemy or smoke," he repeated. Her eyes rolled, and he quickly added, "The smoke will signal where the enemy has found a passage into Greyshelf."

Clahdi blinked. Waelon found those reddening cheeks and the emerald eyes above them fetching. Not the smoky, delicate stunners Haeda possessed, but they had a rugged loveliness that both alerted and allured him.

"A passage into Greyshelf?" Several rangers swore or whistled. "As in, the wheezers had their slaves burrow through the mountain to worm their way in?"

Waelon nodded, but his beard refused to cooperate since it was held hostage by the dragging wind. "No. We think the tunnel was always there," the big dwarf replied, wishing he knew more than what Klaus had told him.

"How did the wights know about it?" one of the other rangers asked, maintaining his squinting vigil. "How did *we* find out about it?"

Waelon frowned at Clahdi as though her inquisitive spirit had proven catching, and the dwarfess shrugged. Waelon looked away, fearing she might see a blush on his cheeks that had nothing to do with the wind.

"I'm not sure how the wights knew," he lied since the truth

wasn't common knowledge. "As to how we knew, we got the information from a grem that was trying to slip in to open the passage."

Another chorus of whistles and curses.

"What's with the smoke?" Clahdi asked with a frown. "The ondwan's going to set something on fire and expect us to follow the trail and tromp on over? If this force is set to invade Greyshelf, they've got to have enough people to take whatever we can dish out without paying us much heed. It's not like a typical sharpshooter's run where you can hope to catch a few officers with a bolt. Wights don't go down like that."

But they do go down, Waelon thought, trying to push thoughts of his brother from his mind, only to have them replaced by a vision of Ober's other self wreaking havoc. *Wights most certainly go down.*

Waelon's hand strayed to his belt, and he caught himself and forced his eyes to sweep the scene again.

Still no smoke.

Waelon turned his attention back to the dwarfess again. "We're supposed to reconnoiter and report. We note where the passage is while avoiding detection, then head for the Lake Gate. There's a supporting force there we will guide here so they can initiate a flanking assault."

Some of the Rangers bobbed their heads, and Waelon couldn't help smiling. There wasn't a ranger worthy of the name who didn't appreciate an ambush.

"That sounds canny," Clahdi called after the wind had died down. "Why did we get saddled with you then, Red?"

Nicknames were common among the rangers. He supposed that, given the possibilities, he should be glad the one she'd settled on was innocuous.

"I suppose the ondwan doesn't think me a former mad lad quite yet, Magpie," Waelon shot back, then savored the feel of basking in the dwarfess' smile. It was striking and radiant, even with a bit of cabbage tucked between her teeth. He almost had enough time to cement the memory in his mind when the air was rent by a shriek carried by the wind.

"What was that?" Clahdi called, her duabow in her hands. The other rangers grabbed their weapons.

Waelon had hunted, fought, and killed most things that walked, crawled, or flew, and he'd heard that cry before. He'd sincerely hoped never to hear it again.

Axe in hand, he scoured the mountain's face.

At first, his eyes slid past it. The second time, he thought it might have been Torbjorn's signal. That sparked a third glance, and he saw its ungainly approach. The wind was battering its body, and judging by the patches and scabby portions of its coat and plumage, the abuse of the elements had been exceptional since it had been displaced by the forces hiding among the crags.

If Waelon had thought they could communicate with the creature, he would have told it they were here to clear out the interlopers. He couldn't, so he braced for the reality that was about to come crashing down on them.

Clahdi's eyes had followed Waelon's gaze, and when she spotted the creature, the rosy color vacated her cheeks. That was followed by yet more questions. "Is that a—"

"A mountain griffin?" Waelon nodded. "You bet your wagging tongue it is."

"Is it—"

"Looking to line its nest with our bones?" The big dwarf sighed and hefted his axe. "You bet your inquisitive arse it is!"

CHAPTER SEVEN

"Where's my fire?"

Torbjorn's battlefield voice cut through the din in the cavern as he hewed another walking dead man with his *cwellocs*. The descending head clove leathery flesh and splintered bone, and the clacker crumbled as the lights in its eyes blinked out. As it fell, two more skulked forward. One had a slab-like shield, and its axe was raised to hack, and the other stalked behind a spear.

"*WHERE'S MY FIRE!*" the ondwan roared as he advanced to meet the attackers.

He drove his cwellocs' butt spike forward to check the advance of the shield-bearer, and the hardened point shivered in aging wood held together by corroded metal bands. The clacker's axe stroke fell, but Torbjorn just ducked to allow the jagged blade of the weapon to scrape the slope of his helm before rebounding off his spaulders.

Swiveling his hips, he brought the head of his weapon around, his axe head tearing the clacker's shield to one side before he thrust forward with the spear-like crown of his polearm. Tempered dwarvish steel rammed through the rictus grin to split the skull of the unliving soldier.

The cold eyes of the clacker dimmed, and its desiccated remains returned to their original state. Torbjorn squinted through the visor of his helm, knowing there was another clacker, and was rewarded by a spear thrust to the face.

The dwarf commander staggered back, trying to get his balance as the enemy drove at him. The faceplate of the helm took the worst of the blow, but the force rocked him, and sparks from the probing point on Sablestone had nearly reached his eyes. Disoriented but taking pummeling thrusts across his armored bulk, Torbjorn made a sweeping block so he could right himself. The maneuver connected with the haft of the enemy spear, and the body on the other end lurched.

His vision cleared, and his head was getting there when the clacker came for him again. There were two more on its flanks, one with a pyramid-headed mace that seemed far too large for its emaciated frame.

"WHERE'S MY FIRE!" Torbjorn repeated as he braced to face this next challenge.

The unliving came on, jaws flapping in a mockery of a war cry. Their bodies suddenly spasmed and fell to one side, lights blinking out in quick succession. As they toppled to the floor, the ondwan saw the bolts that had pierced them.

"Tweldwan!"

Torbjorn barely registered the warning before another foe hammered his flank, hefting a long-handled maul in tireless hands. The first blow struck hardest, slamming into his back. His Sablestone couldn't keep the force of the blow from reverberating through meat and bone.

Instincts honed on dozens of battlefields had the dwarf commander pivot and catch the second blow on the horn of his axe and shove it aside. The dead thing snapped its teeth in his face as it launched a crossbody check, and they locked weapons.

In life, this creature must have been a titan. Even with his strength-enhancing armor, it was an even match. As he jockeyed for a better position, the clacker matched his movements twist for twist and shove for shove.

Then Torbjorn lurched forward, his foe swept to one side by a wall of Sablestone armor. The ondwan righted himself and saw Gromic's hulking form looming over his attacker, which he had shoulder-checked to the floor. The huge clacker's heavy bones and corroded scale armor hissed and rattled on the rocks as it fought to right itself, but Gromic's armored boot descended. The verdigris-veined skullcap it wore buckled, and the skull came apart in a spray of teeth and bone dust.

Gromic spun from his handiwork to check on his ondwan and saw the waiting salute. The fordwan returned the gesture with his notched magsax before hoisting his shield to shove back a pair of probing sword strokes.

Torbjorn looked around the lantern-lit cavern to assess their situation. The Sablestone bulwark had borne the initial onslaught of unliving, and the heavy armor and bloody-minded tenacity of the dwarves had carried the effort. The next line of dwans was forming a battle line that had alternating dwarves hoisted on shields by their fellows to pump duabow shots into the enemy's ranks.

At first, it had felt like spitting into the storm, but it had provided vital relief that allowed the Guard to advance a few steps at a time. As the space expanded and lanes began to open, a wall of dwans formed behind the guard, offering more crossbow support and magsaxes to hew down the dead men who lapped around the Guard.

As they drove the clackers back, fresh alchemical lanterns were brought forward, and long burning flares were launched into the cavern. In the glaring lights, Torbjorn saw that they'd claimed a third of the chamber from the enemy, but the rest of the rocky hollow was filled with hungry eyes, and fresh columns of fiends were marching in from a tunnel.

"GRIMMOTH'S GRIN! WHERE'S MY FIRE?"

Another clacker lunged, axe whistling, but the ondwan's *cwellocs* parted its arm, and the reverse swing parted the outstretched neck. Madness seized Torbjorn, and he beat his chest with a gauntleted fist amidst the shower of vertebrae.

"FIRE! FIRE! FIRE!"

The duo of foes advancing on him succumbed to a flurry of bolts, but on their heels were three more.

"FIRE!"

Torbjorn's voice was raw and ragged but no less potent for that as he fended off his enemies. Blow after blow rebounded off his armored form as he swiped, stabbed, and swatted, parting armor and animated carcasses as he went.

"FIRE!"

A downward chop cleaved a rusted helm and a moldering head. He threw back his head to give another frustrated roar when he heard a ringing clank to one side of him, then a thrumming hiss like a firedrake's snarl.

"Fire down the tunnel!" barked a gruff voice from within a cowl, and dawn struck the cavern.

PFFWOOOM

Torrents of flame lanced through the ranks of advancing dead men, driven with so much pressure that many of those caught in its path toppled, their burning bodies casting gobbets of clinging flame in every direction. Those not in the direct path of the flaming cascade found that the heat was enough to split and splinter the more desiccated and delicate portions of their unliving anatomy. Leathery joints gave way under the tension, bones blackened, and spare bits of flesh crackled and smoldered. Before long, the age-worn weapons and armor warped and distended.

The backwash of heat from the terrible salvo drove every dwarf, including the Sablestone Guard, back a step, hands and shields raised and helmed heads bowed. Blinking back tears, Torbjorn struggled to look out beneath an upraised hand.

The fire had finally come, and with it had come choking black smoke. The stuff was spreading across the cavern. It was no impediment to the unliving, but the dwarves were grumbling, wheezing, and coughing.

"Wind down the tunnel!" the gruff voice called. Gusts of mechanically driven wind drove the smoke from the frontline and across the cavern. Within a few heartbeats, the tunnel opposite the dwarvish position was filled with smoke.

Eyes and nose running, body slack with exertion, and throat aflame with the searing smoke, Torbjorn couldn't help smiling. He saw the teams carrying the Shaper's Breath weapon alternating between keeping their pulley-cranked fans churning out tides of air and preparing for another storm of fiery ruin.

The ingenious invention had come about during the long dark days of the battle with the Dynastics on the northernmost edge of the Wyrmspines. The Shaper's Breath weapon paired dwarvish ruthlessness with dwarvish ingenuity.

In the battle in the Ysgand Vale, the weapons had seen little use. Most battles had been fought above ground, and the wights and their legions of unliving had little to fear from suffocation or blinding smoke since they did not breathe, and sight depended on flesh.

Today the weapon lived up to its lofty name, providing the fiery deliverance they needed.

The clackers reformed and marched over the smoldering, sputtering remains of their fellows.

Torbjorn adjusted his grip on his axe. He had to hope that Waelon and his rangers could lead their Lake Gate relief forces here quickly. Otherwise, they would have a long fight on their hands. As more dead men emerged from the smoke, sockets shining, the ondwan wasn't certain they could win.

Clearing his throat and rolling his shoulders, Torbjorn raised his *cwellocs*.

"Come on!" he shouted in a hoarse challenge. "Neither of us've had enough, so let's get back to it!"

CHAPTER EIGHT

"She's coming around again!"

Waelon looked over his shoulder and saw the looming shadow of the griffin speeding toward their position.

"Hunker down and prepare to shoot!" he barked, looking at a plume of black smoke smudging the clear sky. They had to move, so it was time to take care of this.

The other rangers complied, but Clahdi saw Waelon standing on the ridge crest they'd been skirting when the griffin and the smoke appeared. His duabow tracked the griffin as it flew, shrieking.

"What are you doing?" she demanded, torn between slinking behind a boulder as she'd been instructed and arguing with the big dwarf.

"Keeps making these false dives," he growled, eyes not leaving his target. "Harrying us and waiting until we're vulnerable to lay into us."

Clahdi stole an urgent glance at the griffin's descent and fought to keep a frightened sob from escaping her throat. "Your answer is to stand out here and be vulnerable? Are you an idiot?"

Waelon winked. "It's been said," the ranger admitted with a

grim smirk, then nodded at the nearest boulder. "You better get under cover."

"You're insane!" the dwarfess exclaimed, not retreating. "It's going to snatch your stupid arse off this mountain!"

Waelon steadied his breathing when he saw the griffin's gaze latch onto him and its clawed feet flexed forward.

"Then you better hunker down," Waelon growled as he let the tension flow out of his limbs. "Get ready to shoot the thing, eh?"

The griffin's scream was a piercing assault intended to paralyze fleeing prey with fear before it struck. Waelon of Clan Davish wouldn't run from anything.

The other rangers' shots went wide, monster and bolts tearing past one another. A few did taste blood, slicing fur or striking rigid plumage, but they did nothing to slow the hurtling predator, which was twice the size of the brawniest plow horse.

The wounds were an easily dismissed distraction as its talons strained for the dwarf who had the temerity to stand before it upon its own mountain. The hooked beak stretched wide in anticipation of the flesh it would dine on.

While the majority of the rangers' shots had been wasted, one duabow hadn't yet fired, and it now launched its bolt. The hammered iron point drove through the open beak and up into the skull of the griffin. The griffin choked out another scream while it gagged blood.

Pain and shock had the reaching claws scoring the stone where Waelon had stood moments before. It looked for its quarry as it floundered, the momentum of the diving charge dissipating into an awkward flop across the ground. It tried to roll to its feet with its normal agility, but one of the other rangers' bolts paid dividends as the descending weight of the creature drove it deep into the griffin. The forgotten bolt bit into the shoulder joint, and one sweeping wing buckled.

The griffin hunched on its hindlegs, one wing folded as the

other drooped and dragged on the snowy rock. The fierce beak snapped as it spun, wild eyes still searching for its quarry.

"Finish 'er off, lads," Clahdi shouted as she raised her re-primed duabow to her shoulder.

In quick succession, half a score of bolts punched through the predator's hide, and three heartbeats later, a full score of dark-fletched bolts protruded from the griffin. Blood steamed on the icy stones, and the beast twitched and spasmed, refusing to accept its end.

The rangers stepped from their cover, and Clahdi moved toward the dying beast. The griffin finally slumped, each faltering breath flecking its beak and the stones with fresh blood. Clahdi, her face a grim mask, planted a boot on the neck as the still-defiant beast tried to raise its beak once more. Then the griffin heaved a sigh, and its head rolled to one side.

Clahdi nodded by way of salute, and her duabow twanged.

The griffin shuddered, then went still. Clahdi and the rangers spent a moment in quiet reflection, then some looked at the smoke-streaked sky and others looked at the snow and blood.

"Where's the mad lad?" a ranger asked, and Clahdi looked up. All eyes swept the gouged crimson earth, but there was no sign of the redheaded dwarf.

"There's his duabow," another ranger called, pointing at a stock jutting from a drift near a lip of stone a short way from the griffin's corpse. The rangers moved toward the weapon.

"Where'd he go?"

Clahdi stomped toward the crossbow, understanding how irritating questions could be for the first time. Wasn't it obvious? Did they have to ask? Couldn't they just shut—

"He didn't go anywhere," Waelon growled from just beyond the sunken duabow. "But if you lot don't hurry up, that'll change."

The rangers around Clahdi cried out in surprise and dismay. Scattering snow, they rushed to the edge of the cliff and found a set of red-furred digits clinging to the stone lip.

"So much for the former mad lad, eh?" Clahdi crowed, prompting gruff laughter from the other rangers.

"Former will be accurate if you don't help me." Waelon groaned, and his right arm shook.

Needing no further prompting, Clahdi clamped her hands on the clinging arm while another ranger bent to extend a hand. A few bitter curses and heaves later, Waelon was dragged to safety, then hands slapped his back and fists pounded his shoulder, even the tender right one, in congratulations and celebration. Waelon thought they might have battered him back off the cliff with their exuberance if Clahdi hadn't interrupted with a sharp whistle.

"In case you lasses forgot, we've still got a mission to accomplish," the dwarfess called, her bloody fingers stabbing toward the damning trail of black smoke. "We've got at least a quarter-mile before we've got a good view of it, and then we've got a jolly trot to the Lake Gate before we do it all in reverse. I suggest you leave off with the fordwan so we can get moving."

The clot of rangers around Waelon disintegrated with embarrassed alacrity and sheepish silence, though a few paused to raise a fist and mouth "Mad lad" before shouldering their crossbows and readying for the long trudge ahead of them.

Waelon was last to follow, and he massaged his right shoulder with his left hand as he passed Clahdi.

"Impressive," she acknowledged, her eyes glittering. "Might have made a story if you'd kicked it, though. How are you going to find a way to top that?"

Waelon looked over his strained shoulder at the beast that had nearly killed him. Instinct had driven him to snatch at the rough edge that had cut his fingers, but what had kept him holding on? He couldn't deny Clahdi's point, even if she'd made it in jest. What better end could there be, and what did he have that was worth holding onto?

Klaus' words bounced around his skull, then Waelon met

Clahdi's gaze and shrugged his good shoulder. "Who knows? It's still early."

Clahdi laughed, almost a bray, but it was honest and good. Despite the cold, a knot of warmth formed inside him. It was heady, even disconcerting, but he appreciated it. It *was* very cold out here.

The dwarfess chuckled and held up his duabow. "In case you feel like more heroics." A trio of griffin feathers was bound to the stock with cord.

Waelon stared at the trophy and smiled. "Thank you."

Clahdi turned on her heel to catch up with the other rangers. "Better get a move on," she yelled as she danced over red slush and scored stone. "You're supposed to be leading this rabble, aren't you?"

"You can't be serious." Ober scowled at the pool of slobber spreading on the stone floor, then lurched back as the source of the spittle tossed its huge head. Its ears flopped from one side to the other.

"You bet your perky little arse I am," Haeda shot back as she hauled back on the reins. "You're going to hop on this fine fellow and hold onto him for dear life."

The young dwarf looked from the driver to the blotferow and back and forced out a heavy swallow. "I'll walk, thanks."

Haeda growled and massaged her knotting brows. "That's not an option. We need to get you there quick for when Waelon shows up, and these lovelies will do that, sure as the Shaper's hand."

Ober eyed the trio of blotferows whose reins Haeda held. He didn't think those things had anything to do with the Shaper. Worcsvines, which were used for domestic tasks, were fine. Endearing, even. When he and his sister had lived in their homestead at the southernmost tip of the Vale, their family had kept one of the creatures, a stout sow named Bris. That was short for "Bristle" because of the collection of whiskers on her snout.

Bris preferred Tomza to Ober, and the young dwarf had once been dragged along when the swine had spooked, but he was not opposed to swine as a rule.

Blotferows were something else.

Their proportions were too aggressive. They were not tubular like a domestic pig but bulky about the head and shoulders. Those heads were battering rams of knobby flesh, dense bone, and ripping tusks. Even just standing in place, they radiated menace, and the mad dwarfess wanted them to mount the creatures?

As though sensing his thoughts, the pig with the slobbering maw gnashed his teeth and snuffled the air before Ober.

"He's wondering what I'll taste like." Ober shrank back, then stomped his foot. "No! I don't care if I have to run the whole way. You're not getting me on that monster."

"Keep your voice down," Tomza chided, sounding bored as her eyes roamed over those gathered in front of the gate. The cavalry was at the fore, while those behind were infantry. Despite the size of their burly mounts, the young dwarfess noted that the swine riders looked anemic. They would be moving over rough terrain, and while that might discourage the peculiar mounts of humans, elves, and other longshanks, dwarvish war swine were famously sure-footed. If the enemy forces were as significant as everyone seemed to believe, the charge of this shock cavalry would be hard-pressed to make a dent.

"Shouldn't there be more pig riders?" Tomza asked as her face twisted into a frown. "I mean, all things considered."

"No, because no one has any business being on the backs of those things," Ober replied, only half paying attention to what his sister said. "Anyone who pretends otherwise is a nutter or a liar."

Haeda's fists went to her hips, and her tone sharpened with

maternal disapproval. "Now, just one minute, you dusty-eared whelp," she snapped, her chin jutting out and her nostrils flaring. "Are you saying I'm a liar?"

Ober's arms crossed, and he turned his face away defiantly.

"No," he retorted in anything but an apologetic tone. "I'm not saying that."

The driver's eyes narrowed, daring him to meet her gaze.

"Well, then what *are* you saying?"

"I'd rather ride a horse than that thing." He sniffed.

Haeda gasped, Tomza's eyes widened in shock, and several steps away, a collection of cavalry dwans gave Ober nasty looks. The blotferows seemed disinterested.

Haeda called a prickly "Here" to Tomza and deposited the reins in the younger dwarfess' hands. Tomza stared at her newly acquired charges in surprise while Haeda advanced on Ober like a stalking predator. The younger dwarf tried to hold his ground, but her advance drove him to retreat. The hesitation proved to be his undoing.

"Where are you going?" she snarled, snagging him by the ear as he tried to duck away. "Listen here, whelp."

Ober started to resist, but Haeda twisted harder. The young dwan thought the driver's strong, calloused fingers would rip his ear off, so, struggling to stifle the yelps and groans her grip elicited, he followed her as she dragged him over to the nearest beast. Ober managed one final squeak of protest before he was face to face with the slavering blotferow.

"This magnificent animal," Haeda began, pressing Ober so close that he could feel the hot breath of the swine—and smell a compost pile of pungent odors in that breath. "This beautiful beast has been trained for the battlefield since it was weaned. *It's* the veteran, not you, and from its breeding and its meticulous training, it has everything it needs, knows everything, and is capable of returning you safely. You're going to stop whining, get in the saddle, and hang on tight. Do you hear me?"

"Ow, yes. Ow, fine," Ober groused as he twisted to no avail. "Just let go of my ear."

Haeda obliged, and Ober retreated a few steps to scowl at the blotferow, which gave a low snort in reply.

"What are you laughing at, Drips?" he fumed, rubbing his ear.

For the first time since they'd arrived at Greyshelf, Tomza's face lost its slackness, and she stifled a snort behind her hand. When Ober's glare swiveled in her direction, the young dwarfess couldn't restrain herself.

"Probably you." She chortled, and the sound was so infectious that Haeda and eventually Ober chuckled, his tension finally giving way. The blotferow remained impassive until the sharp blast of a horn pierced the antechamber before the Lake Gate and there was a stir in the procession. The blotferows stamped and tossed their heavy heads.

Tomza, still holding the reins of all three, was inexorably drawn toward their slashing tusks. Only Haeda's quick thinking and sure hands arrested the movement, and the agitated pigs settled.

"What in Erduna's Dug was that about?" the driver swore, looking around as she patted snouts and stroked jaws.

"Somethings coming up from the fortress," Ober observed and pointed at the shuffling lines of dwans.

Something *was* coming, and none of the dwarves were willing to stay in its path. The trio and their borrowed swine had just moved to follow suit when they saw the reason why. A line of dwarvish cavalry trotted up at a quicker pace than seemed advisable, given the close confines. At their head was a dwarf.

Haeda spat as he passed. "Dogordwan Yorm," the driver hissed in answer to the curious looks of the young dwarves beside her. "The 'rescuer' who dragged us back to Greyshelf like common deserters."

The siblings nodded, remembering the retelling of events.

"It's said that he and his dwans are thorns in Torbjorn's sides,"

Ober offered, scowling darkly as the line of cavalry rode their mounts past. "Even heard that last month, he refused an order to join the Sallie sortie when the clackers sent human sappers at the Cliff Gate."

"It's worse than that," Tomza replied. "He was called to deploy to the gate, and he showed up with his entire detachment, ready to follow Dogordwan Finnug out. When the gate finally swung open, Finnug's riders went out. Yorm sat watching, then signaled his dwans to turn tail and ride back into the fortress."

Ober spat and scowled at the dogordwan as he bellowed orders to his forces, driving the line of riders before the gate to one side.

"Traitor!" the young dwarf snarled. "How come Torbjorn didn't strip him of rank and ship him off to Heimgrud for a judgment that would've sent him to the Deeping?"

Haeda matched the pair's scowl at the officer, but when she spoke, her voice was low and measured, carefully pitched to avoid being overheard.

"Because Torbjorn's no fool," she replied. "He knows the Holt'Dwan's only holding up since the command staff caught a case of divine intervention. The tweldwans and dogordwans are in a sort of alliance. Torbjorn comes down on Yorm and his allies, and whoever's stupid enough to fall into that camp pushes back. Then other tweldwans get involved or stake their own claims, and pretty soon, the clackers won't have to kill us cause we'll do it ourselves."

"Yorm seems to know that," Tomza observed, nostrils flaring as though she smelled something sour. "Why are they here? Just to gum up things at the gate?"

Haeda shrugged, then looked up sharply as a gong reverberated over the gate. The ranger team had signaled. The enemy had been spotted, and the gates were opening. With a mixture of irritation and relief, they saw Yorm signal his detachment forward with commendable haste.

"Maybe he's looking to make up for lost time," Ober remarked dryly as the mounted dwarves filed through the grinding doors.

"Maybe, but that's not our concern," Haeda stated in a tone that brooked no disagreement. "*Our* concern is getting something big and hairy up the slope so when the wights show themselves, we can send them to meet their ancestors."

Ober frowned at the pair of reins offered to him.

"I think she means you, brother," Tomza offered as she took her blotferow's reins and brought the beast around to mount.

Ober scowled at the slavering pig, who looked at him with an expectant air.

"I would never have guessed," he grumbled as he gingerly turned the creature's head to mount it. "One beast riding another. I'm sure my ancestors are very proud."

Despite the tremble in his knees and the lurch in his stomach when he heaved himself onto the beast's back, Ober settled into the saddle situated just behind the swine's shoulders. He took a second to make sure he had the lay of the land. All the while, the blotferow stood dutifully.

"This isn't too bad," Ober murmured, feeling the power of the creature beneath him and the steadiness that assured him it would move only at his direction. "You don't seem so bad now. That might just be because I don't have to look at your face."

The blotferow remained noncommittal until Haeda mounted and, turning her beast to the open gate, beckoned.

"Don't forget to hold on," she called, then put her heel to the beast's side.

"Of course we're holding on, what do we look li...*AGH!*"

Whatever remained of Ober's complaint was swallowed in the scream that tore from his throat as his mount sprang after Haeda's steed with violent eagerness.

CHAPTER NINE

"That looks interesting."

All eyes swung to the svartalf who stood on the forecastle, then followed his keen gaze. The waters of Heimlagu were as black and glassy as ever and perfectly reflected the pale sky. A ribbon of black smoke curled and wound upward. The narrowed eyes of dwarf, man, and elf tracked the source of the ribbon to the top of a wrinkle in the mountainside. Beyond that bare glimpse, everything was hidden by the heavy shoulder of rock.

"Looks like a nasty spot o' fire," remarked the dwarf at the helm of the ship. "It's gotta burn hot and use nothin' so clean as wood to produce smoke that black."

The svartalf beside him pursed his lips and tapped a contemplative finger on them.

"Am I correct that the hump of rock ejecting that dark burst of polluted air houses Greyshelf?"

The dwarf's expression collapsed into contemplative creases, and the elf waited patiently. When he was certain that the dwarf had mentally imploded and he got ready to abandon all hope, the helmsdwarf clucked his tongue, then sucked air through his teeth.

"Aye, that would be it, I'm afraid," the dwarf declared, his hands shifting on the spoked wheel that directed the wooden leviathan. "Looks like the fortress isn't faring so well. Suppose we ought to bring her about and make for Heimgrud."

The elf didn't respond, just cocked one eyebrow as he continued to stare out over the mountain lake at the unraveling contrails. His red eyes had an intensity that defied anyone to interrupt the thoughts roiling beneath. However, interruption eventually came in the form of a lanky young human mounting the steps to the forecastle. Bright eyes shining with concern over an auburn mustache, he looked at elf and dwarf.

"Sir Utyrvaul, we need to get over there," the youth declared, jabbing a finger at the smoke. "If Greyshelf is under attack, we have to help."

The dwarf at the helm made a garbled noise, which drew the manling's attention.

"Captain Morb," the lad began, his formal tone unsullied by the dwarf's incredulous grunt. "Where can we land to disembark?"

Captain Morb's nose wrinkled, and he looked at Utyrvaul as though he were expecting the svartalf to attend to his charge. The elf continued to stare at the stony terrain from which the smoke emerged. Seeing no help coming from that quarter, the dwarf turned to the young man and spoke in a patronizing tone.

"Master Reeve, let's be reasonable," the dwarf intoned. "If you've got smoke rising from out of the back of Greyshelf, it means serious fighting. Your little band is not suited for such things. Now, I understand that you've got a connection with those poor souls holdin' the fort, though Shaper knows why, but I can't in good conscience bring you into danger like that."

Mabon Reeve made a sound in the back of his throat that Morb did not seem inclined to ignore.

"Captain, you were paid to deliver us, not to be our nanny," the human stated. One hand settled on his belt. The other motioned at the occupants of the deck. "These aren't simple manservants that Sir Utyrvaul Urivianoc brought along with him. These are warriors who could make a difference if there is fighting going on. You need to take us there *now*."

The captain, who was aware of the dangerous nature of the passengers on his vessel and had charged them accordingly, might have considered the human's words if not for that last sentence.

"Need?" The dwarf bristled, and several of the crew attended to their captain's rising tone. "Listen here, lad. No one, not elf, not dwarf, and certainly not a limp-whiskered longshanks, stands on my ship and tells me what I *need* to do. Do you hear me?"

The Reeve boy seemed ready to contest the point but rumbled agreements rose from the dwarves on deck. That gave him pause, but he refused to shy away from the dwarf's angry scowl. The lad had faced far more terrifying foes than Captain Morb of Clan Eaganger and lived, but he was wise enough to understand that setting himself at odds with the one who he needed something from was a categorically stupid decision. Instead, he turned his gaze to Utyrvaul, the elf who'd spared his life and become his mentor over the past few months.

Mabon still wasn't sure how it had happened, but this was no time for reflection.

The dwarf crew advanced toward the forecastle, and the svartalfs who'd been watching quietly rose. Elves and dwarves eyed one another, each taking what they hoped was an accurate measure. To even the casual observer, it was clear the svartalfs were better equipped and veteran killers, although the dwarves were more numerous and moved with an easy gait on a ship they knew like the backs of their weathered hands.

If things turned violent, it would be an ugly affair.

"Sir Utyrvaul?" Mabon pressed, holding back the instinct that would cause his hand to drift to his family's sword. "What do you say?"

The svartalf blinked and looked at Mabon, then at Morb as if he were confused about why they were staring at him. Manling's and dwarf's brows furrowed with consternation, then a sly smile spread across the svartalf's face, revealing the needle-sharp teeth for which his kind was notorious. His gaze swept to the dwarves and svartalfs squaring off on the deck.

"My, my! An elf can hardly pause to collect his thoughts without friends being at one another's throats. Are we really that eager to start a scuffle that will send blood into the water and see us troubled by the *morgwynoch*, or sumplings, as you dwarves so quaintly call them? I'm not certain that is of particular interest to me, but I suppose we each have our own agendas that need pursuing."

At the mention of the things that lived in the dark depths of the lake, neither elves nor dwarves seemed as keen to engage, though dwarvish scowls still met cold stares.

"Perhaps we should all take a breath," Captain Morb advised, though the sidelong look he gave Mabon suggested he hadn't internalized his message as much as his words suggested. "The fact is that you booked passage to take you to the docks by the Lake Gate, and when we set out, I had every intention of doing so. However, that smoke changes things. Now, you were good customers heading to Heimgrud, and you've been good customers up until now, so I'll try not to hold hasty words against anyone. There's no point in bringing my ship to Greyshelf when the place is liable to be overrun by the time we get there."

Mabon choked back a cry after a look from Utyrvaul quieted him. Morb couldn't hide an ugly grin at seeing the manling silenced, but the jeering expression didn't stick around for long.

The svartalf turned to the dwarf. "I'm afraid that simply will not do, Captain." The elf delivered the words lightly but with a hint of steel behind them. The pointed teeth flashed. "You see, we paid for passage—to the point of extortion, mind you—to deliver us to Greyshelf. You were aware of the ongoing siege, and you should have accounted for the risk in your considerably inflated fares. Since keeping one's word to the letter is valued amongst both our peoples, I insist that you refund the money to us. We will then part ways amicably and immediately."

Morb had dealt with enough svartalfs in his day to sneer at the suggestion that Utyrvaul's people valued their word, but the suggested resolution was peculiar enough that it captured his attention.

"You're suggesting that I give you your money back," the dwarf began, morbid curiosity softening his gruff tone. "Then you all just *swim* to the shore?"

Every eye turned to the svartalf, incredulity or concern etching the faces of man, dwarves, and elves.

"I don't see any other alternative, do you?" Utyrvaul sighed as though this was very regrettable yet inevitable. "We must go and assist our good friends in the Sufstan Holt'Dwan, and we certainly can't allow you to be known as an oath breaker by taking our money and not delivering us where we requested. If you'd please go fetch the fees from your strongbox forthwith, we'll get this done."

The dwarf captain looked around as though he expected a sign that the elf was telling a joke. The grim looks on the face of the manling and the other svartalfs faces did not support his faltering hope.

"Yer a nutter!" Morb guffawed in a tone that suggested anything but good humor. "You get in that water, and you're all as good as dead."

"Needs must." Utyrvaul shrugged before dusting off one sleeve of his armored coat. "I think you'll be surprised to find that, unlike the average dwarf, we are all accomplished swimmers."

After another grating, mirthless laugh, the dwarf sneered at the elf. "Accomplished swimmers, my arse. You don't know the first thing about this lake, do you?"

"Do tell?" Utyrvaul muttered, eyes rolling as he slouched on one hip.

"Where do you start?" the dwarf captain mused. "This water's colder than ice, and only the minerals in it keep it from freezin' over. Even at the start of summer, you'd be lucky to take more than a handful of strokes before the cold got you, but now you'll be dead before you feel wet."

"Cold as all that, really?" the svartalf droned, stifling a yawn. "Sounds rather dreadful."

"I'm just gettin' started," Morb spluttered, a hand coming off the helm to alternate between gesticulating at the elf and pointing at the black water. "Assuming you don't die in the cold in hardly a heartbeat, you'll flounder around as your limbs lock up, and that'll bring the sumplings. Here in the depths of winter, they're especially hungry, and they'll come up quick. Not just the little ones, but big brutes, the likes of which could split this ship in two if they knew we was here."

"How disagreeable," the elf remarked, eyes unfocused and chin idly resting on one hand.

"Disagreeable? It's suicide!" the dwarf captain railed. "You see that if I let you just jump off my ship—"

"After returning our fees, of course," Utyrvaul reminded him helpfully, still gazing into the middle distance.

"Right," Morb continued through gritted teeth. "If I let you and your money just jump off my ship, you're all going to die, either sunk to the bottom of this black Shaper-damned lake to be picked over by blind crabs, or you'll draw the sumplings and be gobbled up, probably along with me and my crew! You understand all of that?"

"Perfectly!" The svartalf chortled merrily before snapping his gaze to Morb with lethal intensity. "Now, are you going to bring us to the dock, or do I have to go get that strongbox myself?"

Captain Morb of Clan Eaganger surrendered to apoplectic shock for another spell that felt agonizingly long to the quicksilver mind of the svartalf, but the answer finally came.

"We should arrive at the dock shortly, sir."

Utyrvaul nodded and turned to Mabon.

"My dearest midge, would you be so kind as to gather our escortee? We shall be disembarking shortly."

CHAPTER TEN

"You going to make it, mad lad?"

The question was almost torn out of the air by the winds funneled between the ridged fingers of the mountain. Waelon, who'd been battered worse by the buffeting of the griffin, sucked in a breath to reply but decided he'd use it to keep moving.

Since they'd signaled the forces at the Lake Gate, the pace to bring the flanking forces to bear had been punishing. The rangers could move across the terrain more freely than the vanguard of swine riders, but the greater speed of the cavalry and the impetuous nature of their commander meant the Rangers were hard-pressed to stay ahead so they could act as both forward scouts and pathfinders. They would hardly clear an area and mark the trail for the riders than they'd hear the pulsing thunder of the beasts' oncoming hooves.

At first, Waelon had kept at the head of the rangers, but his breathing was more labored than expected. He'd attributed it to the air and the elevation, but as he went on, the pain stitching his spine confirmed that when the griffin had sent him tumbling, it had managed to bugger something in his back with the buffeting of its heavy wings. The rough stone he'd rolled across hadn't helped either.

The big dwarf had muscled through the worst of it, but as the dwarvish vanguard pressed them, it was all he could do to keep pace. He'd dropped back to the tail of the formation. They were closing on the concealing crag from which the smoke still billowed, though it was thinner than before. Waelon wasn't certain he'd make it within sight of the place.

His breath wheezed in and out in a way that grated on his ears, and no matter how he willed his legs to move faster, he couldn't seem to gain speed. Every time he looked up from beneath his sweaty brows, he saw that the others were sliding farther ahead. He decided the effort of raising his head wasn't worth the return of getting to see his continued failure.

As a result, when Clahdi appeared at his side after shouting from the head of the rangers, Waelon jumped, or he would have if he'd had the strength to do so. As it was, he only managed a surprised grunt that set half-frozen beads of sweat flying from his mustache.

"A pleasure as always," the spry dwarfess remarked as she brushed the spatter from her cloak, easily keeping pace with him. "Not to tell you your business, but you don't look so good."

Waelon tried to turn to look at her, but the twisting movement sent a punishing lance of pain through him. "Thanks," he managed between gritted teeth as he bent his entire will to remaining upright and mobile.

Clahdi studied him for a moment, then seemed to come to some conclusion as she reached into a kit that was slung across her back. She produced a long-handled axe that he'd noticed that all the other rangers also had strapped to their packs or in their hands. It looked stout, though the end tapered before rounding out to a slight bulge at the bottom that was capped in boiled leather.

The head had no upswept horn to the blade, and the back

spike had more in common with a small mining pick than the killing point of a weapon. Waelon could tell it was as much a tool as a weapon, though he imagined that with a stout wielder, the lopsided smile of the axe blade could be used to deadly effect.

"Take this and lean on it," the dwarfess instructed, holding out the axe. "It'll help a little until we stop and get your back looked at."

Waelon felt a stab of pride stronger than the pain and shoved the proffered axe away. "I don't need a cane," he growled, but it was a wet labored sound, and he'd never sounded more decrepit. "I'm fine."

He wasn't sure what he expected in response to his refusal, but Clahdi just checked him with the axe handle. He realized he hadn't expected that. The force of the blow sent him lurching to one side, feet tangling as he struggled to catch himself. He fell, not hard, his hands and knees sinking into a drift of snow he hadn't noticed until it embraced him with a cool softness. Despite that, Waelon couldn't keep a cry of pain from slipping between his lips as his efforts played havoc with his back.

In the end, he lay in the snow, thankful for its numbing touch on his steaming flesh and throbbing back, but he still found the energy to glare furiously at Clahdi. He sucked air in and out through his bared teeth, but he couldn't get enough to curse her as he longed to. He promised himself he would work toward it.

"You..." he managed to force between his clenched teeth, but even that was too taxing. He sank into the snow to gather strength for the next word.

"You want to finish that thought? I'll be up front," Clahdi observed coolly, then pitched the long-handled axe down next to him in the snow. "Come and find me when you're done being a fool."

With that, she turned and trotted off to catch up with the other rangers.

A stream of invective ran through the big dwarf's mind as he watched her go, but as air wheezed in and out of him, he knew he didn't have the breath to voice a word of it. He lay there for a few moments, then looked up and saw that it wouldn't be long before he lost track of the rangers. He knew where they were going and wasn't particularly worried about any threat to himself despite being left alone, but the shame of not being there to aid the vanguard when they finally came to grips with the enemy galled him.

His eyes fell on the long-handled axe.

Berating himself and fighting back sobs of pain, he stretched out a hand and seized the weapon/tool. Mentally cursing Clahdi with every stab of pain, he began to gather himself around the support as he drove it into the ground. Teeth grinding until he was certain his jaw would break, he pushed himself upward, leaning heavily on the stout haft. To his surprise, it was easier than he expected. As he pressed hard to straighten, he felt several things in his back pop and click in ways that weren't entirely unpleasant.

His gaze settled on the retreating backs of the rangers, and suddenly, with his walking axe and the new vertebral alignments, the distance didn't seem as daunting.

"She's going to be insufferable after this," Waelon mumbled as he set out, staff thumping on stone. "Absolutely the worst."

For a time, he didn't gain on the rangers as they roved ahead of him, but he didn't see their forms shrinking either, which was more than he could have hoped for before. A fresh sheen of sweat drenched the big dwarf, melting that which had frosted over on his flesh, but Waelon welcomed it since the flow came from effort rather than the pain of his tortured back. He still wasn't sure if he'd be of use in the vanguard's efforts, but damn it, he'd get there.

Just one rise before reaching the origin of the now-ephemeral sooty vapor, the rangers slowed, creeping along with carefully measured steps. Waelon realized they'd made contact with an enemy position but hadn't yet been noticed. Understanding that he needed to be careful, he put on as much speed as he dared to close the distance before adopting the cautious and quiet efforts of the other rangers.

It took a few more minutes, but he was able to close the distance. The dwarves had taken up positions amidst a stand of shrunken, scraggly plants that might have been the uglier inbred cousins of spruce and pine. The gnarled and anemic trees clung to the rocks in fitful patches along the slope, which began its descent toward a bowl-like depression cupped between two sweeping extrusions of the mountain. Without the smoke, even veteran Rangers could pass on either side of the sunken location and have no idea it was there.

When Waelon drew level with the rangers, he could see swaying masses of clackers huddling about the wrinkle in the face of the mountain. The seam must have run down to a cleft in which the passage into Greyshelf was, but the ranks of unliving soldiers made it hard to see.

Despite the number of armed dead men, the eyes of the rangers were not fixed on them. Following the dwarvish gazes between the trees, he saw the point where the rocky tendrils of the mountain didn't quite meet, creating a narrow defile into the basin in which the wight's forces stood. Arrayed about this natural chokepoint were teams of humans in rugged furs. Some stood on the path into the basin, spears at their shoulders and ropes in their hands. It took Waelon a moment of squinting beside the other rangers to see that the ropes were attached to lines of sharpened stakes, and their leads ran to iron posts driven into the rock.

In elevated positions just beyond those stood more humans armed with longbows, whose hefty draw and heavy arrows would put even dwarvish armor to the test. It was clear that if there was a flanking attack such as the one the dwarves intended to launch, the humans would haul on the ropes to raise the stakes, then tie the ropes to the posts, creating a crude barricade.

Those on the ground would move behind the barricade, fending off attackers with spears while their comrades above loosed shots into the milling and frustrated ranks of the enemy.

It wouldn't keep out a determined enemy indefinitely, but it wasn't meant to, only to buy enough time for the wight's forces to engage their would-be ambushers.

"This needs clearing," Waelon murmured. Grunts and profanity-laden acknowledgments confirmed the patrol's agreement.

"Glad you caught up," Clahdi called from farther down the line of rangers. "How are we playing this, Fordwan?"

Waelon considered the question, then cocked his head to one side as he heard a distant rumble. A heartbeat later, the humans atop the jutting rocks and on the ground noticed the sound, and shouts rose from them. Everyone prepared for the oncoming enemy. No sooner did that happen than Waelon saw a pair of runners break off and make for the basin.

Waelon realized they needed to act quickly, or things would take a turn for the worse. "Clahdi, I don't want those two to get within shouting distance of their wheezers," the big dwarf instructed, his mind still racing to form a plan. "See to it."

"Yes, sir," Clahdi declared, saluting but tossing in a wink as she darted off.

Waelon had a half-formed thought about her not being able to outmaneuver the longshanks, but then he watched her bound across the slope between the trees. He felt nothing but a twinge of pity for the humans. Those boys were dead. They just didn't know it yet.

Their comrades would join them soon.

"All right, we're dividing into three teams," Waelon growled, breath steaming from his mouth as he assessed the situation with icy calm. "Forwardmost team goes for the far barricade team hanging around the far spike. The middle team will fire on the archers on the far side until they reach a position to engage the other barricade team.

"The far team will fire at the nearest archers until the middle team engages their barricade team. Then just provide general support and suppressive salvos to the archer teams."

Waelon's eyes swept around the assembly of dwarves, and though he'd only met them a few short hours ago, he read each face easily as he'd read Gromic's or Haeda's. They understood not just the plan but what it would mean if they failed.

They were ready.

"What are we waiting for?" he growled, the sound shaking his chest. "Time for rangers to save the day again."

CHAPTER ELEVEN

"Just like old times," Gromic declared as he and Torbjorn fought shoulder to shoulder, their backs against stone amidst a sea of clackers.

The Shaper's Breath weapon, combined with their pressing advance, had torn great holes in the enemy's position, and for a time, they'd had the enemy on the back foot. Torbjorn hadn't ordered the advance so much as it had happened organically. As more forces from within Greyshelf pushed forward, the dwarves' battleline had widened and inched forward. Before he'd known it, they'd taken nearly half of the cavern, and their lanterns had illuminated a graven column in the center. He'd had no time to appreciate the profane artwork on the gleaming stone since no sooner had they pressed past the column than the enemy had redoubled their efforts.

Creaking, rustling bodies surged forward with only the snapping of teeth as their war cry. Cold points of light surged out of the deep shadows of the twilit chamber. Their movements were quicker, their blows swifter and harder, and the tide turned. The common dwans staggered back or fell, some with their stout helms cloven by the terrible strength in the dead men's clenched fists.

Those clad in Sablestone fared better, but they were forced to give ground, else they'd be surrounded and driven to the stone by the sheer number of blows. If they were thrown down, the Guard understood it was only a matter of time before the clackers managed to find a seam, or they'd simply asphyxiate beneath the smothering tide.

Step by bloody step, they'd given ground. However, Gromic's and Torbjorn's steps had brought them back to the central stone column. No sooner had the pair discovered that than the clackers came on like a chattering wave lapping around them.

Yes, Torbjorn thought, unable to keep a cold smile from spreading across his face. *This does feel like old times.*

Such reflections were driven out of his mind as he had to fend off an onrush of attackers. At this point, he was beyond trying to match each opponent and make measured attempts at attack and defense. He fended off blows as they came into his awareness, batting them away without thought of where they came from or where they went. When an opportunity to strike presented itself, he would thrust or hack or smash—whatever could be done before the next round of blows came whistling at him.

Gromic shouted as he shoved from behind his shoulder, "You think they know they left us behind?"

Torbjorn hacked through one bony face, then tore his weapon free to thrust the front spike through the leather harness and crack the breastbone.

"You think they care?" the dwarf commander replied. His mind told him that was not the thing to keep their spirits up, but then he heard Gromic's deep, booming laugh.

"Suppose not." The stout dwarf guffawed as he hewed the legs out from under one walking corpse and then another. "Poor sods don't know what a good time they're missing."

Yes, my good fordwan, this is exactly like old times, and if this is how it ends, I can't say I'll be disappointed.

"Well, Gromic," Torbjorn called as he took a ringing blow on his shoulder, only to powder the skull of his attacker with a backswing. "Can't say I mind so long as you're here to share this good time with me."

A spear shattered on Gromic's armored belly, eliciting a grunt from the broad dwarf before he splintered the shinbones of the attacker with a stomp.

"Wouldn't have it any other way, Tweldwan."

The unliving kept coming.

Torbjorn and Gromic threw them back, often in pieces, but for each clacker that fell, two advanced.

Torbjorn threw himself into a sweeping swing that saw several dead men topple backward, giving him a few seconds of breathing room. He slumped against the stone column, and some of the finer details of the blasphemous art crumbled beneath his armored bulk.

His shoulders burned, and the assistance granted by the Sablestone armor wasn't enough to keep his arms from feeling leaden. More blows were slipping past his guard, though they skittered off the implacable stone plates. He was almost certain he was deaf from the sound of the blows clanging off his armor since the world seemed duller.

Gromic's weight slammed against him, and it was all he could do to stay upright by leaning hard on his *cwellocs*. The fordwan managed to fend off his attacker with a series of savage strikes with his magsax, but Torbjorn noted that the dwarf didn't give chase.

The bright, unfathomable lights within the unliving faces swirled around the dwans as they leaned upon one another. Torbjorn tightened his grip with his wooden hand, the only part of him that was immune to the exhaustion that threatened to collapse him.

I wonder how long it'll keep going after the rest of me dies? Torbjorn mused, a perverse smirk preceding a mad chuckle. *I hope it gives the wight fits when he can't find a way to stop it from trying to tear him to pieces.*

The unliving were a solid wall of death, shuffling closer to entomb the stubborn but exhausted dwarves.

"Well, Gromic," the ondwan grunted, marshaling what little strength remained to face the end standing upright. "Got anything to say worth remembering?"

Gromic's breathing boomed like a bellows, but eventually, he straightened too.

"I would have loved her well," the stout dwarf. "Would have loved her and made a life with her if things were different."

Ignoring the enemies coming to seal their fate, Torbjorn looked at the dwarf he'd known for almost as long as Klaus in bewilderment. He supposed he should have expected that a mountain-blooded dwarf like Gromic might have had an object for his affections, but by every oath before the Shaper, Torbjorn had never thought about it.

"Who in Grimmoth's Grin are you talking about?"

The unliving seemed to be taking their time, their jaws chattering in cruel taunts unheeded by either dwarf.

"Haeda, sir," the stout dwarf declared, managing to sound sheepish while shouting. "Loved her since the day I set eyes on her, and every day since that one, I've found ways to love her more."

Torbjorn had to shout over the clattering of jaws descending on them. "Does she know?"

Gromic took a heavy breath as he hefted his shield. "Don't think so, sir, and don't suppose she will."

Torbjorn's body was still burning, but he found that it wasn't just fatigue that surged in his muscles and churned in his bones.

"Grimmoth take that!" the dwarf commander bellowed, hefting his poleaxe. "You're going to live and tell her. Come on!"

As one, the two dwarves threw back their heads and roared, then leaped back into the fray.

"*BAD BADGERS!*"

The bony faces were ill-suited to expressing surprise, yet Torbjorn could've sworn those clacking jaws hung open in shock as the pair crashed into them, hacking left and right. He knew they couldn't win. Knew this burst of furious energy would be spent before they could make anything like a dent in the enemy numbers. However, it felt good to swing his weapon with abandon.

Just give me one more, he begged after each foe fell, though whether he spoke to the Shaper, the Wyrd, or his own failing body, he couldn't say. *Just one more.*

His *cwellocs* rose and fell, stretched out and swept back, time and again, until he realized with a start that there were no more enemies within reach. The dead were still around him, but their attention had been claimed by fresh enemies.

Torbjorn blinked through sweat and what might have been tears to see that, like two gilded black pincers, the Sablestone Guard had driven in from either side of the column to engage the enemy. In their wake came the dwan infantry, shields interlocked as their duabows menaced from across the rim.

"*Gefarer!*" came the old dwarvish shout signaling the attack, and dozens of duabows spoke as one. The dead toppled to the floor, so thick that when Sablestone boots descended, there was a storm of cracks as bones snapped.

The enemy was pressing back upon their ranks, crumbling before sinking back to repeat the process. The Sablestone Guard formed a hardened wall about their ondwan and his fordwan, allowing them a moment to unclasp their helms and slurp sips of water. On either side of the Guard, dwans pumped bolts into the reeling enemy.

Torbjorn stood for a moment, letting his breath slide in and out, watching the runnels of sweat dribbling off his nose, beard, and hair as he let his head hang. Then, with a groan of effort, he raised his head and grinned at Gromic.

"Haeda, eh?"

Gromic, who'd been sucking on his waterskin like a runt who finally got the front tit, looked away, staring longingly at the shrinking mass of foes.

"I'd rather we forget that, Tweldwan."

"Not on your life." Torbjorn chuckled, chest aching as the sound sawed its way out of him. "When this is over, you're going to tell her the truth."

For perhaps the first time in his life, Gromic balked at the instructions of his commander and friend, head wagging from side to side.

"No, sir, please," he began, looking paler and more terrified than any other time he'd faced certain death. Given what the two of them had been through together, Torbjorn knew exactly how frequently that had been.

"Fordwan Gromic of Clan Dwynkoth," Torbjorn intoned, drawing the blue eyes of the stout dwarf. "That's an order."

Gromic's body quivered. He was a dwarf at war with himself, but little by little, he mastered the trembling. With a last sigh, Gromic nodded, admitting surrender.

"Yes, my Tweldwan," he intoned, his face pale and his eyes watering.

Torbjorn grinned at him. "Hohoho, don't look at me like that." The ondwan clapped a gauntleted hand to his fordwan's shoulder. "It's not that scary. After all, you've gone toe to toe with skinchangers, demons, and wights and always come out on top."

Gromic's nose crinkled at the description, but after a pregnant pause, he thought better of correcting his commander's evaluation of the situation.

"I'd prefer the wights, sir."

As though summoned by his words, the air in the cavern chilled the skin and breath steamed. Torbjorn's mind and senses rebelled against what he knew that heralded, even as mechanical instincts driven into this meat and bones had him slamming his helm into place.

"Looks like you're getting your wish," he growled, working the clasps with a speed that defied the dread trying to seize his heart and stiffen his limbs. "Though I'll say that if we were going to wish for things, I'd prefer you conjure up something a little friendlier next time."

Gromic had replaced his helmet, so he nodded at his commander with a grim faceplate instead of his honest features.

"Noted, sir," Gromic replied, and then his gaze swung to the enemy's ranks. "At least we won't have to wait around."

Torbjorn followed Gromic's gaze and saw the lines of clackers part to allow a towering figure to pass. Towering a head and a half over the tallest of his unliving servants, the wight loomed over all within the chamber like a dark tower. From within its helm shone a pair of glowing points that were brighter, colder, and more piercing than the sockets of his servants. The dark, desiccated flesh around those eyes made it seem as though they looked across a vast and terrible gulf of space. An alien will piercing time and space.

Torbjorn thought that given what they'd learned about the wights and their origins, perhaps it wasn't a stretch to believe.

"Where is she?"

The wheezing voice sent a tremble down Torbjorn's spine, but he compelled his weary body to obey. He stepped to the front and center of the line of Guards, *cwellocs* in hand like a staff of office.

"Don't know who you're talking about," Torbjorn lied as jauntily as he dared. He fought not to flinch when the bright eyes flared before assuming their previous gleam.

"Liar," it hissed. "She entered this mountain, sealing her away from us, but I can feel her close."

Torbjorn allowed himself a small smile at this declaration.

Despite their claims of godlike omniscience, this wight was out of his element. The ondwan had wisely, if nervously, sent the child with the golden eyes, the object of every wight's desire, across Heimlagu to be sheltered at Heimgrud until arrangements could be made to transport her to Torvgrud and possibly beyond.

The effort was not just to protect the girl or thwart the wights but also to placate the savagelings, who swore by a prophecy about the child bringing about an apocalypse if she were to fall into the hands of the wights.

For the first time in his encounters with the wheezers, the dwarf commander had the insufferable monsters at a disadvantage.

"Well, then you're as stupid as you are ugly," Torbjorn shot back. "All we've got here in this mountain are dwarves of every stripe and shape, looking to plant dwarvish steel in your skull and dwarvish iron up your back shaft."

The wight scowled at the dwarf, glowing gaze sweeping over and through him. Torbjorn bore it, but a shiver crept up his spine and had him gripping his cwellocs to keep his arm from quivering.

"No," the wheezer whispered. "No. Something has changed."

"A lot has changed since you took a nap, wheezer," Torbjorn pressed, wondering if his hastily laid plans were now coming to fruition or falling apart. Surely the forces he'd deployed would move into position soon? Had he been foolish in wading into this fight without the one sure way he knew to kill a wight?

"No! Not here, but..."

The lingering word sent panic racing through Torbjorn. But what? The girl should be on her way to Torvgrud if she wasn't there already. But *what*?

The gleaming eyes flashed, and the wight turned away, then swept through the unliving ranks the way he'd come.

"Yes. Close."

Torbjorn knew that wasn't possible, yet as he watched the

wight retreat, he felt a spike of dread in his gut. Could it be? How? What had happened? Why?

Voice rising ahead of his conscious mind, he loosed a bellow, issuing a command through presence alone—a command that required no words to be understood.

The Sablestone Guard fell in behind him, and the dwans flanking them launched a savage salvo. Torbjorn charged into the ranks of the unliving in a desperate attempt to prevent something he knew wasn't possible.

CHAPTER TWELVE

"Are we there yet?"

This was not the first or even the fifth time Ober had asked his desperate question as they made their way up the mountain. Clinging to the humped, heaving shoulders of the blotferow, the young dwarf looked more like an overgrown hairy-faced tick than a rider.

Amusement rocked Haeda and Tomza as their mounts trotted in the wake of the cavalry vanguard, but as they drew close to the enemy position, they got busy looking for signs of the enemy.

Up ahead, the skirling war pipes of the vanguard sliced through the tumult that filled the mountain air.

"What does that mean?" Tomza called to Haeda, attempting to rise in her saddle for a better view.

"Not sure," Haeda admitted, thankful to find that much of her work with worcsvines was transferable to blotferows. She pulled on the reins and the mount readily responded, adjusting its course to clamber up a spur of stone until she saw what lay ahead of the surging line of cavalry. Squinting through the stinging wind, she called back, "We're moving into a little valley and—"

Her words caught in her throat as she glimpsed a flurry of

motion just ahead of the vanguard. It was hard to see, but it looked like a series of barriers were going up, spurs of sharpened wood rising like a hedge of spears held together by thick ropes. The quavering line of wooden points seemed flimsy, and it would disintegrate quickly on contact with the forward ranks of the dwarvish cavalry, but by then, the damage would be done. The impaled and tangled line of the foremost riders would snarl up those charging behind, and the full weight of the rest of the vanguard crashing in would inflict more damage and chaos than the stakes.

More important than the damage to the mounts and riders was the delay. The cavalry forces would be lucky to reorganize and reform their lines by the time the infantry arrived, and by then, the enemy would be able to engage them at the choke point or execute a retreat. Either way, what would have been a resounding blow for the Holt'Dwan would be blunted at a huge cost to lives, morale, and time.

"Haeda," Tomza called to the other dwarfess. "What's going on?"

"There's…" The driver struggled to reply, unsure of how to convey the disaster that was unfolding before her eyes. Her gorge rose and her heart hammered in her ears as the distance between the front line of riders and the sudden barricade decreased. The riders didn't slow. Couldn't slow. Haeda told herself she should look away before the final impact to spare herself the sight of the carnage coming for both dwarves and faithful beasts.

"Haeda!" Tomza shouted, and hooves scrabbled up the slope.

The older dwarfess felt an irrational twinge of irritation for her compatriot. Couldn't she tell Haeda was witnessing a tragedy? Suddenly, the small figures milling about the barricades twisted and began to tumble. The driver squinted over the rough, snow-covered slope and watched as more of the figures fell and shorter, broader forms rushed across the space. From both shoulders of the narrow pass, people she hadn't noticed until they tumbled and fell, stricken by barely perceived missiles zipping through the air.

"The rangers!" Haeda crowed. "Waelon, you beautiful bastard!"

"What's going on?" Tomza asked, appearing a few boar's lengths downslope from Haeda. "What about Waelon?"

"There! Look!" Haeda shouted, pointing at the dwarvish rangers slashing the ropes of the barricade. "No minute like the last minute, but there they are!"

As Tomza followed her finger, the barricade gave a final quiver and came down. War pipes skirled a warning to the surging ranks, and riders expertly vaulted over the downed barrier and rode into the sunken valley.

"That was close," Tomza muttered, shaking her head as she struggled to come to grips with what had nearly happened. "I can't tell you how badly that might've gone."

"I could," Haeda growled, and she shivered, though she wasn't cold. "It looks like Waelon and his lot sorted it so that grempucker Yorm will be useful for once. He's got a clean run to ram his armored pigs into the clackers' back door."

They heard another swine laboring up the rough hillock, but the porcine chuffs and snuffles were nothing compared to the wheezing of the rider. Tomza and Haeda looked over their shoulders to see a trembling, panting Ober lolling in the saddle.

"What happened?" he croaked, lurching forward as his mount came to a stop just behind the other two blotferows. "Who's a bastard?"

Haeda and Tomza shared a look before rolling their eyes. Then a rending crash drew their attention back to the unfolding battle. The dwarven cavalry had made contact with the main enemy position, and as hoped and expected, the result was utter devastation.

Hurtling comets of armored pig flesh festooned with iron-shod tusks smashed through the unliving's ranks, crushing and ripping, while on their backs, dwarvish riders splintered lances in impaling strikes before sweeping their axes and hammers. The devastation was absolute as the first several ranks of clackers vanished under the onslaught.

"Let's hope he doesn't overplay his hand," Haeda growled as she watched the lines of dead men condense and thicken. "Don't mess this up, Yorm."

The driver need not have worried. To his credit, Dogordwan Yorm saw that his force wasn't sufficient to ride through the enemy to the face of the mountain and return. The cries of the war pipes echoed through the valley, and the three dwarves watched as the riders used the last of their momentum to cut laterally through the enemy ranks. The maneuver sheared off a stubborn portion of the enemy who'd managed to muster something resembling a cohesive resistance and allowed the cavalry cohort to trample them as the riders withdrew. In the space of a few heartbeats, the cavalry vanguard crushed several ranks and carved off a few more and were now cleanly extracting themselves.

Haeda wasn't sure she'd ever seen it done better, and she gave a low whistle. Yorm might have been a bloodthirsty, self-serving bully, but the dwarf was a dogordwan worthy of the name.

"A dirty dwan is still a dwan," she reminded herself quietly. "Can't take that from him."

"What was that?" Ober asked, squirming to tend to the parts of him tenderized by the ride.

"Nothing," the driver replied, then shook her head and looked past Ober at the first ranks of the infantry forces that were trudging up. "Best get a move on, or we're going to be next to useless in the show."

After a quick kick, Haeda let her mount to pick its way down the hillock toward the gaping mouth of the bowl-like depression. Tomza nodded and followed, looking less sure as she thumped her mount's sides. True to Haeda's promises, the beast knew its business.

"What are you talking about?" Ober demanded from behind, not putting his heels to his snuffling mount. "We're vital lookouts. There's no need to go bouncing about anymore, is there?"

Tomza looked at her brother. "You can stay up here, brother," she offered. "I'm sure that when we pass Waelon down there, he'll understand that you wanted to stay up here and keep watch."

Ober imagined facing the big dwarf's scowl and gulped reflexively. Intellectually, Ober knew that, given his condition, he shouldn't be afraid of any mortal creature or most more-than-mortal creatures. However, the grim intensity of the sour redheaded dwarf's face was enough to make him want to duck and scurry away. It was like the worst of paternal disappointment and filial disapproval bound up in a smoldering frown that felt like the searing heat of iron from the forge.

"Oh, bugger that." The young dwarf spat and angrily drove his heel into his mount's flank. In response, the swine gave an exuberant squeal and lunged forward to join its fellows, nearly pitching Ober off his perch.

"Shaper take me!"

"How do you always manage to get yourself all battered like this?"

Waelon couldn't answer the question since the young ascedwan drove her palm into his spine. Tears welled in his eyes, and it was all he could do to keep from snarling curses.

"He makes a habit of this?" asked the sharp-faced and bright-eyed ranger they'd heard Waelon call Clahdi.

They'd taken up a position just inside the valley, sheltered by one of the rocky shoulders. Beyond them, the dwarvish cavalry was still making wheeling charges at the edges of the clacker formations. The main body of infantry had filtered in and taken an offset position to the ranks of dead. The tweldwan who was in charge of the block of dwarvish infantry had cleverly set it up so they could pour duabow salvos into the enemy position while allowing lines for the cavalry to retreat, taunting the unliving to pursue. When that happened, the lines of infantry squeezed the attackers and wiped them out. It was a tried and true method of fighting the clackers, used to good effect judging by the number of leathery corpses littering the valley floor.

The only remaining question was when the wight would emerge and order a real counterattack or a forced retreat. That, unknown to the rangers except for Waelon, was precisely what young Ober and his companions were waiting for.

"Let me guess," Haeda began from atop her blotferow, reins in hands. "He did some fool heroic thing that managed to be very impressive and almost get him killed, and now he's been limping around, whining about how he hurt himself."

"I ain't been whining!" Waelon snarled, finding enough breath and will to loose his venom at the driver. "Pig-loving harridan."

"Ha. That pretty much sums it up." The other ranger chuckled. He glared at her. "Though, to be fair, the griffin was a big one."

"Griffin?" Ober asked. He squatted to work out the aches in his thighs and buttocks. "Where'd you see a griffin?"

"We didn't just see a griffin," Clahdi corrected. "We killed it. Put enough bolts in it to take down near a cohort. It's dead and we're not, so I'm not complaining. Hero over here used himself as bait and then put a bolt through the thing's eye."

Ober and Tomza looked at Waelon with wonder and bemusement. Haeda just shook her head.

"That's nothing," the driver declared. "I once watched this fool clamber up the back of a swamp wurm in the Wallow with nothing but an axe in one hand and his trousers in the other. Wouldn't you know it, he put the thing down even though the beast was near on thirty feet long."

With everyone's attention diverted by Haeda's story, Tomza pricked her thumb and pressed it against Waelon's back with a hissed incantation. The resulting grinding, sucking, and popping noises were stomach-turning, and Waelon gave a tight yelp, but after staggering forward a few steps, he realized he had done so without pain or the need to hunch to one side.

For a heartbeat, he looked at the healer in confusion. Understanding flickered across his features with the barest nod from Tomza.

"Finished?" he asked, assuming his usual sour expression. "Or you not done playin' yet?"

"That'll do it," the young dwarfess declared, covering her bloody thumb. "A thirty-foot swamp dragon bare-cheeked, eh?"

"Not wyrm, wurm," Waelon explained, adjusting his tunic and gambeson. "Nasty things. More like bony-plated maggots in the Waellafens, but it weren't no thirty-footer. More like ten."

Haeda spat. "It was thirty feet if it was an inch."

"Who killed it?" the ranger asked, hoisting his mail off the low boulder he'd set it on.

"I'm not concerned with ten or thirty. I'm wonderin' why you were naked," Clahdi remarked with a quizzical eyebrow waggle. Ober started to express his interest in the subject as well, but he caught the big dwarf's eyes, and one scowl shut his mouth.

"Not much to tell, really," Waelon grumbled as he fiddled and flicked the mail, trying to wrestle it into place. "I was going to take a kak in the bog, and the damned wurm decided I was showing off me goods as an invitation to dinner. I tried to fight and ended up tumblin' balls over brains, so I just decided to yank 'em off and sort the maggot out first."

Amused and bemused expressions greeted Waelon wherever he looked, with chuckles and mutters of "mad lad" from the other rangers.

"You kept hold of them on account of not wanting to lose

them in the mud, then?" Ober offered gingerly. He was relieved when the big dwarf nodded gravely.

"Aye," Waelon agreed, finally shrugging into the mail. "They were a good pair with only a few patches all told."

"Couldn't let the wurm cost you such a fine article of clothing, I'm sure." Clahdi chortled as she helped the red-haired dwarf get his armor situated and the back laces tied. The look Tomza and Haeda exchanged might've made Waelon spit one of his more inventive curses, but he was trying not to blush at the dwarfess' touch.

"Don't want to be wandering around with your dang…uh, that is, being indecent," Waelon coughed sheepishly. He had lost the battle to stave off the flush in his cheeks.

"I don't know," Clahdi cooed in his ear as she stepped around him. "Might have been a fine sight to see."

Before Waelon could respond, the ranger joined the rest of her patrol as they pretended to keep watch for stragglers while listening to the banter. The big dwarf was left staring after the light-footed ranger, his mouth hanging open.

Tomza and Haeda rolled their eyes and stifled chuckles as the oblivious Ober sidled up to Waelon. When he spoke, the proximity of his voice made the fiery dwarf jump.

"What do you think drew the wurm?" the younger dwarf asked, his face creased in a curious frown. "Your bare bum or the kak?"

"What? I don't know!" Waelon barked, then shoved the young dwarf away from him. "Who knows, and who cares? Get away from me!"

Ober staggered back, looking wounded. A sharp whistle went up from the rangers.

"Look alive," one growled, and more than one dwarvish finger stabbed across the snowy bowl. "The wheezer's making his appearance."

Every eye swung toward the battlefield and converged on a knot of open space around a looming figure.

"Why are they always so much bigger?" Clahdi mused, unable to keep the dread out of her voice.

"Don't know." Waelon came over and stood at her side. "Makes it easier to know what you're aiming at."

The crowds of clackers parted like reeds before a river barge as the wight moved toward the front line. Even from this distance, every dwarf felt as though the air got more frigid each time the looming figure's gaze swept toward them. A brooding alien intelligence emanated from the towering being as it surveyed its lifeless servants.

"Does no good to shoot 'em," one ranger muttered. "Thing's just too powerful to die."

The shabr'dwans felt a not-so-subtle shift in the rangers around them. Hands tightened on the hafts of their long axes or duabow stocks, and eyes looked at the battlefield but didn't see the conflict of this day playing out before them.

"They say baelgeld artillery can kill 'em, but I don't believe it," another ranger whispered. "Watched one of 'em take a shot from a long-hurler, runes burning on the stone like they were written in fire. Struck the wheezer square in the chest with a flash of light like a new sun, and it just rocked on its heels for a second before laughing in that damn cold voice, then went back to butchering. A hurl like that could have caved in half of any keep's thickest wall, and the thing shrugged it off like it was nothin'."

The rangers paid rapt attention as the wight raised a huge mace that crackled with pale blue fire.

"Whole campaign's been doomed from the beginning." Clahdi sighed, and a hard, bitter sheen coated her green eyes. "Armies and fortresses are just decorations for the real fight we ain't goin' to win. How do you kill gods of death?"

Bolts dropped around the wight and clackers fell, but if any struck the chanting wight, there was no sign. The slush-speckled stone in front of the deathless commander twitched and rippled as the cold flames shrouding the mace spread over the wight's frame.

"What a bunch of kak," Haeda spat, and for the first time since the wight was spotted, dwarvish eyes left the terrible sight.

"W-what?" one of the rangers stammered.

"They're not invincible, and sure as my arse is fine, they aren't gods," the driver replied with a sharp throw of her hip to one side. "Don't know about all yer stories, but the Bad Badgers have seen three of 'em put down, never to get back up."

The incredulous looks among the rangers might have been comical if not for the fear and fragile hope there.

"Go on, tell another one." The eldest rangers scoffed, and several of his fellows snorted in agreement.

"She's not lying," Waelon cut in, his dark gaze challenging each dwarf to meet it squarely. "My brother gave his life to put one of 'em down." The big dwarf's words carried enough weight to turn back the worst of the scowling suspicion, but it was replaced by an insistent, almost feverish curiosity.

"How? How did you do it?" several demanded at once.

Under their scrutiny, Haeda and Waelon balked, looking at each other. "Well, the first was a trial and error sort of thing," Haeda began, shoulder bunching in a helpless shrug. "We lured it into a fight, and then we, well…"

"Dropped a burning building on it," Waelon finished. "Didn't hurt that it was full of flaming liquor. Also meant my brother got to go out like a dwan, surrounded by everything he loved."

The rangers gave appreciative nods and grim chuckles, then cast fretful looks at the wight. As they spoke, the stones cracked, and from their cleft depths came skeletal giants, stooped and bent brutes with arms dangling nearly to the floor but three times taller than any dwarf. Duabows sang, and bolts rattled off the bones to clatter across the broken stones. It seemed the wight was preparing to make its counterattack.

"That's all well and good," Clahdi pressed, her voice sharp and urgent, "but we don't have any flaming booze huts or any more of your brothers to throw at the thing, so how did you handle the other two?"

Haeda and Waelon looked at Tomza, who in turn looked for Ober. She felt a flutter of panic at the absence of her sibling, but from a short way down the slope that led into the basin came a thundering ursine roar.

"You're about to find out," Tomza answered with a toothy grin.

CHAPTER THIRTEEN

"That sounds familiar."

Mabon looked up from the path he'd been picking along the ice-glazed docks, one hand held out for balance and the other clutching a small mittened hand. He was about to say he didn't hear anything, but a second later, he heard a low, rolling sound like thunder but wilder and hungrier. The eldest Reeve might not have had the svartalf's keen ears, but he wasn't certain that he'd forget that sound as long as he lived.

"Things must not be going very well," he observed, pausing to lead his charge around a treacherous-looking set of boards.

"That or they are about to go very well," Utyrvaul offered, long fingers drumming on the basket hilt of the saber at his hip. "Though at this rate, I don't suppose we'll find out before next season."

"The boards are slick, and dwarvish rails are barely above knee level," Mabon countered. "I've already told you that you and the mercenaries can go ahead. She's not going to get there any faster just because the elves fume about her short legs."

"Indeed." The svartalf sniffed irritably. "It seems that our attentions only make her all the more recalcitrant."

The young girl holding Mabon's hand looked up at the elf with brilliant golden eyes, her former fear replaced by pugnacious defiance.

"I'm going as fast as I can," she archly declared a moment before she would have stepped between two boards if not for Mabon's guiding hand. "See! It's dangerous."

Utyrvaul's face twitched, but when he spoke, his voice was all honey.

"Terribly sorry, my dear," he replied, sketching an elegant bow. "If you would like, Mabon or I could carry your lovely self off this treacherous dock."

A bit of the old fear surged to the surface as the elf extended his hand to the child, and she shrank against Mabon. He looked up from the boards, saw the svartalf's extended hand, and shook his head.

"It's no use, Sir Utyrvaul." Mabon sighed. "I'm telling you she's just like my sister, and that means trying to convince her is just making things take longer. Maybe you could, I don't know, see if the people at the gate are ready and willing to open up. I wouldn't mind getting out of the cold."

Utyrvaul looked at the other elves, who stood a few of their long strides from the docks, longing in his eyes. Fingers drummed once more upon the hilt, and the elf shook his head.

"I'll admit that I'm no initiate when it comes to handling small children, mine all having been whisked away to be fostered in other houses as befits any noble's child, but I would like to point out that the dock only presents a veneer of safety. The creatures the good captain feared might come if things grew too rambunctious still might appear if they detect boots thumping across the pylons. I just want us to reach our destination safely, is all."

Mabon's face wore a bemused expression, and Utyrvaul had to suppress a spike of frustrated rage. He knew that despite his seemingly understanding manner, the human was just a human, so he had to lower his expectations. What had he said that was so difficult to comprehend?

Mabon didn't seem to register the rage that swept over and just as quickly vanished from the svartalf's expression. He helped the child across a few more boards before looking at the svartalf with genuine surprise and concern. "You've got children?"

Utyrvaul lips parted in a curdled smile, but he forced his voice to remain steady. "Obviously. I'm a virile son of a respected house. I've done my duty four times over, in point of fact, but none of that means one whit to anyone here or in Greyshelf if we are devoured by the things that infest this frigid puddle. Now can we please accelerate our progress before we are all consumed by aquatic monstrosities?"

Utyrvaul thought he might collapse with relief when Mabon bobbed his head and hunkered down to have a sincere conversation with the golden-eyed child. "I think it's time for me to carry you, little one," the young man explained, holding the child's gaze steadily. "It's not safe."

The girl shot the svartalf a less than friendly look, but when she met Mabon's eyes, there was only a sincere desire to be understood. "I can do it. I'm not a baby."

"You most certainly aren't a baby," Mabon agreed sagely, "but Sir Utyrvaul has a good point. We need to get to the gate quickly, not just because it's cold out here but because it is very dangerous, too."

The child considered Mabon's words, and despite his desire to study every minute detail, Utyrvaul made a point of looking the other way. The little banshee might have lived to thwart him, but at this point, he just wanted her off the dock.

An understanding must have been reached because when the elf looked back, Mabon gave a soft grunt and said, "Up we go."

Without further ado, Utyrvaul led Mabon, with the child clinging to his back like a limpet, across the dock as quickly and carefully as possible. Mabon had grown up in the shadow of cold mountain ridges, so the ice was not a problem. He did stumble once when his feet skittered over a section of frost-glazed boards, and the child on his back bleated in alarm, but Utyrvaul didn't even have to extend a hand before the young man righted himself.

"Whoa," the human muttered, his breath a puff of white. "That was close."

"Verily," Utyrvaul replied stiffly, his eyes straying to the glassy surface of the lake. There didn't seem to be any disturbances, but he wasn't going to hang around longer than necessary, so their pace quickened.

Mabon didn't have a chance to ask his question until they stepped off the dock, their feet crunching on a layer of snow over crushed rock. They paused just long enough for him to detach the golden-eyed child so she could resume what had become her customary place between them, holding Mabon's hand.

"You've never mentioned that you had kids," Mabon stated, then cleared his throat when Utyrvaul didn't seem to understand the implied question. "I guess it is just strange that you have four children, but you haven't mentioned them once."

The waiting svartalfs fell into place behind them as they advanced toward the looming mountain face on which the tall gate of stone and iron stood. Mabon had become accustomed to their silence, which Utyrvaul stated was one of their charms, but the looks they gave him, as though looking through him, always made him uncomfortable.

"Why would I talk about them?" the elf asked, finding the observation curious.

Mabon looked at the golden-eyed girl for assistance, but she was alternating between staring at the looming gate and throwing scowls at the elves. He accepted that he was alone in this and, not for the first time, wished some of the dwarves were around to help him forge on. "I just thought people talked about their families. You've heard me talk about my family, so I assumed that you never talked about yours because you didn't have one."

Utyrvaul Urivianoc frowned. He had never thought that he'd meet someone of even moderate intelligence who would not understand such things, but he comforted himself with the thought that Mabon was still young and Paelon's Watch was, if not a backwater, certainly a rustic point of origin.

"Well, amongst my people and almost all civilized races, that is common," the elf began. "My children were bundled off before they could string more than a few words together, and that, combined with my adventurous lifestyle, meant that I probably couldn't pick them out of a random collection of svartalf children. Even if I was inclined to talk about them, I would have next to nothing to say."

Mabon's eyes widened at the declaration. "That sounds awful."

Utyrvaul frowned, perplexed by the young man's consternation. A quick look at the other svartalfs confirmed that they were as perplexed as he.

"How does the children's mother feel about that?" Mabon asked after a moment of pensive silence.

"My wives?" Utyrvaul mused, arched brows rising in consideration. "Well, at least one of them is insisting that I come back and give her another child, though I suspect that has more to do with her trying to jockey my first wife out of her position."

"Wives? First?" Mabon muttered in confusion, but Utyrvaul had warmed to the subject and wasn't paying attention.

"I told her in the last letter that she'd have to wait until I'd settled this business here in the Vale. There's a good chance that she'll grow impatient and take things into her own hands—and bed, the impetuous creature that she is. She's had an eye on Jethial's chateau since I took her on, but I warned her that despite her demure affectations, Jethial is my first for a reason."

They were now in the shadow of the mountain and coming

up to the gate. Mabon noticed the signs of very recent movement by many feet and hooves, all coming out of the fortress. He wasn't certain if that boded well, and Utyrvaul seemed more concerned with relaying the peculiarities of his marital situation.

"Though if the two of them want to lock horns, I don't suppose I mind," the svartalf opined with an airy toss of his head. "It keeps them entertained while I am gone and gives me a reason to stay away, which is agreeable to all involved."

Soft laughter swept through the elves. Utyrvaul basked in it, but Mabon frowned and continued to look bemused. The child just gave them a look of suspicion and disgust, though Mabon didn't think it was because she understood Utyrvaul's cynical assessment of his domestic life.

Before more could be said about the matter, a sharp call rose a dozen or so strides from them. "Who goes there?"

Utyrvaul seamlessly transitioned from gossip with aplomb, sketching one of his elegant bows. "My good dwarf, do you not recognize us?" he called, searching for where the voice was coming from. "We are friends and allies of your good ondwan Torbjorn of Clan Cyniburg. I am Sir Utyrvaul Urivianoc, and this is my young friend Mabon Reeve, Esquire, formerly of Paelon's Watch. We are accompanied by friends and reinforcements on the return journey to the company of the ondwan."

There was movement near an arrow slit, and the elf saw the glint of dwarvish eyes trying to see who had come to call. Utyrvaul wondered if he could pitch a knife into the spot and come out with a spitted dwarvish eye for his trouble.

"The ondwan is otherwise occupied," was the flat reply.

Utyrvaul had to keep another surge of irritation from playing across his features. "Yes, the siege," the elf stated in what he hoped was a grave tone. "Serious business, which is why he sent us to your fair city of Heimgrud to see about getting help."

The svartalf felt this might be the situation where he would throw in a gesture of gumption and candor, but nothing came to mind, so he just stood there and looked dashing, which was not difficult for him.

"I'm from Bandegrast," was the reply, accompanied by snickers from within the gatehouse.

"That's lovely," the elf observed. "How—"

"You said 'my lovely city' about Heimgrud," the gate dwan interjected. "Just thought you'd want to know that before you call that festering canker in the mountains 'my city' again."

"Terribly sorry about the confusion," Utyrvaul remarked, one eyebrow rising before he continued. "Since we've returned from our diplomatic liaison, it would be much appreciated if you would let us in, even if it was just to wait on the ondwan's pleasure. You see, we have news of Heimgrud and the wider world."

The agitated sounds from inside the gate and barbican were hardly encouraging, even before the dwarf within spoke in a sharp, accusing voice. "When you left, you went out with two envoys from the Holt'Dwan," the obscured dwarf replied. "Where are they?"

That was a prickly matter Utyrvaul had hoped to avoid. "Why, they are still in Heimgrud," he declared, chin rising. "Laboring long and hard to make certain the Sufstan Holt'Dwan receives all the assistance they deserve. Now, can we ple—"

"When are reinforcements coming?"

Utyrvaul heard Mabon swallow and desperately hoped the sound wouldn't carry up to those above. "Presently, I'm sure," the elf lied. "I'm sure you understand I can't discuss the details of this out here, so the quicker you let us in, the quicker I can deliver my message to your commander and my very good friend Ondwan Torbjorn of—"

Spittle was hawked, and the answer was distinctly less friendly.

"I know who he is," the gate dwarf growled. "If you want to see your very good friend, you and your myrklings can prance your pretty toes around the mountain to where the ondwan is fighting off a fresh attack by the invaders."

"The smoke," Mabon muttered.

Utyrvaul nodded, but he hushed the lad with a wave of his hand. "Well, I'm glad to hear the defense of Greyshelf is as vigorous as ever," the svartalf called up to the gate. "Now, would you please let us in? Even if your ondwan is out and about, I very much doubt he wants us left standing at the doorstep."

Voices hissed and rumbled before the answer came. "Maybe he wouldn't," a new voice declared, "but I'm not sure he'd much like the idea of us letting in a bunch of armed myrklings without anyone to vouch for them."

Utyrvaul's temper rose, and his smile took on a predatory cast despite his best efforts. "My good dwarf," the elf began a long-suffering air. "You and your comrades can vouch for us since they've already noted they saw us depart in the company of two of your Holt'Dwan. That should suffice to shelter us until your ondwan returns, shouldn't it?"

"How do I know you're the same bunch of blade-ears?" asked the voice over snickers. "You all look the same to me."

Utyrvaul was trying to master his mounting fury to form a reasonable objection when he heard the creaking clicks of duabows being primed. A quick appraisal of their position and the number of arrow slits and murder holes before them presented a grim reality.

"Oh, dear," Utyrvaul murmured. Mabon moved to shield the child. The other svartalfs held themselves rigidly, like steel springs under tension.

"You've got your answer, elf," the dwarf replied. "Chase the ondwan up the mountain or go for a swim, but you and yours aren't coming in unless you've got the ondwan with you."

Utyrvaul stood tall and straight for a moment, then without a word, he turned sharply on his heel and motioned for the others to follow him out of the shadow of the gate.

"I'm going to enjoy our next meeting," the svartalf promised as he stalked back up the churned path. "That you can most certainly count on."

Mabon, almost dragging the child in his wake, leaned in close to the elf. "What are we going to do?"

Utyrvaul's eyes followed the clear trail stamped and gouged into the snow and stone before them that wound up the mountainside.

"Well, I'm not keen on returning to the dock, and I don't think good Captain Morb would return even if he heard or saw a signal from us. That just leaves the mountain, doesn't it?"

Mabon's brow furrowed, and his voice dropped to a whisper. "You think it is a good idea to take her up where there could be fighting and one of *them*?"

Utyrvaul's voice was as sharp and clear as a blade as he replied in a furious riposte. "No, I don't think it is a good idea, but seeing as there are no other options, I don't suppose it matters. At least this way, we're moving about so we won't freeze stiff while we wait outside a miserable dwarvish hovel like the worst sort of beggars. Now, do shut up and keep that thing attached to you!"

CHAPTER FOURTEEN

"Where you goin', lads? Don't you want to have a try?"

Gromic's taunts were wasted on the clackers as they shuffled down the tunnel just ahead of the Sablestone Guard. The wight's withdrawal from the battle had caused the ferocious attacks of his unliving servants to slacken, and Torbjorn relentlessly drove the Guard and the rest of the infantry forward.

In the back of his mind, the ondwan wondered what he was going to do if he provoked the wight to return and attend to his advance, but the interaction with the wight had his stomach twisting. What had it meant? The girl was in Heimgrud, wasn't she? They'd received word that Utyrvaul and Mabon had arrived with the girl, along with the envoys from the fortress, those two compromised priests.

What was the wheezer talking about?

The question drove the dwarf commander beyond fatigue and good sense, but the advantageous circumstances, combined with growing momentum as they crushed rank after rank of clackers, kept them going. They'd ground so many leathery corpses under their heels that the dead men were retreating. Torbjorn knew better than to think it was fear or even some brute instinct of self-preservation that drove the unliving before him and his dwans.

The wight had called them back after they'd covered his withdrawal.

Still, Torbjorn and Gromic followed the lead of the doughty Guard, breath rasping out of their helmets. Here and there, a time-gnawed foot in fraying sandals would slip and turn on the rough-hewn tunnel floor, or the back of its skull would meet a *cwellocs* or a magsax and a crushing Sablestone sabaton.

"How long is this damned tunnel?" Gromic wheezed after the ninth time he ground a clacker beneath his boot.

Torbjorn didn't want to waste the air to reply, but then he saw raw daylight glinting off a cavern wall. It was so unlike the wan alchemical light that had defined their existence during the battle in the cavern that Torbjorn's eyes stung from so dim a reflection.

"Light up ahead," he wheezed, then felt the first brush of cold air through the visor of his helm. "And fresh air."

"Also fresh enemies," Gromic quipped, hefting his sword to hack down another that had fallen just ahead. "I think these ones are a bit rotten."

The clacker's head swung around just before the hard-honed blade bit through its temple and socket. It ripped free through the jaw with a spray of teeth. "A bit," Torbjorn acknowledged as he stomped on the remains, splintering bone and flattening the desiccated gristle as they pressed forward.

He idly wondered if the remains behind them, trampled not just by the pair of them but by all the other Guard and the lines of marching dwans, were any more than bone dust on sheets of shriveled hide.

The thought faded as they rounded a corner and were forced to slow when sunlight poured into the passage. It was merely the pale winter sun sliding through a seam in the stone above them, but after hours of false twilight, it blinded them.

Torbjorn shouted a warning to slow and reduced his pace to a faltering trudge. He felt the presence of a large body coming close but not crashing into him as the other guards strove to check their momentum. The last thing any of them wanted was to crash into one another and get stuck in a narrow point in the tunnel.

Torbjorn realized that if they weren't careful, he'd end up getting himself and Gromic stuck behind enemy lines again. The heroic efforts of the Guard had been a pleasant surprise, especially given that until that moment, he hadn't been sure the Guard would serve if he called on them. However, he was not foolish enough to test their dedication again. One valorous intervention per battle seemed a wise choice.

As they continued to the dead men, the passage widened, so he had the Guard create a widening battle line while instructing the dwans behind them to form up when the opportunity arose.

They were five dwarves wide when they came to the passage's mouth. Its low roof was bifurcated by the seam that allowed the sun in. As the retreating clackers vanished down the slope and moved out of sight of the tunnel entrance, Torbjorn felt a prickle at the back of his neck.

If the wight had baited them into a pursuit to turn the tables on him, this would be the moment. He knew the wise and proper thing was to send some of the Guard forward while he stayed back to avoid being caught in the jaws of a trap. If Klaus had been there, he would have insisted on it and gone himself.

Klaus wasn't there, and Torbjorn was well beyond being wise and proper. "We go out at speed, and we form a proper battle-line sharpish," he shouted hoarsely over his shoulder, trusting word of mouth to reach where his voice could not. "Guard at the front and fore, then standard dwans staggered after that. We've got a slope here, so watch your footing."

Torbjorn looked at Gromic, and the dwarf nodded and set to beating his sturdy blade on his shield in an even measure. The rhythm was matched by the footfalls of the Guard. Gromic accelerated the beat, and the Guard's pace quickened.

"Let's go, lads," Torbjorn shouted as they burst out of the passage and rushed down the hill.

Despite their efforts to adjust to the light in the passage's antechamber, the glare of the sun on the snow in the basin had the dwarves blinking and turning their heads this way and that. Weapons and shields were hoisted in preparation for the attack that would take advantage of their befuddlement, but that attack didn't come.

In good order, Torbjorn's forces assembled along the slope, a wall of black and gold armored hulks standing before staggered ranks of professional dwans with their shields in front of them and their duabows resting on the shields. The wind tugged on beards or hair that had worked loose in the battle inside the mountain, but otherwise, the dwarf force was a solid wall before the mouth of the hitherto hidden passage into Greyshelf.

Centering the line, his eyes having adjusted to the bright glare, Torbjorn saw what lay before them as Gromic gave a low whistle. "Well, isn't this odd?"

Like a thick streak of filth, the wight's forces spanned the basin at its widest point, their backs to Torbjorn's force. Opposite the ondwan and the clackers were several blocks of dwarvish infantry in an offset formation. Formed up along one side was a squad of dwarvish cavalry, their mounts stamping and pawing the ground eagerly in anticipation of the enemy flank being exposed.

Bolts sailed through the air to pepper the unliving and the few living men and goblins who stood with them. The wight's fighters were caught between two forces, each nearly a match for it on its own, and they could expect to be ground by both unless they tried something bold.

Any such move was likely to end in doom since the cavalry forces would be quick to punish their weaknesses.

This was an interesting sight, but even more striking was what lay between the dead men and the dwarvish force that had come up from the Lake Gate. In the little valley, a handful of bowed, bony giants did battle with an enormous bear.

The death-scorned giants, their bones having absorbed the shade and strength of the rocks in which they'd been encased, threw themselves at their massive opponent with reckless abandon. Huge fists swung like knobbed cudgels while bared, jagged teeth gnashed, eager to rend. There was no art to their movements, no suggestion of anything than a primal desire to batter and crush, rip and tear.

Had their quarry been a mere animal, the end would have been a foregone conclusion, but the bear was anything but. Larger than even the most hulking of ursine kind, when the embattled bear reared on its hind legs to pummel and scythe with sickle-capped paws, it stood head and shoulders over its opponents and displayed a chest wide as two giants. Bony hammers struck its thick fur, sending up dull, reverberating claps that only enraged the beast further. Each blow struck was answered in kind, and jagged shards of petrified bone flew from the giants.

One of the unliving brutes hurled itself at the ursine terror and leaped upon its back to pound its spine, neck, and skull. In response, the bear reared again, forcing the clinging attacker to hold fast or be thrown off. The giant's rock-hard claws dug into its fur for purchase, prompting the bear to initiate the next step by rolling.

The giant threw itself to one side. Still clinging to the bear with its apelike arms, the skeletal creature slammed into the unforgiving stone of the mountain. The force of the impact knocked its grip loose, and the great bear, still rolling, came to its feet and pounced on the foe. The bear's heavy clawed paws pressed down on the giant's chest, and for the barest second, it seemed it would absorb the impact. Then, in a chorus of cracks, the ribs splintered, and the chest caved in.

The bear rose in a plume of rock dust, batting aside the inert fossil and bellowing a challenge to the remaining giants.

"Wasn't sure about not having the lad with us in there," Gromic admitted as he nodded at the titanic clash. "It seems he's made his own fun out here."

Torbjorn nodded, but Gromic's words reminded him that there was still a wight to manage. For all their size and danger, he could tell by their movements that the bony giants were mere extensions of a stronger and more malignant will. The giants were just a threat to keep Ober busy while the wight made his escape.

As he searched the ranks of the clackers, Torbjorn's stomach churned. This wasn't only about stopping the wight from escaping or destroying it in a much-needed victory after a long siege. The wight had sensed the presence of the child they'd been hunting for so long. The child Torbjorn and his companions had fought and bled to keep safe. What did it sense, and what did that portend? He had to know, and at the very least, he had to stop it from achieving its aims, whatever they were.

Despite being prepared to fight the wight to the bitter end, under the pale sun, he struggled to tell one dead foe from another. He sought the towering figure, the tall helm, and the menace, but the glimpses he caught were only shadows of what he had seen before that, upon scrutiny, revealed nothing.

Frustration mounting, he decided the only choice was to order his forces to attack. They gained nothing by watching the battle between the huge champions from either side, and in the meantime, the wight's scheme came closer to fruition.

"All right, lads," he roared, his voice less hoarse after the brief rest. "We can't sit around expecting the beast to do all the work for us. Shape up and *ADVANCE!*"

The command struck like lightning, spurring the dwans to action. They began their grinding march down the hill toward the enemy ranks at the bottom. Their bolts flew before the clackers even started to shuffle about, ripping down the slope to bury themselves in lifeless foes. Bones cracked and leathery ligaments snapped as the dwarves trudged down, a descending curtain of metal come to crush all in their path.

The dead men formed a semblance of a battle line, rows of animated corpses broken up by nodules of sweating, shivering goblins to fill the gaps. Javelins flew from these quivering pockets, but they might as well have been rain pattering on Sablestone and upraised shields.

Two dozen strides from the enemy, Torbjorn was still searching for the wight when he heard the shouted warning that the dwans were nearly out of bolts. He swatted aside the wistful thought that someone from Greyshelf might think to resupply them as they closed to less than a dozen strides from the enemy.

Even with the advantage of elevation, he was losing his chance to spot the wight as their lines loomed like a sprouting forest of bone and moth-eaten war gear. He made one final sweep, knowing it was hopeless...but *THERE*!

Like a dark cloud driven by the wind, he felt as much as saw the wight sliding through the ranks with well-armored clackers around it. It was heading for the far end of the basin to skirt the rim and make for the mouth, in which Torbjorn saw only a small collection of dwarves standing watch.

Whoever they were, they would be no match for the wight when it came.

Brandishing his *cwellocs* like a conductor's wand, Torbjorn directed every duabow at the wight. A storm of bolts tore through the clackers, even taking down a few of the elite entourage, but if any found their mark in the wight, there was no sign. Torbjorn howled and ranted for them to fire again, a sixth sense telling him this was the last chance before something dreadful was set in motion.

A few more bolts flew, hurried and ineffectual. Then the shout came back that the last of the bolts had been expended.

Torbjorn screamed and swore, but they'd engaged with the enemy, so the only thing left to do was pour out his impotent fury on all those in reach as the wight vanished.

CHAPTER FIFTEEN

"That thing is your brother?"

Tomza tore her eyes from the ferocious struggle between the bear and the bone colossi. Ober ripped the head off one of them with three jerks, then spun to club flat one who was springing at his flank.

She couldn't lie and tell herself she wasn't concerned for her brother, but she also couldn't deny that she struggled to imagine anything being a true threat to him. He'd been powerful before, a storm of strength and rage laying waste to everything around him, but after making peace with the spirit that now shared his skin, he was even more potent.

The fury and power of a force of nature had harnessed itself to a will and a mind, a dwan, a fighter trained to be mindful of the world around him. Ober was almost a demi-god of war, even if he failed to realize it.

You. You could have been more. You still could be.

Tomza shook off the intrusive thoughts. They had been a nuisance at first and were now a crushing tax levied on her mental will. Jaw clenching and head wagging, she tried to focus on the question she'd just been asked.

When she'd batted her brain around enough in her skull, she looked at the questioner, the ranger Clahdi, and her tongue tripped over an answer. "In a way, yes," she offered lamely. "He's in control if that's what you mean. We're not in danger or anything."

The other dwarfess nodded, then turned fierce, narrowed eyes on Tomza. "In a way?" Clahdi asked, cocking her head to one side. Her sharp features made the movement hawklike. "What does that mean?"

"Wait, what?" Tomza asked, stalling for time. "I don't understand what you are asking."

Don't you see? The disrespect, the questions, the suspicions! You are more than that. You deserve more than that.

Dark, thorny incantations came to her mind for the thousandth time in the past few months. With a weary sigh, she batted them aside with the same will that birthed them. Another tax on her depleted resources.

She wondered if a day would come when she could no longer resist. No longer drive the insidious voice that sounded like her own away. Yet, if she broke, how could she summon the potency she'd need to drive the magic out into the world? If she surrendered and tried to bring it forth with a sunken, emaciated will, what would happen?

She knew, and the answer sent a chill through her to beat anything the mountain wind could do.

"Tomza," the ranger growled, seizing her shoulder and pinning her eyes. "Where did the bear come from?"

No one else noticed what was playing out between the two dwarfesses as they watched the cataclysmic fight below.

"Uh—"

"They're on the move!" someone shouted, and with a final squeeze to assure Tomza that this was not over, Clahdi released her. Both turned their attention back to the scene in the basin and noticed for the first time that a new host of dwarves had emerged from the tunnels and was engaging the enemy forces.

Not to be outdone, the dwans who'd left the Lake Gate also moved to engage, though they were careful to avoid the struggle between the great bear and the fossilized brutes. In response to the dual attacks, the unliving host broke in two. One was determined to keep Torbjorn's company mired in their fight on the slope to the tunnel, while the other tied up the Lake Gate forces.

"What are they doing?" Waelon rumbled, face bunching up as his gaze swept the basin. "They're going to be torn to shreds."

Her thoughts were still syrupy from the back and forth with Clahdi and her internal struggles, so Tomza was confused by what she was seeing. "Maybe…" she began, thinking she should shut up before she embarrassed herself. "Maybe they're just trying to keep from being flanked."

A few rangers scoffed at the idea. Haeda explained. "If they're looking to avoid being flanked, they're doin' a piss-poor job of it." The driver pointed at the dwarvish cavalry. "They don't have enough in either section to tie up both infantry forces and screen for cavalry charges, and now they've got twice as many flanks. Yorm's going to swing his lads around, and then he's got his pick of which one force he's going crash into one side and out the other."

Tomza saw what Haeda was indicating when the riders kicked their mounts into a trot to skirt the advancing line of dwans.

"Should've surged back up the hill and enveloped the ondwan's forces," Clahdi mused. "There's enough clackers to box 'em in, and on the higher ground, they could hold out for a good while, especially since the dead don't get tired."

Waelon's head bobbed as he tracked something across the basin.

"It wouldn't win them the battle, but they'd hold out for a good long whi—"

The big dwarf jabbed a finger at a small knot of fighters that didn't seem to belong to either of the two enemy formations. "Looks like we've got runners!"

An eager cry went up from the rangers, who dispersed to snatch the best vantage points. Tomza looked around, stunned at the rapidity with which the group of dwans had dispersed.

She saw Haeda holding Waelon's arm and the two in an urgent conference. "What is the one thing the clackers are going to sacrifice themselves for?"

Waelon didn't respond. The grim look on his face was answer enough.

The wight, Tomza realized, and when she looked at the approaching cluster of tall figures, she felt the dark presence.

Tomza's eyes swung to where her brother, bloody but still rampant, grappled with the last two giants. Even if they could summon him, it was unlikely he could break free quickly enough for it to matter.

He's not the only one with power. That which heals can also kill, and the tools to mend are tools to destroy if the will is there. The thought sent an icy spike through her mind, and she shoved it away. She'd told herself that the blade-ear's warning about her corrupted workings were only the words of the jealous scion of a dying people, nothing but spite and lies.

Then the siege had come, and she'd been using her magic surreptitiously to assure that dwans lived and could be made whole again. That was when the voice she so often mistook for her own came, and it would not go away.

She glanced at the ranger patrol. *Maybe just this once to save them. Why should they have to die?*

"We can't just let the damn wheezer get by," Waelon growled, the force of his words snapping Tomza back to reality. "Maybe we'll get lucky, or barring that, we'll slow it down enough that Ober can get over here to finish it off."

Tell them! Tell them you can stop it. You can do it!

Tomza's voice spoke without her consent and a garbled cry formed, though whether in protest or offer, she was not sure. No one heard her since the Rangers shouted to one another, calling their shots as the tireless collection of lifeless figures came within duabow range.

"Southwest limpers mine."

"Northeast bugger with the shield."

"Big bastard at the very front is mine."

"Oy! He's big enough to share, don't you think?"

Waelon, Haeda, and Tomza looked at the rangers splayed across the passage out of the basin, and their tongues stuck to the roofs of their mouths, and their voices dried in their throats. They'd learn the truth, but what would that matter if their only choice was to hold out as long as they could?

Clahdi's head rose from the stock of her crossbow, a jest on her tongue until she saw the pained look the trio wore. "Waelon? What is it?"

The big dwarf pried his jaws open by force of will, but it was too late when the first bolts flew. "Wight!" he shouted. "It's the damn wheezer!"

As though determined to put paid to the claim, the looming figure at the head of the knot of unliving warriors raised the recognizable mace and pointed at the rangers. Despite the many yards between them, its hiss carried across the snow and cut through the general rumble of the battlefield in the basin like a blade. "Kill them."

Some bolts found their mark, but not a single figure fell or even slowed. On they came, adjusting the path of their flight to rush the rangers. Tomza wondered why they would waste time on the small force, but then she understood that they were trying to make a clean break, and if the rangers pursued them, the whole of the dwarvish forces or Ober could be drawn down on them.

You're their only chance! The barbed thought coiled in her mind as the Rangers panicked.

"A wheezer!"

"Shaper preserve us!"

"Grimmoth's Grin! We can't fight that thing."

"It's coming right for us."

The rangers lost precious seconds as they scrambled back, clustering together in confusion.

"What do we do?"

"Run?"

"Run!"

"*HOLD!*" Waelon's roar cut through the yammering and beat every other voice into silence. "We're going to hold as long as we can," he shouted, glaring at every face to prevent contest or argument. "I want a loose line standing with me at the base of these rocks and the rest putting bolts downrange. Right *NOW!*"

Some of the rangers responded immediately, driven either by the power of the big dwarf's voice or their instincts. The others, nearly half of the patrol, only milled about, torn between stubbornness, suspicion of the newcomer, and fear of the monster bearing down on them. Vital moments slipped by as they stared at the oncoming horror.

"What are you waiting for? Move yer arses!" Clahdi's sharp rebuke was like a spurred kick in the side of a recalcitrant swine. The rest of the rangers sprang into vigorous action, quickly sorting themselves.

Waelon centered the line of dwarves with Clahdi's long-handled axe in one hand and the axe from his belt in the other. She formed up with those launching bolts, and with her keen eye coordinating their fire, one of the wight's entourage crumpled.

"Haeda, Tomza," Waelon shouted over his shoulder as he set his feet wide. "Get on those pigs and get Ober's furry bum over here."

Tomza saw Haeda open her mouth to tell the big dwarf what he could do with his order to abandon them, but the protest didn't emerge. The older dwarfess looked around her, eyes filling with tears, and she understood that without something besides dwarvish steel and will, there would be no hope.

Cursing beneath her breath every step of the way, the driver went to the agitated blotferows. By whispering softly and stroking their snouts, she settled two beasts enough to gather their reins. Haeda mounted her swine, then looked at Tomza and gestured at the other blotferow. "Come on, lass." Emotion thickened her voice. "Get over here! We've got to go!"

Tomza shook her head, but Waelon shouted, "Get going! You need to get clear before they get too close!"

"Damn it, Tomza!" Haeda snarled as she kicked the swine into movement, dragging the other along by its reins. "You heard him. Get on the pig!"

"I can help," Tomza croaked, finally finding her voice. "Go without me. There's no time!"

"Ober won't listen to me," the driver shouted. "Mount up!"

"It's not like before," Tomza countered, her voice stronger and clearer as she accepted her fate. "Go, and he'll listen. I need to stay here. *Ride!*"

Haeda looked like she would have given her right arm to argue further, but another bellow from Waelon settled the matter. Screaming curses at everyone and everything, Haeda drove her mount into a full gallop, and the other blotferow kept pace.

Now. It is time.

Tomza felt the brambly incantations in the forefront of her mind. Workings she'd only glimpsed in books took shape, and she knew that if she called on them, they would answer without fail. A vast library of potent hexes and savage curses was hers to plunder and exploit and was begging her to do so.

Two more of the wight's corpse retainers had fallen, their heavily armored forms sinking to the ground with several bolts embedded in each. The wight came on, seemingly untouched, with two vassals in tow.

"We die as dwans," Waelon bellowed, and every ranger shrieked his lusty answer.

"*AS DWANS!*"

Let them die. You will live. You will conquer!

Tomza retrieved her flint knife as Waelon hurled his axe at the oncoming wight, and the creature swatted the spinning weapon aside with contemptuous ease.

Waelon and the other rangers were already in motion, long-handled axes raised high. They whistled as they carved through the air to hack into armor and desiccated meat. Outnumbering the wight and his remaining warriors two to one, the rangers fell on them in a frenzy.

"Come on, lads," Clahdi shouted, raising her magsax as the others drew their long-handled axes. "Can't let the mad lad take all the credit."

Silly fools. They don't know you'll save them.

The incantation slithered from her mind to her mouth, each word piercing her tongue until she tasted blood.

It hurts, yes, but that is the price of power. You know that.

The rangers' axes were still rising and falling when the first of their number crumpled. A vassal had torn his throat out. Another was transfixed by a revenant guard's spear shaft. The clacker had only one arm left, and its jaw dangled from a few wizened tendons, but it tore the impaling spear free and rammed the blade through another throat before a deluge of blows bit through armor and hide to cleave its bones.

He's toying with them. Even in flight, they can't keep from their sport. Inspiring.

The last clacker's sword was slivered and his shield splintered, but with crooked claws and gnashing teeth, he fell on one ranger, then another, gouging and shredding. The dwarves screamed until their throats were clogged with blood. Waelon left off hammering the wight to slam the axe's pick into the gore-smeared face of the savage dead man.

Tomza's lips, then her chin, got wet as the incantation continued to cruelly ravage her mouth and throat. A shudder ran over her body, touching her everywhere at once, then slid between and within her.

Almost there! Just a little longer. Yes. That's what real power feels like.

The last of its retinue gone, the wight was done with its sport, or maybe it was certain they had nothing that could harm it. Brushing aside blows that would have felled an armored dwarf at a stroke, its mace swept out.

Dwarves were scattered after the stroke, their limp bodies rolling across snow and stone. One landed next to Tomza, and she heard the bones in his body break at the impact. With the magic thrumming through her, her awareness swelled, straining to encompass what was growing inside her. She felt the ranger's life leave him as surely as she would feel the warmth of a candle's flame vanishing as it was snuffed out.

She cried out when she remembered that she was supposed to be saving them. She was trading everything to spare their lives. Yet, they were dying before her, and she felt every one.

The mace, slinging blood and trailing chunks of ragged flesh and hanks of hair, rose and fell over and over. Like a demonic workman with a bevy of fleshy pegs to hammer, the wight kept striking, pivoting to snag a retreating ranger and strike again.

In a few heartbeats, only Waelon and Clahdi were left, staying one step ahead of the crushing bludgeon through instinctual teamwork. Waelon would dart in for a strike to allow Clahdi to duck away, and the dwarfess would spring back with a blow to buy the big dwarf a life-saving instant to zip to one side. The wight seemed frustrated, but then its laughter rose, a tidal wave of hissing ice shards threatening to burrow through flesh to freeze their hearts.

Another shudder wracked Tomza, and she knew what it meant.

Now! You are ready. NOW!

Clahdi had been too slow. The mace was about to come down, but Waelon viciously tackled the wight. The wight lurched to one side, and the crushing head missed the dwarfess. However, a twist of the wrist laid the pommel across the bridge of her nose. Staggering and spinning as tears ran from her eyes and blood from her nose, the ranger looked at Tomza as she loosed the final damning syllable of the incantation.

Burning motes of blood flew from the young ascedwan's mouth to fall upon the earth and the bodies of the dead. Clahdi looked on in horror as those sorcerous fireflies set the skin of the mountain and the bones of the dead to twisting and spinning like clay in a potter's hand.

The ranger gazed at Tomza in dismay, but the young dwarfess bent her will upon the wight as it tore Waelon from where he clung and prepared to smash him on the rocks. Waelon kicked and punched, but he might as well have been beating his fists on the walls of Greyshelf for all the good it did.

The wight laughed like a malicious child smashing a doll on the floor, but with a flex of will, Tomza sent lances of stone and bone into the wight's frame.

The barbed shafts pierced and bit when the axe blades and pick points had failed. For a moment, the wight stood there, Waelon still held in one outstretched arm, pierced in a dozen places.

Yes! This is power. This is what you've denied yourself. Now, make him suffer.

With the barest exercise of her will, the jagged spurs twisted and pulled. She felt its resistance, the terrible will fighting hers, but she was certain she would win. The advantage was hers; her adversary had been caught off-guard. She just needed to press harder.

A deep, raw dwarvish voice cried out, cutting through the hiss of the incantation and the throbbing of her heart in her ears. Tomza came back to herself, and her gaze found Waelon, hanging in the wight's grip with a lance of bone driven through his back and out his belly. As she'd set the magical darts twisting, she'd been ripping him open. Dark blood ran down his legs and dripped from his boots.

"Waelon!" Tomza cried. "No! I'm sorry!"

NO! He doesn't matter! Finish it. Finish him before—

Like the proverbial knot meeting the famed blade, Tomza's magic did not unravel so much as it was shorn from her in one brutal stroke. The lances sprouted blue flames as she staggered back, colder and emptier than she'd ever been. The ache in her was so deep and absolute that she prayed that death would claim her.

Her legs gave out, and she sank to the snow, the cold forgotten in the numbness creeping over her.

So close. You were so close.

Tomza groaned when the wight dropped Waelon and strode toward her. She didn't retreat from the gore-smeared mace in its hand.

"Impressive." The wight chuckled coldly. "I'd forgotten that we'd taught some of our slaves the lowest spells."

As it spoke, it traced the places where she'd punctured its armor and decay-blackened flesh.

"Thank you for the reminder." The wight seemed lost in thought. "It is good to see that the *tozelchaun* remembered some of what we taught them."

Tomza stared into the merciless light within the helm, hoping to see a jest or a jeer. Her magic had been passed down to her by her mother, carried in that line of their family for generations. It couldn't be born of this looming horror, this vengeful vestige of ancient blasphemies.

Yet, as she stared into the unflinching, unwavering light as alien and distant as the stars, she understood.

"Rejoice, daughter of Earth," the wight declared, straightening and resting the mace on its shoulder. "For your daring and the gift of a memory, I will let you live a little longer."

Tomza looked at the hideous face and wanted to scream that she would never give herself to sorcery again, but her throat was aflame, and her tongue still bled in a half-dozen places. She managed a defiant croak, not words but an animal sound of rejection and denial, but this only provoked another laugh from the wight.

"May you survive to grow to be a real challenge one day."

Tomza was struggling to form a rebuttal when a figure rose behind the wight, long-handled axe clenched in both hands.

"How about you both just die!"

Clahdi's swing had her whole body behind it and was driven by grief and rage caused by the blood of her entire patrol. It was aimed true, committed without fear or reservation.

It didn't matter.

With viperish speed, the wight spun the mace to bat the axe away. Unbalanced, the dwarfess staggered into the path of wight's sweeping fist. The preternaturally hard bone collided with the side of the ranger's head, and her skull gave way with a wet crunch. Clahdi's eyes rolled up and she fell to the ground, body spasming.

The wight flicked the remains of the dwarfess' skull from its hand. There was a thunderous roar, and it glanced back with what might have been fear.

"Until next time, brave *tozelchaun*," it intoned. Then it was off, long, swift strides carrying it away.

Sobbing, Tomza crawled to where Clahdi still seized and twisted. When the young ascedwan reached the fallen ranger and wrapped her arms around the trembling form, she saw the state of her skull, and fresh tears stung her eyes. It was an ugly, brutal wound of the type that brought certain death, but not quickly enough. The dwarfess' head and body lolled independently, eyes unable to focus. The mind behind them was unable to make sense of the death creeping over it.

Tomza wanted to look away, but she stayed, refusing to let the brave dwan die alone.

"Shhh, it's all right," she managed in a coarse whisper. "I'm here. It's all right."

Clahdi's spasms were growing weaker, but the eyes rolled to Tomza, and for an instant, they cleared. Then another spasm struck, the worst yet, and the ranger's body rejected whatever comfort the healer could offer. Tomza bore that too, her embrace firm but gentle as tears rolled down her face.

"It's all right. I understand," she murmured, cradling the dying dwarfess like a sister in the grips of a nightmare. "It'll be over soon. It's—"

"No!" The word wasn't loud, but it had a force that would not be denied.

Tomza looked up to see Waelon clawing his way toward them across the ground. His legs hung limp and useless behind him, and the blood from his wounded limbs looked almost black against the snow.

"Waelon," Tomza groaned, the ache in her chest deeper than any physical pain. "I'm so, so sorry."

"No!" Waelon growled through gritted teeth. "Save her."

Tomza looked at him, his dark eyes full of tears of pain and desperate pleading.

"Waelon, I can't!"

"Save her," the big dwarf was about to succumb, the trauma and blood loss too much even for his iron constitution and implacable will. "*Save her.*"

He was close enough to clutch Tomza's sleeve. Her denials died as she looked into his eyes.

"Save her."

CHAPTER SIXTEEN

"What sort of madness follows you, Torbjorn Cyniburg?"

The ondwan didn't have to answer the question since the questioner had asked it as he rode by on a sweating, bloody blotferow. Even if he'd had an answer, he couldn't have offered it before Dogordwan Yorm had galloped beyond shouting distance.

"I don't like that dwarf," Gromic rumbled between gasps as he leaned on his shield. Torbjorn was inclined to agree with both. He didn't like the dogordwan either, though he was glad the petulant dwarf's defiance had reached its limit. He also couldn't deny that the dogordwan's question was a fair one. What madness, indeed?

The remains of scores of clackers covered the battlefield as the ondwan took stock of the situation. They'd emerged from the melee as the bulk of their forces drove into the vacuum created by Yorm's most recent flank charge. The clackers were still fighting, but their battle order was collapsing as the grinding pressure from the Guard and the dwans was paired with hammering attacks by the cavalry.

Torbjorn had stepped back from the battle line, and Gromic had stuck with him. With Yorm's riders past, the ondwan could see that the wight's forces had been split, and both knots of resistance were near the point of collapse. That should cheer him, but as his gaze swept the basin, he saw no sign of the wight, and at the mouth of the sunken valley, he couldn't see the dwarves who'd stood watch there. Curses rose in his throat, but they died when he saw only the fractured remains of the fossilized brutes where Ober and the wight's conjured hulks had fought.

"Where's Ober?" Torbjorn hissed, tearing his helmet off after struggling with the clasps for a profane moment.

Gromic removed his helmet as well, though without any curses. "Hmmm, I don't see him," the stout dwarf offered, squinting across the basin. "Never would've thought something that big would be easy to lose."

Torbjorn clenched his teeth as he fought the surge of hope that was springing up in his chest. If Ober had given chase, there was a chance that the wight might still be within reach.

The hoofbeats and snarls of swine snapped Torbjorn out of his thoughts. He realized that a rider drawing two additional blotferows with them was coming up from the basin, dodging between the boulders. When Torbjorn shaded his eyes against the sun, which was going down, he realized it was Haeda.

Gromic came to the same realization a moment later. "Torbjorn, my tweldwan," the doughty fordwan muttered. "Please, please don't say anything about…"

Torbjorn glanced at his faithful subordinate. It took him a few heartbeats to realize what Gromic was talking about, and then a wry snort escaped him. He clapped a hand on the dwarf's shoulder.

"Priorities, Gromic." He chuckled as he willed his weary body to shuffle down to meet Haeda. "Your secret is safe…for the moment."

Gromic let out a long, sputtering breath before squaring his shoulders and following his commander.

"Torbjorn!" Haeda shouted as she hauled on the reins to bring her blotferow skidding to a halt. "The wight! Ober's after it, but the others…"

"Where are the others?" Torbjorn demanded, eyes darting to the mouth of the valley even before the driver's finger pointed in that direction.

"Waelon and the Rangers were going to try and slow it down," the dwarfess explained, her voice trembling. "Tomza stayed, saying she could help."

Brave lass, Torbjorn thought. *Suicidally stupid but brave.*

"I rode over to Ober and shouted at him until I got his attention," Haeda continued, frustration sharpening her tone. "I told him about the wight and his sister, and I thought he understood, but then he roared while he was finishing with those *things*. The swine spooked, and I was thrown."

Torbjorn could see her pained irritation, and if they'd had time, he would've assured her that if *she* had been thrown, even the finest rider wouldn't have kept her seat. Instead, he ground his teeth together and let her continue her report.

"By the time I'd gotten things sorted, Ober was thundering after the wight," she stated, her voice flat. "I thought about going back to Waelon and Tomza, but I didn't see anyone moving over there."

The ondwan nodded, then fought to stay upright with his shoulders squared. Her report should have propelled him into action, but as it stood, he felt hollow and weighed down. He was an empty vessel in danger of collapse as his burdens mounted.

"What do we do?" Gromic asked, drawing Torbjorn out of his brooding. He could contemplate his frailties later. Right now, he must decide, for good or ill.

Torbjorn's eyes shifted to the blotferows that stood twitching and snorting behind Haeda. "Gromic, help me get this shell off," he growled, letting his helmet drop to the snow and starting to unclasp his gauntlets. "We're going after them."

Gromic obeyed the command but asked, "What are the three of us going to do to stop a wight?"

The ondwan let one heavy gauntlet tumble free and braced himself as the web of alchemically driven current weakened through the war harness. The weight settled with a soft, grinding groan, and he was reminded why removing one's armor in the field was not done. Get careless, and he'd be knocked flat by the shifting weight. With such heavy armor, that could have bone-snapping consequences.

"It won't just be us," Torbjorn growled as he worked at the other gauntlet and nodded at Yorm and his riders as they wheeled. "First things first. No beast is going to carry us wearing this harness. Tell me when you're ready to clear the cuirass."

"I don't understand what we're doing."

Torbjorn wanted to ignore that statement like he'd ignored the first when Haeda had dragged the dogordwan to attend Torbjorn. On its face, it was an honest confession, but its delivery as they pursued the ondwan's commands annoyed him.

"You don't have to understand," Gromic shouted over the clattering blotferow hooves. "You just have to obey."

Torbjorn appreciated the support, but before the words had finished coming from the dwan's lips, he knew they were unlikely to satisfy Yorm.

"That's all well and good for fordwan," the dogordwan shouted back, "but I've got my dwarves, their mounts, and most of all, our honor to think about."

They were near the mouth of the basin, and Torbjorn hauled on his boar's reins to check their speed while holding up his hand to signal to the piper. The war pipes issued a few sharp notes, and the entire assembly slowed from a gallop to a trot.

"Are you trying to suggest something about our ondwan's

honor?" Gromic roared, his voice not having yet adjusted to the lower ambient volume. That or he wanted to let Yorm know exactly how he felt about such insinuations.

"I said nothing of the sort," Yorm countered, the smirk in his voice revealing that he thought he was about to score a point. "The ondwan's history is known throughout the Holt'Dwan and beyond, and it can't be ignored."

"It's also known that the Shaper himself plucked me out of the Gauntlet," Torbjorn reminded him in the low and sharp tone that he knew unnerved even brash bullies like Yorm. "After striking down the last ondwan and all those who stood in judgment over me. Or have you already forgotten that?"

Yorm's mouth clamped shut as he chewed on several replies that didn't make it past his teeth. Torbjorn hated to use the fraud as a counterpoint to what might have been legitimate concerns, but shutting the dogordwan up so they could attend to the matter at hand was a worthy aim, even for a lie.

Torbjorn tried to blot Yorm's glaring presence from his mind when he spotted the first ranger lying face-down in the snow. Something about the way he lay looked odd, and Torbjorn realized it was because his chest faced the reddening sky while his bloodied face was buried in the snow. The unsightly bulge in the skin on the neck provided the final clue, and it struck the commander's heart like a mallet.

Wight hit him hard enough that his head twisted backward.

As his eyes went from that ranger to the others littering the ground, a flood of what-ifs and self-flagellating questions rose in his mind. Experience told him to let them wash over him. He'd let them all come at once, then shrug them all off with a breath and a shake of the head. He couldn't bring them back with self-accusations. He could only compromise his ability to avenge them.

"They're all dead," Yorm observed, his tone smug. "Killed either by the wight or that beast."

Torbjorn fought the instinct to argue about what the "beast" had done since that was not a conversation he wanted to have at the moment. It was just as well that he was silent since his ears picked out a weak voice from behind a knot of boulders.

"Not all dead," the voice called. "The beast was too busy to bother with us."

Torbjorn hauled on the reins to bring his mount around and make for the boulders. Out of the corner of his eye, he could see where the path trampled by Ober led out of the basin. He knew that should be his priority. Whoever had survived was fortunate, but he shouldn't take precious time to find them.

Yet, he'd not seen a corpse that looked like Waelon or Tomza, and so he was inexorably drawn by hope even as he cursed himself for a fool.

"Wish the wight had been too busy for us," the voice behind the boulder groused, the voice familiar now that they were closer.

Torbjorn nearly sobbed with relief when he rounded an intervening lump of rock to find Waelon leaning upon the stone. Blood crusted his tunic and trousers, but he stood on his own two feet, dark eyes meeting every gaze with surly fortitude. Torbjorn thought to ask if he was well, but then he smelled the faintest whiff of smoked herbs in the air and saw Tomza kneeling behind him. A dwarfess, a ranger by her gear, was lying in front of the young ascedwan, head in Tomza's lap.

"She going to make it?" Gromic asked as his mount shuffled nervously, snuffling the air.

Waelon followed the stout dwarf's gaze to the prone dwarfess, then nodded.

"You're saying one wheezer did all this?" Yorm pressed, nudging his mount forward until its tusked snout was inches from Waelon's face. "Killed a whole patrol except for you three? You expect us to believe that?"

"Aye," Waelon replied icily, looking past the boar at the rider. "If you'd ever fought a wight, you'd know that's not surprising."

Yorm bristled, but before things could devolve into a greater waste of time, Torbjorn raised his voice to an authoritative boom.

"I saw the trail the bear left, but is that a good guide to where the wight headed?"

For a heartbeat, Waelon held his glare at Yorm, then nodded at a spot that was particularly trampled. "Good enough for a start, but I'd watch for tracks. He seemed frantic and spent a bit of time fretting like he was trying to sniff the wheezer out. In that sort of state, he's liable to make a mistake and follow his nose down a false trail."

Torbjorn nodded, uncertain that the light would hold long enough for them to have much more success, but it was a fair warning. He was about to turn his mount with a call of thanks to the big dwarf, but Yorm's grating voice cut in.

"He?" the dogordwan cried, incredulity making his voice even more peevish. "Do you mean the beast?"

"Aye," Waelon answered coolly, then turned his back on the officer to nod at Torbjorn. "Good hunting, sir."

"Did you just turn your back on a superior officer?" Yorm snarled, and his blotferow gave a sympathetic snort.

"Dogordwan Yorm!" Torbjorn snapped in a tone so sharp the cavalry officer flinched. "Kindly shut your mouth or relinquish your command. I've no more patience for your suspicion or your vanity! *Do you understand?*"

Yorm met Torbjorn's gaze, and after a measuring moment, understood that now was not his moment to play the defiant hero. The dogordwan muttered his understanding as he ducked his helmed head in a show of deference. Torbjorn didn't miss how the hinged cheek plates flexed with Yorm's jaw clenching as the helm bobbed.

This isn't going to end until I do something drastic. You won't back down until someone puts you down. Knowing that was coming did nothing for Torbjorn's flagging energy. He could only manage one crisis at a time.

"You heard the dwarf," Torbjorn called, dragging his blotferow's head around. "We follow the bear's trail, keeping an eye out for where the wheezer's path might have branched off. If we come to that, I expect I'll send half of you to follow the bear. The other half will come with me after the wight."

There were stiff nods all around him, and Torbjorn got the distinct impression that these dwans were not the sort to ride to his rescue should he find himself cut off and surrounded by the enemy. They were no Sablestone Guard.

"Let's go."

"Follow, but don't engage. We won't fight the creature if we don't have to."

Before long, they had found it necessary to divide the riders, one group to follow Ober's trail and the other with Torbjorn to follow the long stride of the wight. He'd just issued a warning about how to handle the "bear" if the secondary force encountered their quarry, provoking more than a few questioning frowns but, thankfully, no criticism.

Not that it would do them any good, Torbjorn thought as they trotted after the footprints. *I'll just have to hope Ober has control of whatever part of him makes him that way.*

The commander had once had an opportunity to talk privately with Ober about the events that had taken place when they were separated, particularly this new "understanding" he had with the force inside him. Torbjorn had admitted at the time that the explanations the young dwarf had offered made no sense to Torbjorn, but Ober had insisted that he was again united.

Torbjorn hadn't the slightest idea what that meant, but that Ober had remained in control throughout the siege and had not changed and devoured a garrison's worth of dwarves was evidence that *something* had improved. The ondwan hoped that "unitedness" would see Ober spare any overzealous riders.

The one silver lining was that Torbjorn had a near-perfect justification for sending Yorm with the second group. There was a risk in letting the dogordwan off his leash, though he'd surreptitiously motioned for Haeda to follow them. What was the worst Yorm could do, attack a transformed Ober? Torbjorn almost laughed as he imagined the look on the rebellious officer's expression just before Ober removed said expression, along with the head that was wearing it.

"Is it wrong to hope he runs into the lad?" Gromic rasped as he pulled level with his commander. His voice was pitched for the two of them. "Like to see him try and throw his weight around then."

"Great minds," Torbjorn mused as they trotted on, leaning over the humped shoulders of their mounts.

"Where do you figure it's going?" the fordwan asked after a few minutes. "To escape, I figure it would've gone back north the way it came from. This way is going to bring it either to Heimlagu or the Lake Gate, right?"

The sun was sinking toward the hungry teeth of the peaks along the Wyrmspines fast, but the night-wise eyes of the dwarves were able to adapt. Torbjorn frowned as he tracked the sharp depression through the trampled snow that marked the passing of the dwarven forces earlier in the day. If the snowy slush hadn't had time to at least partially refreeze, this whole exercise might've been fruitless, but as it was, the pockmarks left by the retreating wight were easy to follow.

Retreating? Torbjorn pondered. *It didn't feel like he was running away in the cavern. It was like he'd found something more worth his time.*

"I don't rightly know," Torbjorn admitted, eyes narrowed and knuckles white on the reins. "I just know we need to find the bastard."

"What do we do if we come up on it?" Gromic whispered, concern if not fear in his tone.

Torbjorn looked up from tracking and offered Gromic a grim smile.

"I suppose we'll have to figure it out." The commander shrugged, trying to force an energy and flippancy he didn't feel. "If nothing else, we tangle with it until Ober shows up and does what he does best."

Gromic nodded with a wan smile before settling back in the saddle, eyes down and brows crinkled in consternation. "Doesn't seem like that strategy worked out so good for the ranger."

Torbjorn, having no answer, went back to picking out the wheezer's tracks. Silently, he prayed to the Shaper and whoever else was listening that he would find a better answer before they came across the deadly creature.

A short spell later, Gromic rose in the saddle, prompting a squeal of protest from the blotferow at the shift in weight.

"Do you hear that?"

"Yes. I think the poor beast wasn't ready for that," Torbjorn replied irritably, the distraction threatening to make him lose track of the prints. The path was narrower here, so the passage of the dwarves had been compressed. The snow was now more difficult to read, and that, combined with the onset of darkness, was making reading the trail tenuous.

"Not that." Gromic huffed, then cocked his head to one side. "It sounded like metal on metal. You know, fighting."

Torbjorn was about to observe that if the wight was fighting Ober, there would not be the sound of metal on metal, when a keening cry tore through the air.

"That's a blade-ear," one of the dwarf riders called. "I'd know the sound of them dyin' anywhere."

"Savagelings here in the mountains?" a fellow rider retorted to the grim declaration.

"Too soft and high," a third interjected. "Not enough bite to it. That's a myrkling screaming, that is!"

"Myrklings!" The second scoffed. "Where did the ol' bruised biters spring from? I didn't spot any myrkboughs on the way here."

Another piercing cry shivered the mountain air.

"Pale or purple, they're dyin'," the first observed, disgust thickening his voice. "Hate how they make that noise. Just die quietlike, why don't you? No need to make such a fuss."

Further discussion was put to rest as Torbjorn put his heels to his boar, then the whole group thundered down the slope. Slush and shards of ice flew up from the blotferows' hooves, creating a clinking rain on the armor of dwarf and beast, adding to the noise.

Despite that, just before they rounded a twist in the path, Torbjorn did hear metal clashing.

Elves doing something useful for once, Torbjorn considered. *That caps the day off.*

Then they were around the bend, and Torbjorn's mind reeled.

In the middle of the path, the wight was engaged with a troupe of well-armed svartalfs led by Sir Utyrvaul Urivianoc. Two elves lay on the ground, one clutching its shoulder, from which the arm hung bonelessly. The other svartalf was flat on the ground, body curled around a chest that looked as though it had imploded.

A short distance from the fallen elves stood Mabon Reeve, with his family blade in one hand. He shielded the golden-eyed child with the other.

"Grimmoth's Grin," one of the dwarf cavaliers swore. "What is this?"

Before Torbjorn could produce an explanation or command, the wight swept its mace in a wide arc that sent the nimble elves darting back. Seizing the opportunity, the wight rushed toward Mabon and the child. The two elves in its path were knocked aside by its lowered shoulder.

"Mabon!" Utyrvaul shouted, springing after the charging wight. "Look out!"

Torbjorn urged his mount forward, but he knew he wouldn't get there in time. Worse still, the swine only made it a few hesitant steps before it screamed and began to buck in terror. The commander shouted for the others to engage, but they were all in a similar predicament.

Utyrvaul managed to close the distance and lashed out with his saber. The curved blade swept toward the legs of the racing revenant and managed to notch the bone. The wight hissed but hardly slowed, then swung blindly at the attacker at its back. The svartalf's blade swept up for a parry, but the cudgel battered the saber back upon its wielder. Poleaxed by the blunt spine of his blade, Utyrvaul staggered, long legs tangling, then toppled to one side. The elf managed to turn it into a graceful roll, although blood ran from his crown to the bridge of his nose.

The wight was out of range. It reached for the girl, not concerned by the trembling man-child in its way. The lifeless tyrant learned the error of its ways when Mabon swept his family's sword up and the blade flared with white-hot light. Bones that had barely been marred by an expertly placed sword stroke parted like rotted wood.

With a howl of rage, the wight staggered back and glanced at the arm that now ended just below the elbow. The wound smoked, bone charred and metal bowing like it was fresh from the forge.

"Stay back!" Mabon cried, shifting his feet into a respectable fighting stance with the point of the blade aimed at the wight's face. "You're not going to touch her!"

The wight recovered from its shock and fixed eyes on the golden-eyed child. "Impressive," it droned with a voice of stolen breaths. "Finding a slave that can wield the ancient arms after a *tozelchaun* with sorcery. What a wonderful day! Playtime is over, little one. The Matron calls, and we're done waiting."

The wight took a step forward and Mabon leaped to the attack, but the step had been a feint. Pivoting, the agile corpse avoided the glowing blade and punched out with the hilt of its weapon. The coat of plate the manling wore spared him a crushed sternum, but the blow sent him rocketing back to land on the ground, gasping.

"You're coming with me, little sister. It is time."

Torbjorn would have sprung clear of his boar to go to the child's aid, but the creature's movements were so wild and frenetic that it was all he could do to keep from being thrown off and gored or trampled. He wanted to shout for the child to run, but that proved impossible when the impact of the blotferow's head against his body knocked the wind from him.

The source of the swine's terror was made manifest by a tremendous roar. Off a ledge crumbling under his weight came Ober, wearing the titanic form of the bear. The ursine terror landed with a heavy thud, scattering elves who dove to avoid its bulk. Some of the swine in the ondwan's retinue bolted, taking their riders for a merry jaunt.

Through the yawing and pitching, Torbjorn watched as Ober swatted the mace aside with disdain and plunged his claws through the center of the revenant's mass. The wight shrilled as they pierced armor, flesh, and bone like cloth, but the cry cut off when the heavy head plunged. Everything above the wight's chest was between the bear's huge jaws.

With a crunch and a ripping twist, the wight came apart. The head and shoulders hung from Ober's maw, and the rest collapsed under the weight of the claws in the torso.

Ober shook his paw free of clinging remains and sat down on his haunches. A huge yawn stretched the lethal jaws, then, as before, the semblance of the bear fell away. From the shrinking torso appeared Ober, wearing the peculiar collection of hides that served as armor. The young dwarf shuffled about for a moment, taking in the bizarre scene before looking at the golden-eyed child with a sleepy grin.

"Well, hello there," the young dwarf murmured. "Didn't think I'd get to see you again." Eyes half-lidded, Ober looked up at Torbjorn, whose mount, along with the rest, had finally stopped screaming and flailing.

"Hey, Commander," Ober called with a cheery wave. "Mission accomplished, sir."

With another yawn, Ober started to lower himself to the ground, then collapsed in the snow. A moment later, his snores sawed through the unnaturally still air.

Torbjorn murmured, still coming to grips with what he'd seen, "Ober, sometimes I envy you."

CHAPTER SEVENTEEN

"What are you talking about? Of course it should be destroyed! Kill it now while we have the chance."

Gromic stepped forward, looming over Dogordwan Yorm since they were both on their own two feet.

"His name is Ober," the stout dwarf rumbled, arms crossing, "and he, like everyone in this fortress, serves at the ondwan's pleasure."

The hall within Greyshelf used as the central command station was a barebones affair compared to the previous administration's. The scattered gilded plates of finger foods and copious offerings of drink were gone, replaced by a single table where plain biscuits sat next to salted pork, practically untouched. Beside the table, a stout barrel full of fresh snowmelt was the closest thing to luxury.

Torbjorn was thankful for it as he dumped another ladleful into his cup. *All this about Ober*, the commander thought. *They don't understand that the lad might be the least of our problems. Well, maybe not the least, but certainly lower tier.*

"This is not a question of the ondwan's authority," Ghedau explained with forced patience. "This is a matter of understanding the practicalities of keeping someone like that in the fortress. If he loses control, there is little to stop him from killing dozens of dwans."

"There's no need to be hysterical," Klaus replied. "He's still a creature of flesh and blood, and one creature couldn't kill—"

"Hundreds," Torbjorn stated, his flat tone cutting off the chatter. "Thousands, even."

He faced those gathered in the hall, meeting the eyes of all in attendance. "It's not an exaggeration to say that if he wanted to, Ober could tear apart every dwarf in this fortress. Certainly, some could retreat to the lower levels where he wouldn't fit, but if he stalked this fortress in his bear shape, every dwarf who tried to fight him would die."

Torbjorn recalled the slaughter in the Picket tower. The twisted iron and cracked stones of barred doors smashed in. The blood on the walls, the floors, and the ceiling. He shook his head and took a drink of the icy water.

"If you could draw him out into the open, maybe you'd be able to wear him out," Torbjorn mused, verbalizing thoughts he'd considered a time or two. "Keep him rushing back and forth between skirmishing bands, hope he exhausts himself and changes back. You'd still lose scores of dwarves, and if he could, he'd wise up and run off, but that's the best you could hope for."

Torbjorn emerged from his musing to find every face gray and grim. All except Utyrvaul, whose practiced expression of nonchalance and condescending amusement was as affixed as ever.

Gromic's mouth opened to support his leader, but the stout dwarf could offer nothing.

"Knowing all that," Yorm snarled, stalking forward a step. "Knowing how dangerous that thing is, you are still going to let it live?"

"Not just live," Ghedau added as she moved alongside the

dogordwan. "You're having it live in this fortress with us, though you admit it would be unstoppable. Why would you do that?"

Torbjorn looked from the cavalry officer to his supposed betrothed and couldn't keep a wry smile off his face. Grinning over his cup, he nodded at Ghedau before taking another swallow.

The dwarfess realized where she stood, and with an embarrassed start, she shuffled back.

Almost forgot, didn't you, darling? Torbjorn's smile melted as he considered the remaining water at the bottom of his cup along with the questions they'd raised. As with most things, he knew the answer, but forming it into something audible and clear would be no small task. His brow furrowed as he sought to fit the last pieces together, but one dwarf was not content to give him the time.

"If the ondwan doesn't know his mind," Yorm declared, his voice an unwelcome interruption of the silence, "maybe he would do well to listen to reason before the demands of many voices make up his mind for him."

Gromic, much quicker than his rotund mass should have allowed, moved before anyone could react. Well, anyone except Utyrvaul, but the svartalf was watching the events with glee.

"Guards!" Yorm shouted as he fumbled for the magsax at his belt. The dogordwan proved doubly unlucky since the Sablestone Guards within the chamber remained motionless, and his unsteady hand bound the weapon in its scabbard with his panicked draw.

Gromic moved with mechanical precision, one meaty paw snaring the sword arm's wrist as the other hand smashed into Yorm's face. The dogordwan's head snapped back, one cheek beginning to swell and discolor. The smaller dwarf gave a cry as the hand gripping his sword completed the draw. A sharp twist of Gromic's hand sent the blade to the stone floor.

"Stop this," Ghedau shouted, shrinking back another step. "Torbjorn, tell him."

Gromic struck again, and Yorm went to his knees, blood dribbling from split lips. The stout dwarf hand left the cavalry officer's wrist and seized his collar to keep the dogordwan upright, and his fist pumped like a piston to punctuate his next words. "Don't. Ever. Threaten. Him. Again."

Yorm had tried to fend off the first few blows. By the last two, he was limp in the fordwan's grip, head lolling after each impact.

"Torbjorn," Klaus whispered.

The ondwan nodded and raised his hand. "That's enough." He turned to fill his cup from the barrel behind him.

Gromic released the dogordwan and walked over to stand before his ondwan. Yorm flopped to the floor and lay there wheezing and burbling through his mashed face. Torbjorn waited, his gaze on the battered officer despite feeling Ghedau's burning stare.

You made a dwan the ondwan with poison and a lying priest, Torbjorn mused. *Then you expect he'll not have to rule with an iron fist? Oh, my dear, you're the most dangerous kind of fool.*

Little by little, Yorm gathered himself, eventually managing to rearrange himself into a slumped sitting position. One eye was swollen shut, and the rest of that side of his face had adopted the shades of the night sky.

Torbjorn hid his wince, remembering his beating at the hands of Tweldwan Jozef Merihn, but he reminded himself that his abuse had come from obeying orders, not threatening insubordination. That and he'd been tied up, then laid into by two dwarves. He wasn't sure why, but he was certain that made it different. He dismissed the thought as he knelt beside Yorm.

The dogordwan's good eye widened in fear and he tensed to scuttle backward, but Torbjorn took his shoulder in a firm but gentle grip. "Steady now." Torbjorn's voice carried the gentle tones he'd heard Haeda use with frightened swine. "Steady."

Yorm stopped trying to scramble away, then noticed the cup in the ondwan's other hand. With shaking fingers, he took the cup, his commander's hand helping steady his grip.

"I need you to listen very carefully," Torbjorn began, his tone still soft. "I've tolerated your insolence and insubordination patiently, hoping to win you over by demonstrations of my competence and goodwill. I've given you months to come to grips with me. As you now understand, that time is at an end."

Yorm choked as he sipped the water, and red-steaked spittle splattered his beard.

Torbjorn waited for the fit to end before he spoke again. "I don't have to explain myself to you, but I'm not a tyrant if I don't have to be. I hope you are listening now. We will keep Ober alive, first because he is a good dwan who has proved faithful and true despite great trials. Second, his bear form is one of the only ways we know we can consistently kill wights, and they fear him if they can fear anything. That will be vital to breaking this siege.

"Third and perhaps the most practical point, if we attempt to kill Ober out of fear and fail, we will not only betray a good dwarf, but we will also have lost our chance to wield a powerful weapon against our enemy. Finally, we'll assure that a large number of good dwans die when they should not have had to."

Torbjorn studied Yorm's brutalized face, wondering if, even without the split, swollen skin, he'd be able to read the dwarf's thoughts. "Do you understand?"

The dogordwan's head bobbed, but when the ondwan looked into his eyes, all he saw was fear. Torbjorn heaved a sigh, then rose to his feet and motioned to the nearest Sablestone Guard.

"Assist the dogordwan to his squadron's barracks," Torbjorn instructed. "See that he is brought an extra measure of liquor from the stores to aid his recovery."

All stood in silence as Yorm was helped to his feet and led out of the chamber. Only after the doors boomed shut and the stomp of heavy sabatons echoed on the steps beyond did anyone dare to speak.

"That was foolish," Ghedau hissed. "Do you think with everything as precarious as it is, you can have your bully batter a senior officer without consequences?"

Gromic opened his mouth to respond, but Torbjorn silenced him with a wave of his hand. "Yorm has defied me on multiple occasions, often in a very public fashion," the ondwan explained, realizing with a sigh that the pummeled officer had taken his cup. "This time, he was openly speaking of leading an insurrection against me. This helped him understand that will not be tolerated without me having to shame him in front of all of the other senior officers."

Ghedau crossed her arms, unimpressed. "Some will not see it that way, especially when they see his very public bruises."

Torbjorn shrugged as he fetched a fresh cup, his wooden hand scraping the vessel. He clenched his teeth at the sound. "If you're so concerned, why don't you chase after him? I'm sure you could soothe his wounds if you could find the right thing in that bag of yours. Who knows, he might even take you up on whatever else you have to offer."

He saw the dwarfess' cheeks redden and felt something twist in his chest, half shame, half disgust. He was being petty, and he hated it. He ladled more water into the cup and took a drink. Maybe the cold water could wash away the hot venom that welled up any time he talked to her.

"My only concern is you, my Ondwan," Ghedau countered after taking a moment to compose herself. "I know you are doing everything for the sake of the dwans in Greyshelf, but there are more diplomatic ways of accomplishing tasks."

Where do poison, treachery, and blasphemy fit into that statement?

Torbjorn's wooden hand spasmed in irritation, and the tin vessel crumpled. Words that burned on his tongue and would cut through the air to bite deep sprang to mind, but he forced them down, albeit with an effort.

Klaus stepped forward to reply for him, but a sharp look from Torbjorn made the lardwan step back with a submissive nod.

"I will take that into consideration," the ondwan replied, looking at the water dribbling from the ruptured cup. "For now, what's done is done. It's not just dwarves that are my concern."

Taking his cue, Utyrvaul stepped forward to sketch a courtly bow as Torbjorn turned to regard him. "I wish I could say I was glad to see you, elf," Torbjorn grumbled, then thrust his chin at the chambers beyond the hall, "but there's a manling and a lass in my halls you were supposed to see to Heimgrud and beyond. I didn't expect you back until you returned with Waegur and Rothi at the head of a relief force. While I'm sure your little band of myrklings are proficient murderers, they're hardly what I asked for."

The svartalf rose from his bow, flashing Torbjorn a knowing smile.

"Oh, they most certainly are, and upon compensation from the Holt'Dwan's coffers, they're yours to command as you see fit, most mighty of ondwans."

Torbjorn frowned as he pitched the crushed cup behind him and groped for another. "Cut the kak and explain yourself. Why are you back, especially with your current company?"

Utyrvaul struck a noble pose, shoulders back and chin raised as though he were sitting for a painting. The bandages on his brow somehow made him look even more dashing, a valiant officer fresh from the field. Torbjorn rolled his eyes.

"It is a truly harrowing tale from which a great saga could be composed to entertain generations. Where to begin?"

Torbjorn heaved an intrusive sigh that stymied the elf's carefully composed recitation. "Utyrvaul, for once in your life, would you please cut to the chase? As you've already seen, I've got quite enough to sort through."

The elf's posture relaxed, and his smile became unctuous.

"Ah, yes. Heavy is the head that wears the crown," the myrkling quipped, then raised a hand to flutter at his mouth. "Oh, my apologies. We're not quite there yet, are we? Terribly sorry."

"Utyrvaul," Torbjorn growled. "Report. Now."

"Of course, Torbjorn, anything for you," the elf replied with a wink and squared his narrow shoulders. "We arrived at Heimgrud without much incident other than extortionary rates by the ferry captain. Very impressive…well, I'm not sure you'd call it a city. Is there a dwarvish word for a massive citadel atop mountain-ravaging mines? Anyway, thanks to your clerical envoys, we were soon brought into the court of Stendwan Assface."

Torbjorn almost reminded the myrkling that the name was Stendwan Ashfer, but he didn't want to derail him. That, and "Assface" wasn't an inaccurate description of the stendwan, whose teeth and braying laugh reminded him of a beast of burden.

"Once there, your representatives did a passable job of presenting the current predicament, though they proved somewhat indiscreet. I'm afraid they did not conceal the recent changes to the power structure in this Holt'Dwan. Assface—am I saying that right?—was, as expected, very surprised to hear who had risen to the rank of ondwan since your infamy has reached well beyond the Holt'Dwan. Even with the priests providing thorough and, at times, impassioned propositions about your divine selection, the stendwan didn't seem convinced."

Torbjorn was not surprised by that, and the burden settled on his shoulders. He'd known this was all going to come to an end. Known they'd eventually come for him to finish what Glastuc had set in motion. He'd told himself he was at peace with it since, either way, it meant that forces would come and help drive back the wights. He just wished the end didn't have to come so quickly since those he was responsible for were still in precarious circumstances.

"We knew this might happen." The ondwan sighed. "Assf...I mean, Stendwan Ashfer won't leave Heimgrud, but he'll contact the Cefstan Holt'Dwan who are patrolling the Wyrm Way between Heimgrud and Torvgrud. They'll get rid of me, but at least with another Holt'Dwan, they can drive back the wights. Hell, they might even be able to launch a new campaign if things go well."

Utyrvaul's head wagged, but before he could explain the gesture, Ghedau's voice rose in a sharp cry. "They can't! You were chosen by the Shaper."

Torbjorn didn't even try to hold back his bitter laugh. "Our missionary priests were unsuccessful in their efforts to convert others."

"I don't understand," Gromic admitted, brows knitting in confusion. "Cefstan's going to come over here to remove you? Can they do that?"

"They most certainly can." Torbjorn chuckled. "That and much more."

Ghedau's eyes were bright with fear and fury. "What are you laughing about? Don't you understand what's going to happen to you if they come and remove you?"

"Excuse me," the svartalf began, but the dwarves hardly noticed.

"Oh, I'm quite aware," Torbjorn declared with another sour laugh. "Everyone has shown their hand, and we've lost. There's nothing to do except let things play out."

"If I could just..." the elf attempted, but Klaus cut him off.

"Even if they've come to remove you," the lardwan began in his most reasonable voice, "they're not going to just show up and drag you away in chains. You're the acknowledged and sworn ondwan of the Holt'Dwan, and you hold the oaths of a dozen veteran tweldwans."

"You think they are going to care about that?" Torbjorn snorted. "They accepted me because they were caught between a rock and an army of walking dead men. With a relief force and a legitimate command staff, those tweldwans will forget their oaths faster than Yorm's going to forget the beating Gromic gave him."

The ondwan turned to his faithful fordwan with a conciliatory hand. "No insult meant. There's just no teaching some dwarves."

Gromic nodded grimly. "Yorm's got kak for brains."

"Just so." Torbjorn nodded and turned back to his lardwan and his betrothed. "Honestly, I don't understand what either of you expects me to do."

"You just won a great victory against the enemy," Ghedau protested, her words gaining momentum as she spoke. "If you planned another sortie, a true counter-offensive, you could catch the wheezers off-guard. Get that beast back on the field and tear through the enemy, crushing one wight after another. Then when the relief force gets here, they'll have to see."

"There is no relief force coming!" Every dwarven eye swung to Utyrvaul, who stood rigid, glaring at the assembly.

"What?" the question sprang from enough mouths that no one was certain who'd said it.

"As I was saying," the svartalf resumed archly. "The stendwan was not impressed by the priests' arguments concerning the ondwan, but when he learned about the request to bear the child to Torvgrud and eventually to Mount Smarthdun, he became very curious about the provenance of the little one."

Torbjorn was about to ask why that much information had been shared with the stendwan, but the myrkling held up his hand. "As I said, the fretful priests were indiscreet. Regardless, once Assface heard that, he was like a dog with a bone. There was nothing we could do but watch as he wrung out the fact that the wights were in pursuit of the child, and no one was able to convince him that the consequences of the wights acquiring the child might prove apocalyptic. A very cynical sort in all the worst ways, that Assface."

Torbjorn was inclined to agree, but he remembered that only a few months ago, he too would have found all of this beyond belief. Decades of war and surviving in an ugly world, and in the relative blink of an eye, the world turns upside-down.

"Well, once he'd ferreted out that point, the stendwan had a better idea than having armies march off. It seems many of those in power now see the efforts in the Southern Vale to be a losing wager. Since the rising of the dead, even those settlements still under dwarvish control have proven to be less profitable than hoped, and there is increasing pressure on the Cyniburgs, both without and within the dynasty, to cut their losses and establish a stable border with the wights. Stendwan Assface saw the chance to accomplish that in the child."

Torbjorn rocked back on his heels at the news as if it were a blow, yet it refused to be relegated to a matter of the physical. The dwarf commander's mind reeled as anguish threatened to rise and choke him.

"Oh, no," Gromic muttered. "They're going to just hand her over."

"No relief army, just a task force to remove you and then broker the exchange," Utyrvaul expounded. "Needless to say, I knew you wouldn't approve of this turn of events. While the stendwan was putting things together, Mabon and I worked in secret to acquire the services of some of my kind to help us extract the child and return her to you. I provided several false trails as we absconded, so I imagine we have at best a ten-day. More likely half that before the stendwan's task force arrives, looking for our little bundle of doom."

Torbjorn nodded, his mind racing as he turned to meet Klaus' gaze.

"Maybe a counterattack isn't such a bad idea," the lardwan

opined, reading his old friend's thoughts. "The wights don't act like living things, but they do seem to have some understanding of self-preservation. I need to go through the lookout reports on movements now that we've bloodied their snouts."

"Were there any serious attacks on the Cliff Gate while we were gone?" Torbjorn asked, the first hints of a plan forming.

"No," Klaus answered. "Nothing worth noting."

Torbjorn smiled. "Then they are either weaker or at least less coordinated than we thought. If they'd been able to, they would have launched a real assault down there, either to assist the forces inside here or to divide our attention if their efforts were thwarted."

"Wait!" Ghedau shouted, hands raised as though she were prepared to swat down any other ideas flying about. "What are you two talking about?"

Both dwarves turned to her. "A counterattack, my dear," Torbjorn replied, then cocked an eyebrow. "Just as you suggested."

"Why?" the ascedwan spluttered. "The only reason we've kept that brat safe is because there was nothing to be gained by handing her over to the wights. Now that we know you could beat Stendwan Ashfer to the punch, why shouldn't we?"

Gromic gave an incredulous chuckle, and Torbjorn rubbed his throbbing eyes to buy time to compose himself. "Because, my dearest darling, if we give the child to the wights, they'll use her, quite possibly lethally, to restore themselves. After they do that, what is to stop them from marching forth and taking the entire valley and then the Wyrmspines and beyond?"

Ghedau saw everyone's expressions and retreated a step. "You don't believe that nonsense."

"Of course we do." Torbjorn sighed. "After what we saw in the tunnels beneath the valley and what those wolves told Ober, Tomza, and Utyrvaul, it all makes sense. Especially combined with the wights' goal and what little the child can tell us."

Ghedau laughed harshly. "Do you hear yourself? Some old ruins and tall tales from a couple of savagelings, and you buy into all this? Be reasonable, Torbjorn. Make a deal with the wheezers for the brat, and this can all be over."

Torbjorn's hands clenched, and he was forced to speak very slowly to make sure his words didn't come out in a bellow. "Ignoring the fact that you are telling me to offer up a child to monsters, it was *your* idea to launch a counterattack to change minds about me. I'm not sure a counterattack will do that, but it *will* change the Empire's plans for the Southern Vale."

"If we succeed," Klaus added.

"Yes, if we succeed," Torbjorn agreed, his expression pensive. "If we fail, there's a chance that we'll all have died for nothing."

"Not for nothing," Gromic stated, shoulders squaring. "We'll die doing what's right. That's all any dwan can hope for."

Torbjorn's heart kicked hard in his chest, and he slapped a hand on Gromic's shoulder. "That, old friend, is why you are my fordwan."

Gromic cheeks flushed over his golden beard, but he nodded appreciatively after a gulp.

"You're all mad!" Ghedau shrieked, moving toward Torbjorn, hands held out beseechingly. "Torbjorn, my betrothed, please, listen to me! You don't have to do this. It's a stupid risk, and worse, it won't save you. If you win, they might continue the war, but you will not be the ondwan. If you broker the peace to end a fruitless war, you can return in victory, resigning your position as Ondwan in honor. Then we can return to your family to start the life we should've had."

Torbjorn's icy glare made her back up before she could rest her hands on him.

"Even if it doesn't begin something catastrophic," he growled, eyes burning through her, "it will cost the life of an innocent child."

Ghedau's outstretched hands curled into fists and shot to her sides. "In war and in peace, there are casualties," she hissed. "Are you going to risk our future, your life, and the lives of every dwan here for the sake of a single human child?"

Torbjorn glanced at Gromic, who nodded, and Klaus, who shrugged, then looked Ghedau in the eye.

"My betrothed," he rumbled from deep within his chest, "you should know by now I'd risk more than that for the right thing."

CHAPTER EIGHTEEN

"You need to eat." Waelon had been careful to keep the broth from dripping on Clahdi as he held the spoon out to her, but he nearly slopped some on her as she twisted away.

"I'm not hungry."

Waelon frowned and withdrew the proffered spoon, to then put it back in the cloudy contents of the bowl. Tomza had insisted that while things were still healing on the dwarfess ranger's head, she be kept on a liquid diet to keep vigorous chewing from undoing the needlework there. Waelon had immediately thought stout ale would do the job, but the young ascedwan had insisted that actual food, if broth could be counted as such, be eaten first.

The big dwarf had not wanted to bring that point up to Clahdi as though she were a naughty child in need of bribing, but now, with her lying upon her cot, refusing to eat, he wasn't sure if that might be necessary.

"How can you not be hungry?" the dwarf asked, red brows knitting over his eyes. "You were too rangy for a proper dwarfess when I met you, and now you've gone over a day without eating. You've got to be hungry."

Clahdi's eyes glistened with unshed tears. "No, I *don't* got to. I don't got to do anything."

Waelon's frown deepened as he saw her pained expression. He was not a particularly sensitive dwarf, and that among a rather taciturn species, but something twisted in his chest at that look. Vaulting through unfamiliar patterns of thought, the ranger forced himself to ponder what could be bothering the dwarfess.

"Is it your patrol?" he asked after a moment sitting silently, the bowl of broth in his lap. "Because they...I mean, that you lost them all?"

Clahdi blinked rapidly and swallowed hard but didn't answer.

Waelon fidgeted with the rim of the soup bowl, then, with a heavy sigh, he set it to one side and sank down next to the pallet. One thick, scarred hand stretched out, fingers shaking, but then slowly, gently, he put it against the side of her face. With care for her small cuts and bruises, he ran his thumb over her cheek as his fingers slid into her tangled hair.

The big dwarf braced himself for the violent twist away, the scathing rebuke that he would dare to treat her like this, but it never came. To his surprise, shock even, the only move Clahdi made was to press her face against his hand, and the only sound was a soft sob as the tears finally broke free to trace their glittering arcs. For a good long while, there was no sound except her low sobs as he held her fast and wiped her tears away.

The moment stretched until Waelon felt like he must say something. It wasn't because the quiet bothered him, quite the opposite, but more that he knew he had something inside him that might help. That, more than anything, was what he wanted to do.

"I told you how my brother died," he whispered, his gravelly voice more gentle than it had ever been. "He died a hero, died defeating an evil enemy, which isn't something a dwan can trust will happen. He hopes it will be. Hopes that his death will mean something."

Clahdi didn't speak, but her breathing steadied, and she gazed at him, still tearful but focused.

"It's what every one of us thinks about." Waelon sighed, his gaze sliding beyond her, recalling places and faces she'd never seen. "We ask the question of what that death means to us, not what our death will mean to others. At least, I didn't."

The big dwarf's eyelids fluttered. The shimmer under them might have been mistaken for the reflection of the flames that day at Ipplen's Ford.

"Then my brother died," he continued, and a lump he hadn't expected formed in his throat. "Suddenly, I knew I'd never asked the right question. I'd never wondered what it would mean to others if I died, even a hero's death. I never thought about what it would mean to my brother, the only family and blood that mattered to me."

A fresh sob welled up inside Clahdi, and the dwarfess let it roll out, unashamed. Waelon's hand still caressed her face.

"He beat me to the punch. That's it, really," Waelon croaked, his voice tightening as those events replayed in his mind. "He was always like that. Smaller, quicker, and more reckless, if you can imagine it. Things were burning all around us, and one of the eaves was coming loose as the framing split. I saw my chance. I knew if I could just catch the wight off guard, I could send him crashing into the blaze. Then the eave would swing down and smash us both, fire and force in perfect harmony to snuff out the wheezer."

The tears would not be denied any longer, and his hand stilled on the dwarfess' cheek as he watched the moment unfold with grief-born clarity.

"Raelon saw it too," Waelon growled, the pain tightening his chest, his heart, and his soul. "That crazy bastard, the real mad lad? He saw it, then saw me, and he winked and tore across the burning boards right into the damned wight."

Waelon made to wipe the tears from his eyes to dispel the

weakness he despised in himself, but Clahdi held his hand, lips pressed to his scarred knuckles. Even more surprising were her eyes, huge and intent, drinking him in without scorn or pity for his tears. The shining remains of her tears were still in the corners of her eyes, and that sight eased the crushing pressure around his heart.

"I wondered why it was him and not me," the big dwarf admitted, shoulders bowed. "Even though I knew that's a fool's game. I asked every stupid question—every one that doesn't have an answer. They ran in circles around my head."

He remembered the whirs of axes and blades thudding into a broken mill wheel.

"I can't say I learned anything," he confessed, his gaze wandering away from her face. He still felt her watching him, but it wasn't unwelcome. "No great mystery solved or wisdom. I'm a simple dwarf who's pretty good at killing things and living for the next battle. Always had a knack for survivin'."

For an instant, he remembered the blade passing through his neck, his lifeblood flowing over his chest. He felt coldness descend as the world darkened, and he remembered the stinging sound of the incantation and the smell of burned honey. His eyes darted to the stitches on the dwarfess' head, the thin rents in the skin the only evidence that the wight's fist had cratered her skull.

He looked away quickly, his stomach turning and his mouth tasting like ashes.

"I'm just saying I know what it's like." He sniffed, then coughed, trying to clear the burn of bile from his throat. "That's all."

He still felt her eyes on him, and suddenly he felt naked. He didn't dare look at her lest she peer into his eyes and see the damnation that united them.

Her lips pressed his hand, and she breathed deep. Could she smell the scalded sweetness of the sorcery on him? Tomza had put him back together so many times he was amazed he didn't reek of it.

"I'm sorry about your brother," Clahdi whispered, then her hand left him, and she patted his shoulder. "But I'm glad that you're here with me."

Drawn by her touch, Waelon turned to face her, his mouth dry and his heart hammering in his ears. He saw the deep longing in her gaze as she drew him toward her. A heartbeat later, he was close enough to feel her breath on his cheek, and her lips rose to meet his.

Waelon pinched his eyes shut as they kissed, trying to will himself not to see where the bone had buckled or remember the sounds she'd made as she'd flailed and contorted in the snow.

"Did you hear?"

Tomza looked up from her untouched meal to see her brother settle across from her on the bench. They were the only ones eating at the moment, but after everything that had happened the day before, the dwarfess didn't imagine there would be many in Greyshelf who'd willingly sit by either of them.

Word about Ober had gotten around quickly after Yorm and his detachment returned. Tomza was now guilty by association, along with the rest of the Bad Badgers, though, as his sister, she was even more tainted. She might have laughed at the irony, Ober being considered the source of corruption and her a victim of proximity, but since returning from the battle at the hidden basin, she could do little more than the bare minimum to keep herself upright, much less afford something as luxurious as a laugh.

"Hey, are you listening?" her sibling pressed. "I said, 'Did you hear?'"

Tomza was surprised to see that he was angry. Not just angry but fuming. She might have been sunken in heart and spirits, but the young dwarfess felt life trickle back into her at the peculiar revelation. Ober didn't get angry very often. Irritated or heated, yes, but genuine anger like that which smoldered in his eyes, she'd rarely seen.

"What happened?" she asked, leaning toward him.

"Torbjorn's drawing up plans for a counterattack and soon," her brother growled. He tore up his bread yet didn't bother to put the pieces in his mouth. "Seems we have to get out there and strike a real blow before some band from Heimgrud comes to kick Torbjorn out and take over."

Tomza nodded, her weary mind trying to catch up with the implications. More, she tried to understand why that course of events had driven her brother to outrage.

"You don't think that's right?" she ventured, her chin lowering as her brows rose.

Ober threw down the shredded remains of the bread he'd been savaging. "What? No! If we can hit the wheezers where it hurts, all the better. Now that the secret's out, it will honestly be easier. Torbjorn and I talked, and he's planning to make good use of my abilities."

Tomza nodded, amazed that her brother's condition would officially be included in battle plans. How this would all play out when word reached beyond the Holt'Dwan or once control was taken from Torbjorn, she could only make dark guesses, but for the moment, it was a bewildering if welcome development. That day when they'd been shuffling along in chains, each trying to figure out how to protect the other, seemed like a lifetime ago, not mere months.

Much had changed, but for her brother, life was better at this moment.

Which left the matter of his rage, which was on display as his square fingers set to twisting a rasher of bacon to bits.

"Then I don't understand," Tomza admitted, shaking her head

to stave off the lethargy threatening to creep over her. "What are you mad about?"

Ober looked up from his vengeful dismantling, then glared at his greasy fingers. "I'm angry because of why the pack of gremlickers is comin' from Heimgrud," he growled, looking around helplessly before wiping his hands on a trouser leg.

"Oh." Tomza nodded, her head swimming as her heart sank. "Because they're coming for Torbjorn."

"No," Ober snapped, the word ripped from deep within his chest with a hint of something more sinister beneath it. Tomza started at the force of the reply, then leaned back and eyed her brother warily. Her gaze swept from the tops of his hands to his eyes and back. His eyes remained normal, and no hair grew on his knuckles, but the violence of his sudden temper made her cautious.

When he registered her posture and scrutinizing stare, Ober blushed and hung his head. "I'm sorry." He sighed. "Torbjorn being removed when he's done such a good job? Better than Glastuc, for sure? That's bad."

She watched her brother's hands and eyes as he spoke. "We don't know what they'll do with him after he's been removed, and that's bad too. Torbjorn doesn't think a counterattack will change anything, but that's not what's got me so worked up. I'm fine, by the way. I know it's hard to believe, but things are different now. Bela didn't just show me that I *could* speak to it, but also how to, and we've come to an understanding."

Tomza felt the prick of a bitter thorn of jealousy at the mention of the savageling who'd proven so vital to Ober's newfound "understanding." She could've sworn from the way he talked about the furry waif that he had forgotten it was his sister's vigilant application of mona root that had kept him from transforming and murdering everyone around him before the elf had pranced into their lives.

"I wonder how they're gonna feel when they find out the girl's back?" Ober mused, not noticing that his sister's face twisted at more references to the elves.

"How about you tell me what's got your danglers knotted, eh?" the dwarfess snapped. "Rather than coming in here and tearing up your food like a savageling and scaring me by growling like an animal."

Her brother's chin dipped at the rebuke, and Tomza felt the urge to hide her face. An embarrassed silence stretched between them. "Look, Ober," the dwarfess began. "I'm sorry. I just—"

Ober's shaking head cut off the apology she was about to muster.

"No, it's all right," he replied, then let out another long sigh. "That's fair, and with everyone knowing now, I need to be even more careful, so this is good. I'm glad you said it. I needed it."

Tomza felt the urge to throw her food-laden platter and also to scream and reach across the table to hug her brother. In the end, she settled for sighing and sinking into her chair. "Okay, then what's bothering you?"

Ober's hands interlocked, knuckles whitening before he slowly set both hands on the table and looked at his sister.

"The ones coming to kick out Torbjorn are also coming to take the girl and trade her to the wights. Seems the feeling in the rest of the Empire is that the Southern Vale isn't worth taking back."

The news struck Tomza like a hammer blow, but as the impact reverberated through her mind and soul, it became clear that she'd become so hollow there was nothing beyond a dull sort of ring through her.

"Oh," she managed, which was all she could summon.

Ober's gaze sharpened as he waited for more. When she spoke no further, he growled, "Oh? That's it? That's all you have to say? Oh?" His knuckles ground against each other as he wrung his hands. "You do understand what this means, right?"

Tomza nodded, desperate to muster an outrage to match her

brother's. If not for her sake, then to make up for wounding him earlier. Yet, try as she might, there was nothing within her that could produce anything close to the anger she needed. In truth, she feared that she was satisfied, if not quite happy, about the prospect.

How could she explain that to Ober?

"I know it means an end to the campaign," the dwarfess began, straining to soothe her distraught sibling. "It also means that unless there are new borders set, our parents' home will stay in wight territory."

"*Our* home," Ober corrected, eyes aflame with indignation. "And not just our home. If they hand the child over, everything, everything from Shore's Ditch to Crempelwash will belong to the wights. That means every homesteader in the Southern Vale was lied to and will never, ever get their life back. It means the reason that we and thousands like us became dwans was based on a lie!"

Ober's hands unlaced, and he raked his beard as he stared at the table. "That's not even considering if what Bela said was true," he muttered, pausing to look at his sister. "Do you believe everything she and Hukka told us?"

Tomza's mouth opened and closed on several responses. Each time, she was incapable of forcing the words out. "I don't know, Ober," she finally admitted. "We've seen enough to believe it's not worth the risk."

Ober nodded vigorously and put his hands on the table.

"Yeah, not that anyone outside the Badgers has seen that," he stated. "Since those passages under Paelon's Watch collapsed, I don't think anyone's going to see it for a long time. Maybe ever."

The pair lapsed into silence again, their thoughts shifting between awful pasts and dark futures. Tomza distracted herself with considerations of the kind of effort it would take to uncover the tunnels below Paelon's Watch and even wondered if the tunnel system's collapse had adversely affected the Reeve homestead. That speculation kept her from having to consider the yawning vacancy Ober's outrage had thrown into sharp relief.

"What's happened to you?"

Tomza was so deep in her mental retreat that the question emerged out of thin air. She looked up, eyes darting around for two panicky heartbeats before she realized Ober had asked the question.

Another trio of heartbeats passed before she understood that her brother was determined to wait for her answer.

"What do you mean?" Tomza gulped. Ober's gaze remained fixed on her as she squirmed internally, but instead of anger, there was only concern and perhaps disappointment.

"Something's been wrong for a while. Since before the siege," her brother replied, pity seeping into his voice. "First, you were angrier, and then you started being sad and distracted, like your mind was always on other things. If you were less of an ascedwan, you might've ended up hurting someone, but as usual, you managed. Now you've changed even more, and it's not good."

Tomza groped for something to fend off this line of questioning. There wasn't much, so she settled on a worn-out device. "Stop worrying about me." She snorted. "I'm your *older* sister, remember? It's my job to worry about you, not the other way around."

"Don't do that," Ober warned, the words firm but without anger or malice. "Don't pretend you don't know what I'm talking about or that I'm just going to shrug my shoulders and ignore what I see happening."

"What *is* happening, Ober?" Tomza countered, leaning on another familiar tool of sibling conflict, her tone vitriolic. "You're so smart, so wise, so why don't *you* tell *me* what's going on? Is this another new trick you learned from your precious new sister, Bela the savageling slut?"

The words burned on her tongue like acid as she loosed their venom on her little brother. To her dismay, she saw that those stinging jabs weren't going to dissuade him. They found their mark and wormed their way under his skin, but his gaze didn't waver.

"What happened in the mountains?" Ober asked. The question lay between them like an unearthed corpse. For a time, Tomza couldn't respond because she found it hard to breathe. Her chest felt like it was in a vice, and her throat felt rigid and prickly, every breath hurting while going in and out.

Ober's stare got more concerned as his sister began to breathe rapidly. He looked ready to come around the table and wrap his arms around her to comfort her, tend to her, and she rebelled at the thought. At first, it felt like pride, but it washed over her, and she realized it was disgust with herself. She didn't want comfort because she didn't deserve it, and in her bones, she knew it would be a travesty to accept it.

She had to keep Ober on the other side of the table, and she realized what would do that.

The truth. "The wheezer—the wight who killed all the rangers. It told me some things."

CHAPTER NINETEEN

"I'd hoped I'd find you here."

Klaus looked up from his reports with red-rimmed eyes. "I can't say I'm pleased." The lardwan sighed as he set the latest collection of reports down. He'd been working feverishly with little sleep these past few days. Torbjorn's scheme had grown from a haphazard idea to something requiring a degree of coordination and intelligence that the lardwan could truly appreciate, but by the Shaper's hand, it was an enormous effort, especially for Klaus.

It didn't help that since taking command, Torbjorn had not been able to elect members of the Holt'Dwan to serve in the other senior offices of kuadwan and vindwan. Many of the tasks which would have fallen to those officers had to be divided between the two old friends, and Torbjorn, for all his character, prowess, and leadership qualities, was a mediocre administrator at best. He was at his best when he delegated those tasks to others, but in this case, "others" was Klaus.

"Have I done something to offend you?" Ghedau asked as she sidled into the room, producing a jug and two goblets from behind her back. "I thought we might talk."

Klaus frowned, then burst out laughing. "You can't be serious!"

Ghedau froze halfway across the office, drawn up short by the amused question.

"I don't understand what you mean," she replied, eyes flashing with irritation even as her brow furrowed. "What's so funny?"

It took the lardwan a moment to stop chuckling and snorting every word. He assigned the problem to his fatigue, but after a few false starts, he was able to respond succinctly. "In case you missed it, Torbjorn and I are more than just friends and compatriots," Klaus explained. "My family has been serving the Cyniburg dynasty for generations, and I was charged with serving Torbjorn when I was barely a whiskerling.

"Things have not gone according to plan, but I know that dwarf better than any other living soul in or out of this fortress. Even the bitch who bore him is an amateur at Torbjorn Hralson of Clan Cyniburg compared to me."

Ghedau's eyes glittered in the candlelight, and a teasing smile formed on her lips.

"Oh, I'm counting on that," the dwarfess replied, advancing across the room once more. "I still don't understand why you're laughing at me."

Klaus stifled another snort and leaned back in his chair. "You're not stupid, dwarfess, so you can't think there's anything that Torbjorn doesn't eventually tell me. Not one thing. That means that I know how Torbjorn's little miracle worked and the sort of damage you can do with a few sips.

"Now you show up bearing refreshments, so I have to assume this is either a joke or perhaps the worst insult I've ever been given. Since I don't have the energy to be insulted, I chose joke."

Ghedau reached his desk, and she gave a throaty laugh as she leaned forward to place jug and drinking vessels on the edge of the desk. The ever-observant Klaus noted that the laces of her bodice had been adjusted to afford more room for things to bob about as she tilted forward.

Klaus tapped his foot, a sign of his irritation, but it was lost on the dwarfess.

"If I'm as smart as all that, I'd surely want you as an ally, not an enemy, and certainly not as a martyr," Ghedau replied as she straightened. "Why would you think I want to hurt you, Klaus?"

The lardwan frowned, then moved a few pieces of parchment to a safe distance from the jug and goblets. As he did so, his eyes remained fixed on the dwarfess' face, which he noted provoked no small amount of irritation on the part of Torbjorn's betrothed.

"I've given up on understanding why anyone does anything," Klaus remarked dryly. "I simply try to figure out the what, where, and when of other people's actions. The whys are someone else's problem, as are you, so perhaps you should scurry off before this joke runs its course."

Ghedau studied Klaus, then came to a decision. Her posture and movements changed, and she wandered around the office. "No need to be catty," she remarked, pausing to peek through the bars at the huddled goblin in the cage, who was wrapped in a ragged blanket. "Is that the goblin that revealed the secret passage in the assembly hall?"

Klaus, who'd leaned over to examine the contents of the jug, didn't bother to look up.

"No, it's the one I caught sneaking biscuits and cream out of the pantry," the dwarf replied. "Now, if you don't mind, I have work to do, and it doesn't involve giving tours to intruding murderesses."

Ghedau's lips pressed together in a thoughtful pout as she turned away from the unmoving prisoner and strolled to the desk. Still thinking, she lifted the jug and poured its contents, a sweet, aromatic red liqueur so dark it was almost black. She filled one goblet, then the other.

"You don't expect me to drink that, do you?" Klaus asked, one eyebrow rising over a wry smirk. "That will be when the joke runs aground."

"Drink, don't drink. I don't care as long as you listen," Ghedau stated with a shrug before quaffing a big mouthful of the liqueur. "You can do *that*, can't you?"

The lardwan eyed the dwarfess but nodded. "For a moment."

Ghedau smiled and drained the goblet in one long pull. "Good," she said, placing the cup down and putting a hand over the other goblet. "Despite all of your plotting and strategizing with Torbjorn, we both know this counterattack business is merely a very dangerous way for Torbjorn to assuage the demands of his martyr complex."

Klaus carefully watched the dwarfess as she hoisted the second goblet and took a hearty swig.

"On most days, we could humor my betrothed in his eccentricities," Ghedau continued, sipping between each sentence. "Those around him who are more practical-minded understand what's going to happen. Torbjorn is going to use up most of the time that myrkling bought us in preparing for a fight he can't win. Then he's going to engage in that fight, and if he doesn't manage to get himself killed, he will retreat into Greyshelf with our garrison compromised by losses. We will then hold out, hoping the wheezers don't come in after us before the group from Heimgrud shows up at the Lake Gate to bring everything crashing down. How am I doing so far?"

Klaus' mustache twitched, and he drummed his fingers on the desk. "You paint a cynical and grim narrative. I'll confess that I'm interested to see if you are going to pull off a surprise ending, so please continue."

"'Grim' and 'cynical' are pejoratives used by fools allergic to being reasonable," Ghedau pronounced with a sniff before finishing the second goblet. "I'm not here to talk about fairytales or the chest-beating rhetoric that excites little dwarves who want to be real dwans. The attack will fail. We don't save Torbjorn from himself, and we are, at best, summarily dismissed out of sheer embarrassment. At worst, we share his fate. Either way, our chance to salvage this situation is slipping away."

She filled the two goblets again, taking up the first she'd drunk from and pacing around the desk. "The point I hope is clear is that we need to act now to protect Torbjorn and ourselves, even if it means doing something he couldn't or wouldn't do. It's up to us to be the reasonable ones when he can't."

Klaus had listened intently, not moving to follow the dwarfess' path as she circled his desk. After she fell silent, taking sip after sip from the first goblet, he retrieved the second one.

"May I assume you're done?" the lardwan asked, then smiled over the liqueur after a nod from Ghedau. "Good."

Klaus sampled the drink, and after letting it mellow on his tongue, he decided it was worth a more substantial test. "Very good," he mused, looking over to see that Ghedau had paused in her pacing to watch him but continued to sip. Klaus imbibed one more time before setting his goblet down.

"Must have been from Glastuc's collection," he remarked, drumming his fingers on the desk next to the goblet as he glanced at the waiting dwarfess. "You plan to abscond with the child to go strike a deal with the wights before the task force from Heimgrud arrives so Torbjorn can take credit for it."

Ghedau stepped to the desk and set her goblet down, then placed a rounded hip on the edge. "I might've thrown in a few thrilling nuances, but you've got the general picture."

Klaus nodded, leaned forward to settle his elbows on the desk, and steepled his fingers before him. "You've been praised for being practical, and there's much to be said for that, so let me respond in kind."

The lardwan's brow lowered even as his gaze quickened. "Torbjorn will *never* go along with this, so your plan is doomed to failure. Even if we could accomplish what you said, Torbjorn

Hralson would rather be dead than hand over that child, and he'd rather face execution than take credit for her being handed over.

"Even if he has nothing to gain and everything to lose, he will not comply with any part of this and will work actively to prevent it from succeeding. What's more, I'm not going to put him in that position. Simply put, I'd rather die with Torbjorn than have us both live and know I willingly betrayed as good a dwarf as I've ever met."

Ghedau nodded slowly and withdrew from the desk to resume pacing.

"While not entirely practical, that is better than all this business about the human being handed over resulting in some world-ending event. If you'd cited that, I might've poured the jug over your head on principle."

Klaus chuckled as he toyed with the goblet, one finger tracing the foot.

"Torbjorn seems to believe it, and I can't discount that." The dwarf shrugged and took up the goblet again. "As you said, we're more practical creatures, so the facts about Torbjorn's nature have to be the bigger reason I'm going to turn down your offer. In return for this fine liqueur, I'll hold off on mentioning the conversation until after the counterattack."

Another swig. He savored the sweet burn as it passed down his throat. "That should give you time to compose good enough excuses to keep him from pitching you off the parapets."

The dwarfess' voice sounded behind him as he took the last swallow from his goblet.

"Such generosity makes me regret this next part."

Klaus felt a prick like the nip of an insect on the back of his neck.

"What d-d-di…"

The lardwan sank back against his chair, then slid bonelessly to the floor. His eyes were still open, though moving his eyeballs was strenuous. Every breath he drew was a pained wheeze, and they grew labored.

"I meant what I said," Ghedau insisted as she moved over to Klaus, carefully arranging him in a peaceful position on the floor. "I don't want you as an enemy or a martyr, but someone has to do something. I know it's frightening, but your breathing shouldn't be affected any more than it is, and the effects of the entire thing should wear off in a day or two. I'm just going to have to find someplace to store you until then and someone to help me get you there."

The dwarfess' eyes returned to the cell set into the wall, only this time she started when she found the goblin staring at her between the bars.

"Did you understand everything this dwarf and I just said?" she asked, scrutinizing the goblin's expression. She'd only had limited experience with goblins—a few kept as slaves on her father's estate—and they were simple creatures, easily directed if one was clear and forceful.

The goblin nodded, tracking her every breath and twitch.

"If I let you out will you help me get the child your masters are looking for?"

Another nod.

"We both need this to work," the dwarfess stated, hoping to impress upon the goblin how vital their cooperation was. "Your masters will know you revealed their secret plan, and only the girl will excuse you for betraying them. Your only hope of getting to her is for me to help you. We need each other, understand?"

The goblin nodded, his expression unchanged.

That would have to do. She fixed the laces of her bodice before retrieving the key to the cell from Klaus' belt. She went to the cage, and after a moment's hesitation, she unlocked the cell and threw the door open.

The goblin stalked out, seeming to expect a trap to be sprung, but when nothing happened, it straightened, lips parting in a jagged-toothed grin.

A combination of fear and gorge tightened Ghedau's throat, but she forced it down as she motioned for the goblin to follow. "Hurry up. If we move him into your cell and cover him with the blanket, there's a good chance no one will be the wiser for a day or two."

The goblin hesitated as Ghedau went to stand over Klaus' paralyzed body. "What are you waiting for? Get over here and help me!"

The goblin's grin became a grimace, but it complied, and they managed to drag Klaus into the cell. Ghedau had a moment of terror when she realized that the way they'd entered, it would be a simple thing for the goblin to shove her back and slam the cell door on her, but to her relief, the goblin shuffled out of her way to let her pass.

She scurried out of the cell and turned back to see the goblin kneeling over Klaus, splayed hands passing over the recumbent dwarf.

"Nothing fancy," the dwarfess called, looking nervously over her shoulder. "Just cover him with the blanket, and let's go. The longer this takes, the harder it will be."

The goblin ignored her, and irritation sharpened her tone. "Hurry up," she growled, moving away from the cell to the lardwan's desk. "There's nothing you need now that I've got his keys."

In response, the goblin gave a sharp tug. Then its large, strong fingers clutched a dwarvish dagger. Since she was rifling through the disturbed contents of the table for a seal and wax, Ghedau could barely hear the goblin's low snicker.

"Has something for Traz," the goblin cooed, testing the keen blade with a finger before licking the blood off. "Traz needs a souvenir. Something to remember dwarves by."

CHAPTER TWENTY

"Don't they know that some folks are trying to sleep?"

Haeda sat up, the golden-eyed child resting against her chest, having heard a lively conversation outside the girl's chamber. Since her return, Haeda had not left the young one's side since the child clung to her for dear life most of the time. Also, Torbjorn had told her she was to take over the child's care.

Given that there were guards posted just outside the chamber, Haeda could have gone to her bunk, but the little one had asked the dwarfess to stay the first night, and since then, Haeda had stayed every night.

It didn't hurt that the child had one of the plushly furnished rooms, most likely housing for visiting envoys and other important guests. The room was more open than was common for dwarven construction, but floor-length velvet curtains helped portion them off. The girl was still dozing despite the disruption, so Haeda tucked her in before slipping off the bed and passing through the muffling divider.

When she stood in the common living space before the door, Haeda could hear more of the conversation going on outside. One voice was that of a female dwarf, while the others came from the guards. Instinct had Haeda moving to her kit in one corner of the room as she strained to hear the words filtering through the stout door.

"...need to go...Lardwan's orders..."

"...see that...looks like...orders..."

"Of course! Need to...waiting around.."

"All righ...wait here...Back..."

"Yes...I'll stand...now go."

By the time Haeda had drawn her magsax, considered and dismissed her duabow, and moved to the door, she heard the clop of boots retreating down the hall. Again, a potent instinct had the driver raising the blade, ready for a skewering thrust as she yanked the door open.

A figure occupied the doorway, hand raised. By reflex, Haeda thrust, only checking her attack at the last second when she registered a frightened exclamation in Dwarrisc. Haeda's out-thrust blade was poised to tickle Ghedau's throat as she stood with her hand raised in preparation to knock on the door.

"What are you doing here?" Haeda growled, her taut muscles relaxing as her expression hardened. "Do you know what time it is?"

To her credit, Ghedau recovered with remarkable alacrity, using her upraised hand to push the menacing point to one side.

"Do you always greet visitors this way?" the ascedwan asked with a frown as she flicked a finger at the flat of the blade. "Or did you hear me coming and want to make me feel special?"

Haeda lowered the blade but didn't move from the doorway. "I answer the door this way when I shouldn't have to be answering it." She sniffed and pointed at one of the narrow windows behind Ghedau. "I'll repeat. Do you know what time it is? Where are the dwans who guard this room?"

Ghedau shook her head, then recalled why she was there. "Word from the lardwan. Something about another secret passage being found, but it was already open. They need to set up watchpoints at crucial junctions. I don't know. I was just delivering the message."

Haeda's scowl deepened, and she held her position in the doorway. "Why are you out delivering messages?"

"Because along with the message, I am supposed to stay here and help keep watch," the dwarfess explained readily. "Given how important the child is to everyone, they couldn't pull all protection. Tomza's still tending the injured, and the rest of your little company is either on watch or they're preparing for the coming attack. They thought it would be better to have a dwarfess and someone who knew how important the girl was."

Haeda thoughtfully tapped the flat of her blade on her leg, eyeing the other dwarfess. "Instead of two sturdy armored dwans, I get one plump needlewhore," Haeda observed with another sniff. "What's that smell?"

Ghedau looked almost frightened as she sniffed the air, then stopped and giggled.

"I think you're smelling ol' Glastuc's fine liqueur." She chortled. "I'd just started to enjoy a sample of it when I was called upon to help. Everything is happening fast, so I might smell a bit boozy. That's also why I'm unarmed, except for my service dagger. They probably hoped I could wedge my arse in the doorway to keep 'em out if things got desperate."

Haeda didn't laugh at the joke and continued to glare at the other dwarfess for a moment. Something nagged at her, but it was not concrete enough for her to turn the new guardian away. "From the stink, I'd say you had more than a bit," Haeda remarked as she took a step back. "But who am I to judge? You want to come in or keep watch out there all night?"

"Would that be all right?" Ghedau asked, peering over Haeda's shoulder tentatively. "I don't want to keep the little one up if she needs her rest."

Haeda heaved a sigh and moved another step away from the door, then reluctantly motioned the dwarfess inside. "She's asleep right now." She held the door open and waited for Ghedau to enter. "Keep your voice down. If you wake her up, I'll take it out of your arse."

"Oh, good." Ghedau chuckled as she shuffled in. "That's one place where I feel I've got plenty to give."

"Hardly the only place," Haeda muttered under her breath as she thrust her head out to check up and down the hall outside the room. There was nothing but an empty stone corridor with lanterns at regular intervals. Heaving a long-suffering sigh, she withdrew and made to close the door.

"You must not like me," Ghedau called loudly from behind Haeda. "That or maybe you treat everyone this way."

"What did I tell you about keeping your voice down?" the driver snarled as she drove the bolt home.

"Sorry," the other dwarfess apologized, now very close. "Haeda, I have to tell you something."

The driver turned from the door with a low growl and caught the butt of a duabow square in the face. Haeda's head snapped back, but she retained her grip on the magsax. Her vision swimming, she slashed out in a wide arc and felt a jarring impact as Ghedau used the crossbow's stout frame to catch the blow. The magsax hit enough to bind in the stock, and seizing her chance, Ghedau twisted down and drove forward.

Haeda's back thumped against the door she'd just bolted, followed by her head, and her vision went from swimming to swallowing. Everything was gulped down without understanding or clarity. The driver snarled and thrashed, but her movements weren't coordinated since her rattled brain couldn't make sense of anything. She'd lost her magsax, so she beat at anything in reach with her bare hands. Something hit her in the belly, and she folded in on herself as she sank to the floor.

She heard a grinding click she recognized and knew she should be afraid of, but at the moment, everything was confused.

With sticky slowness, bits of the world started to come back into focus as she lay panting, trying to force air into her lungs.

"Do what I say, and this will be over soon," Ghedau hissed, panic giving her words a sharpness that cut through Haeda's fog. "I'm telling you for your own good."

The grinding click ceased, and a deeper mechanical noise followed. Haeda's world was resolved into the form of Ghedau standing back a pace with a cocked duabow in her hands. Haeda realized what the mechanical noises had been as she stared at a crossbow-armed dwarfess whose hands were far steadier than her voice.

"What are you doing?" the driver groaned, the restoration of her senses meaning the return of pain with a vengeance. "What's happening?"

Ghedau took a breath and raised her head from the stock far enough to meet Haeda's gaze, though her aim didn't falter.

"I'm fixing things," she growled, her voice dripping exasperation. "Like I always have to do. I'm doing the hard thing. The necessary thing. I'm sorry if that hurts you, but I can't turn back now."

Haeda blinked, trying to wrap her impact-addled mind around what was happening. "This is about the girl," she muttered, swinging her gaze toward the velvet curtain. "What're you goin' to do?"

Ghedau made a bestial sound in her throat, part whine, part snarl, as she advanced a pace, duabow still in hand. "Haven't you been paying attention? I'm doing what I have to do!"

Someone knocked on the door. Haeda's heart leaped, and she stiffly started to climb to her feet.

"Don't move," Ghedau warned, but she did nothing to stop the dwarfess as she straightened.

Haeda straightened to her full height and looked into Ghedau's eyes as someone knocked on the door again. Haeda tried to keep her exuberance from showing as she imagined the duo of dwans bursting through the door and coming to her aid. The driver felt a twinge of embarrassment since she imagined the kind of ribbing she'd get from the other shabr'dwans, but it would be worth it to see Ghedau of Clan Brydwif shackled and waiting for an introduction to Grimmoth's stone.

Her merry thoughts crumbled when Ghedau spoke. "Open it."

Haeda wracked her mind for a solution, but there was nothing. She could open the door and see what happened next, or the other dwarfess would put a bolt through her. The driver knew what that would mean, especially since she wore no armor. This close, even her standard-issued harness would hardly matter.

Someone knocked three times.

"Haeda," Ghedau snapped, her voice icy with warning, "open the door."

She might miss, and then they could fight again. This time, Haeda wouldn't turn her back. She could scramble for her sword —it had to be close—but she was unsteady, her head not recovered from the hit it had taken. If Ghedau didn't miss, who would be near enough to try to save the child?

"Now!"

Haeda threw the bolt back and was battered back by the swinging door. She saw a wiry goblin rush forward, bloody dagger in hand.

"No!" Ghedau hissed, halting the goblin through sheer venom. "Stop that and shut the door."

The goblin bared his teeth in either a defiant snarl or a winning grin—to Haeda, those looked the same on goblin faces— then turned around and did as instructed. The door thudded shut and the goblin turned back, nostrils flared as it sniffed the air suspiciously.

"Where whelp?"

"She's in here," Ghedau assured him, nodding at Haeda. "She'd never let the girl get far from her, would she? First things first. Secure her."

The goblin's eyes narrowed as it looked at Ghedau, then Haeda, and back.

"Easier just kill," the goblin observed, brandishing the dagger.

He must have stolen the blade since it was of dwarven design, and if the blood smeared on the blade wasn't enough, she saw what looked like a bloody hank of hair tied to the hilt. As close as she was, Haeda saw ragged flesh clinging to the end.

"Traz, this is not a debate," Ghedau growled, gesturing sharply with her chin. "Tie her and gag her, but no more killing. You don't have to come back here, but I do."

"I'm looking forward to when you do," Haeda promised, glaring at the other dwarfess. Her with eyes were alight with emerald fire. "I'm looking forward to watching you slink back, just to have your arse hauled to Grimmoth's Altar, you traitorous—"

Traz's hand snaked out with whip-like speed and efficacy, and Haeda reeled back, tasting blood.

"See?" The goblin sneered and pointed at Haeda. "Easier just kill."

"Do what I tell you to, you stupid grem!"

Haeda's foot shifted back as she wiped blood from her mouth, and she felt something against her heel. Out of the corner of her eye, she saw the impediment, and her heart hammered at the sight of her magsax. The abductors were glaring at each other. Maybe she could—

"Badger bitch!"

Haeda dove and managed to get her hand on the sword's hilt as the goblin pounced. Reflex had the point of the sword whipping up to spit the advancing attacker. Traz saw it, though, and he twisted, then tumbled away with a spider's agility.

Haeda refused to give him a chance to recover. She lunged forward, the tip of her sword darting out.

"Get out of the way!" Ghedau hissed, and her duabow bobbed as she tried to find a line of fire to Haeda that didn't pass through the goblin. Despite the dwarfess' exhortations, Traz was too concerned with keeping ahead of the probing sword point. He was so concerned with keeping his hide intact that he staggered into his partner in crime, knocking the duabow aside.

Haeda seized the opening and drove the point of her magsax into the dwarfess' wide belly. The steel punched through cloth and flesh, and blood welled around the wound. More than half the length of the broad-bladed sword was embedded in the dwarfess when she twisted away with a cry, wrenching the sword from Haeda's hand.

The driver swore as she chased the hilt, but she was thrown hard to one side. Traz, seeing his opportunity, sprang on her, and they went from freewheeling across the chamber to tangled in a curtain. Kicking and scrambling, their feet slid on the thick fabric pooled on the stone, then both went to the floor, the goblin on top.

Haeda's hands formed claws as she saw the bloody dagger rise over her. The point began to descend, and then her fingers closed around the goblin's sinewy arm. The descent slowed but didn't stop as Traz leveraged his weight, one bony knee driven into her belly so each breath felt like an exercise in frustration.

The dwarfess' world shrank to inches as the trembling point of the dagger crept closer to her heart. Her lungs clenched as the goblin's knee compressed her diaphragm, and her arms burned with exertion.

Then someone knocked on the door.

Their struggle ongoing, dwarfess and goblin stole glances at the door. It was latched but unbolted.

"Haeda?" a basso voice called after a heartbeat. The dagger sank a little lower.

Gromic! Haeda recognized his voice, and she felt a flood of relief. She just needed to cry out, and the formidable dwan would thunder in and crush this grem like an insect.

Traz's knee was still grinding into her, and when she opened her mouth to scream, only a thin wheeze passed her lips.

"Haeda, I know it's late," Gromic rumbled from the other side of the door. "I just wondered if we could talk for a minute."

He was very close, but he couldn't hear her.

"There's something," the dwan continued, each word sounding like an anvil he was hoisting. "Something I want to tell you before it's too late."

It was about to be too late for Haeda. Traz leered over her, the dagger's tip very close to tasting her flesh. Her jaws opened as wide as she could manage, and her throat strained until she thought it would tear, but she produced only the barest hiss.

"I understand if this isn't a good time."

That was it! Her savior would stand there in silence until he finally shuffled away despite being mere feet away from saving her.

"Haeda," a soft voice called from opposite the door. Her life now measured in heartbeats, Haeda saw a pair of golden eyes stretched wide in terror.

"What was that?" Gromic asked from behind the door.

"*HAEDA!*"

The child's scream tore the air, high, loud, and as shrill as only a terrified child could manage.

The door flew off its hinges as Gromic burst into the room.

Traz twisted his head with a snarl, and the shift in his weight allowed Haeda to redirect the dagger to the floor. The goblin lurched forward, and the dagger scrawled a jagged line across the stone. Hissing in his guttural language, Traz tried to spring away, but Gromic was on him with the suddenness of a summer storm.

Thick fingers wrapped around the goblin's throat and threw him across the room into a pair of curtains, which helpfully came down atop his head. Screaming in rage and fear, the goblin slashed the dagger and tore with fang and claw and succeeded in ripping his way clear of the heavy velvet. He escaped the fabric's embrace in time to see Gromic's boot before it snapped his head back in a spray of broken teeth and blood.

The goblin toppled to the floor, flailing the air with the gory dagger. The huge dwan caught the wrist and, with a sharp twist, sent the dagger tumbling to the floor.

Haeda had climbed to her feet and swayed as she moved to the child. She scooped her up and carried her away from the carnage.

The goblin had squealed with pain when Gromic twisted his wrist, but that was nothing to the scream he let out when Gromic's foot descended on the outstretched arm he still held. Tendons popped, then the bone snapped with a wet crack.

Traz wailed, arm flopping like a landed fish when Gromic released the limb to seize the goblin's face. The scream was muffled when Gromic's massive hand enclosed said face, but it faltered after Gromic smashed the head into the stone floor. It became a groan, then a moan, then the goblin fell silent. In place of his cries, the chamber filled with the sound of meaty impacts that gave way to stomach-turning crunches.

When Gromic rose from his labor, his breath as even as his cold stare, blood dripped on the floor from his fingers in a soft patter. He turned away from his mangled handiwork, gaze sweeping the room. At the foot of the large bed, Haeda held the little one close. The driver looked at Gromic with a mixture of wonder and horror.

"You both all right?" Gromic asked as he moved toward them, hand outstretched.

Haeda recoiled and Gromic stopped, taking stock of his red hand. He stared at the thick crimson smears, then his fingers curled in on themselves to hide the stain. However, the blood was everywhere.

The ice left his blue eyes, and he was once more just Gromic, bemused and unsure. "I'm sorry you had to see that."

Haeda shook her head, words refusing to come as she fought

to keep the shudders out of her limbs and the sobs from ripping their way out of her throat. She held the child close to her, rocking slowly, shaky shushing noises slipping out from time to time.

Gromic frowned, and his eyes went to the floor, looking for somewhere safe to settle. His gaze quickened when he saw another body moving on the floor. His magsax leaped into his hand as he advanced on the person sprawled at one side of the room.

His steps faltered when he realized that the dwarfess crawling feebly across the floor was Ghedau. Brows furrowing, he saw her grope for a duabow, then saw the magsax jutting from her belly. The floor was slick with blood, the fluid even pooling in some of the stone's pocks and imperfections.

Swiftly sheathing his sword, he knelt and moved the crossbow to one side, then cupped the back of the dwarfess' head.

Torbjorn's betrothed was ghostly pale, and when she looked up at Gromic, her gaze was unfocused, her bright eyes dimming.

"Torbjorn," she called softly as if she feared being overheard. "Torbjorn, is that you, my love?"

"No," Gromic rumbled, sifting uncomfortably. "It's Fordwan Gromic."

Ghedau's eyes welled with tears, and her lips trembled. "I hoped it would be him," she explained. "Can you tell him something for me?"

Gromic looked at the sword in the dwarfess' belly, heaved a long breath, and nodded. Ghedau's hand found Gromic's, her touch icy and her grip softening with each second that passed.

"Tell him…" She shuddered. "Tell him I'm sorry. Sorry about everything. Tell Torbjorn that I'm sorry for it all."

The dwarfess' grip failed, and Gromic prevented her arm from dropping to her side. "I'll tell him," he promised.

Ghedau gave a final gasp. "Tell him about Klaus. I'm sorry."

CHAPTER TWENTY-ONE

An unnatural silence covered the Lake Gate dock.

Even the wind that perpetually keened over the ridged crests of the Central Wyrmspine Mountains was uncannily muted, emitting only a low hum that was not quite beneath their notice. Torbjorn imagined that if he'd been stationed there with nothing but that sound, he'd go mad during the cold and bitter watches.

Looking out over the glassy waters of Heimlagu, he wondered if he would hurl himself into the black water in his madness. He imagined the icy shock and the way it would drive first breath and then life from his body. Would his madness-addled mind welcome the swiftly encroaching numbness and accept the embrace that would free him from the mind-shredding song of the unwholesome wind, or would his fractured psyche attempt to survive and set him straining toward the shore, even though his effort was doomed? How far would he make it before the denizens of Heimlagu slithered up, eager to claim their due for his intrusion?

"Thinking about Klaus?" Gromic asked, breath pluming in the moonlight.

Torbjorn blinked and found he couldn't look at the lake or his fordwan. A blush threatened to betray his embarrassment, but the night was too cold for it to matter. He opened his mouth to say something vague that would suggest he had been thinking about his oldest friend and confidante. In the end, he decided he'd rather not lie, so his mouth closed, and he settled for watching his silver breath roll from his nostrils into the darkness.

The minutes crept by, with no one having much to say. That was just as well since the ondwan had no desire to listen. The silence had a gravity that fit this dire moment, even if the whole mountainside seemed perversely affected by it.

Leave it to an elf to spoil a good thing.

"Not to relay impatience," Utyrvaul whispered at a volume that everyone in the negotiation party could surely hear, "but are we quite certain that they received *and* understood our communique?"

"The message was simple," Gromic replied, not bothering to whisper—if he even knew how. "Remember? 'Meet by the lake at midnight for trade. We have her.' What's complicated about that?"

The svartalf tittered, which provoked dwarvish frowns of disapproval. "Ahem. I've never worried about my dear dwarf companions being too complicated," the myrkling explained. "Obtuse, yes. Obstinate, most certainly, and also irrational but never too complicated. For all your many, *many* faults, dwarves have never been, nor will they ever be, too complicated."

The dwarves might have spat in protest as was their wont, but the idea of disturbing the water held them all in check. They lapsed into sullen silence, refusing to even look at the condescending elf.

"Well then, Sir Utyrvaul," Mabon began, looking at the elf sellsword. "What exactly did you mean about the wights not understanding the message?"

"My dear midge, it has more to do with how the message was delivered," Utyrvaul replied. "See, that magnificently terse message, which even Gromic was capable of reciting from memory, was attached to the skull of the wight slain by our beloved Ober, which was itself mounted on a spear that was thrown at a wight spotted near the Cliff Gate."

"A good cast it was, too." Gromic chuckled. "Waelon pitched her smooth, and she flew straight into the wheezer's ribs. Shame there wasn't much left between the ribs for the spearhead to tickle."

Utyrvaul paused to pinch the bridge of his nose before continuing very slowly. "Impressive as the spear throw was, how do we know that the message on the skull on the spear was received?"

"Simple." Gromic shrugged. "Wheezer took the skull off the spear."

"I recall that as well," Utyrvaul agreed, continuing to speak at an excruciatingly slow pace for him. "The only reason he did so was to hurl said spear back at Waelon."

Gromic nodded vigorously. "Boy, did he! Thing damn near took Waelon's head off. Luckily, he had the gate to hide behind. He was none too happy, as you'd imagine, but by the time we popped back up, the wheezer had slipped into the trees and was out of sight."

Utyrvaul stared at the dwarf, red eyes widening, then narrowing as if he suspected a ruse. Gromic didn't notice since he was staring into the night. Utyrvaul finally shook his head, apparently concluding that Gromic couldn't define "ruse," much less perpetrate one.

"They got the message," Torbjorn stated, halting any further discussion on the topic through his tone alone. "They're just making sure they've got all their pieces in place. Last time we paddled them at their own game. I'm sure they're looking to do the same to us this time around."

Frowning, Mabon looked up from blowing on his fingers.

"You mean they're going to come in acting like they're making a deal and then try to kill us?" the manling asked.

"That is what I would do if the roles were reversed," Utyrvaul remarked.

"Somehow, that doesn't surprise me," Gromic grumbled.

"Why, thank you, good dwarf," the svartalf responded with a wink, then turned back to Mabon. "You'd be wise to learn that lesson, my young protege. Honor is all well and good among those who can be trusted to adhere to fair play in duels and tournaments and the like, but when it comes to matters of statecraft and of business where the stakes matter, you never give up something when you don't have to, and you never pass up something when there's nothing to stop you. That's the only way to make it as a soldier of fortune in this wicked world."

Mabon's frown deepened. "My father always said that it's what we do when we have the most to lose that defines who we are. Any man can keep from stealing when his belly is full and his home is warm, but it is a great man who can starve and freeze without becoming a thief."

"The more I hear about Poppa Reeve, the more I like him," Gromic declared with a nod.

"As if you've ever starved a day in your life," Utyrvaul grumbled. "No disrespect to your father, midge, but the man had at most half a century in Paelon's Watch. I, on the other hand, offer a wealth of experience accumulated over centuries and across more lands than you've ever heard of, which admittedly is a very small list. You'll have to choose whose advice to follow."

Gromic sniffed, then shuffled to stave off the numbness in his feet. "I know which I'd choose."

"No doubt," the svartalf replied dryly.

"All right, you two, that's enough." Torbjorn chuckled despite himself. "Concerning the matter at hand, I'm guessing the wights will want to make sure that we do indeed have the girl. After that, I imagine they'll offer us whatever we want, up to the deed to Cer'Kest, if it gets us to hand her over because once they have her, they're convinced we're all as good as skinned, boned, and sizzling on a spit."

An icy breeze darted down from the mountains and over the docks and rippled across the Heimlagu.

"If you're so certain of our betrayal," a voice colder than the wind whispered from the dark, "why bother with this farce of a negotiation?"

All eyes spun toward someone who materialized out of the shadows on one of the many paths leading away from the docks and up the mountain. At first, it seemed to be a wight, with a gaunt, skeletal face leering from under a voluminous hood, but as it drew closer, it became clear this was not a wight but a tall man, his face bedecked with ornaments and daubed with makeup to make him appear to be one of the unliving. Another difference was that while every wight encountered thus far had worn raiment fit for a warrior, this one was wrapped in billowing black. No breastplate or gauntlets adorned his form, nor did he seem to bear any weapons.

The only thing he wore besides the robes was a copper chain whose taut links bloomed with verdigris. It was hard to observe due to the hood, but Torbjorn saw where the links dug into the human's skin.

"For much the same reason you came," Torbjorn called to the master through its puppet. "Some combination of morbid curiosity, desperation, and opportunism."

The robed figure halted half a dozen strides from the company on the docks. "We're intrigued, *tozelchaun*, and we are never blind to opportunities. We do not know what desperation you believe troubles us. We are deathless, our legions are unending, and our victory is inevitable.

"We might be willing to parley with those who should be serving us to facilitate our return to supremacy to display our beneficence and our mercy, but do not delude yourselves into believing you can win this war. You were doomed to fail, though your valiant efforts deserve recognition and will be recorded in the art and chronicles of our people. We are not so proud that we cannot see value beyond our ranks."

Torbjorn stared at the possessed envoy, then looked at the assembly on the dock. He shook his head. "Well, you heard it here, lads. This whole business is pointless, and we might as well pack up and head back inside where it's at least warm. We are doomed and all, but there's no reason to die cold and hungry when we don't have to. Let's go back inside."

The group hesitated, but Torbjorn's waving arms got them to shuffle an about-face and head back toward the Lake Gate.

"Sorry to have wasted your time," Torbjorn apologized before turning to follow his subordinates. "See you. Inevitably, I guess."

The wight pulling the envoy's strings allowed them to take a dozen strides down the dock toward the gate before it relented. The envoy strode over to stand on the boards of the dock. "Perhaps we should not be so hasty as to speak of eventualities that haven't yet come to pass."

Torbjorn turned regarding the puppet with a cold stare. "I've done you the honor of showing up in person. If we're going to do this, I want to talk to the real commander of the army that's been besieging me for months. I'll only deal with the Matron."

The verdigris-covered links on the constricting necklace twitched and squirmed as the decorated human absorbed his words. The silence and the vacant stare stretched on for so long that Torbjorn wondered if he'd pushed too far.

Then the meaty marionette regarded Torbjorn with a pensive expression. "You've already stated that you expect betrayal," the envoy began. "You've proven that you possess a creature that is dangerous to us. What is to stop you from loosing the beast upon any who come to meet with you?"

Torbjorn shrugged. "What's to stop one of you wheezers from showing up and killing every last one of us? The way I see it, we've got more to fear from you than you do from us, but I'm still willing to venture out here and face the cold, the wind, and a lake full of monsters. Seems like I'm the only one taking this seriously."

Torbjorn could almost feel the wheels clicking and occasionally grinding in the power behind the fleshy automata.

Come on, he willed. *Put some skin in the game.*

The envoy's eyes narrowed, the expression strange on a face that had been made to look like a death's head without eyebrows or eyelids. "Are you considered honorable among your kind, *tozelchaun?*"

"If what you're asking is if I keep my word, the answer is that I've not spoken falsely so far. I'm here to make a deal, and I've got the child. I've no intention of having the bear come out here and gobble up the Matron. That's the truth, and I'll stake my name and my life on it."

More silence and empty stares. Torbjorn was sure that things were falling apart and he'd made a fatal mistake. Then, just as before, the puppet master took up the strings.

"Wait."

"I must say, this was not what I expected." For once, Utyrvaul spoke for all those present.

Coming down the path was a tall, radiant figure that was the antithesis of everything the wights embodied. They were ancient power gone rotten and ugly without losing its potency. They were imposing, terrifying even, but part of that horror lay in how their strange baroque armor and skeletal yet leathery faces displayed a malice that would not die, no matter how long it lay entombed. They were evil, dark, and twisted.

There was nothing dark or twisted about the Matron.

Clean limbs encased in gold armor inscribed with brilliant, artful filigree carried the Matron to the dock. Wearing a hauntingly beautiful mask fashioned from more flawless gold, she watched them with warm eyes that bore the heat of the earth's core, not the sinister light of foreign stars. Flowing from the mask down to her shoulders and across her back was a mane of rich dark hair, ebony and onyx mingled with subtle streaks of indigo and azure. Waves of golden radiance rippled from her, so warm and tangible that the ice-glazed boards began to sweat in her presence.

For a time, everyone on the dock stared at her. When she spoke, those eyes widened.

"I am the Matron, the Mother of Lost Children," the demigod in gold declared in a fulsome voice that resonated through her mask, not within it. "I've come to reclaim one that has wandered far. I've come to negotiate her return to her family."

Torbjorn took a steadying breath. He had not planned for this, but he needed to keep his head.

"Torbjorn Hralson of Clan Cyniburg," the dwarf replied. "It's a pleasure to meet you, but the return of the child is not what we are negotiating here."

The Matron's gaze settled on Torbjorn, which was a peculiar experience. Being a dwarf, he could not recall a time in his life when he'd looked directly at the sun. Dwarves preferred their dimmer life amidst tunnels and caverns and viewed the sun as a strange and dispassionate force. Dwarves would never talk about the sun smiling down on them since their conception of the burning orb in the sky was that it and they had better things to do than consider how one felt about the other.

When the Matron gazed at Torbjorn, it was like the sun was looking down on him from on high, and it despised him with all its infinite burning potency.

"You swore on your honor that you were here to negotiate the return of my granddaughter *Izze'Tepin*."

Izze'Tepin, the ondwan thought. *At least we've got something better than "girl" or "little one."*

Torbjorn moved his shoulders parallel to the dock.

"I did not," the dwarf denied, then held up his finger to the Matron to wait before waving at the Lake Gate, "but just so we know, everything is on the up and up."

From a narrow window set in the barbican over the Lake Gate, a small figure could be seen waving vigorously, as could a stout figure vigilantly standing beside it.

"She may be far away," Torbjorn acknowledged, "but I don't think you need to see her to feel her presence. Tucked away in the fortress, you struggled to sense each other, but standing there, you can sense her just like she can sense you."

The Matron's burning gaze cut across the intervening distance like a dart. The child, *Izze'Tepin*, her granddaughter, stopped waving and was bustled away from the window by the stout figure, which could only be Haeda, her faithful guardian.

"What do you want for her?" the Matron asked, her gaze sweeping back to Torbjorn. "Name it, and it is yours."

Torbjorn shook his head. "No, you keep forgetting," he chided. "That's not the negotiation I'm here to work out. It never was."

The radiance around the Matron shifted in tone, becoming darker and hotter. "There's nothing else that you can offer me." Her voice was both sincere and furious. "Nothing with which to negotiate. She's everything to me and my children, and you've no idea what we will do to see her returned."

"Oh, I think we've already seen a good bit of what you're willing to do," Torbjorn retorted, his tone flinty. "The thousands of innocent dwarves you and your children's legions slaughtered all bear testimony to that."

The Matron inhaled and seemed to grow even taller, more remote, and more terrifying. "Those deaths will be like a single tear in the ocean of weeping we shall wreak upon you, *tozelchaun*. Your mountains will melt, and your holes will flood. You and your entire misbegotten race will be reduced to the crawling, rootless things you were when we found you eons ago, sheltering under hill after hill like insects creeping from one rock to another. Your empire, your people, and your species will not just be defeated, not just broken. They will be *unmade*."

Torbjorn let the furious tirade wash over him, tasting the crackling power and vehemence in the words. He let them touch him and teach him that this is what he fought. The next time he considered surrendering or laying down and dying, he wanted to remember this moment and the true desire of the enemy he and his people faced.

He basked in her glow to fix the memories, then with another steadying breath, he shook his head and met the Matron's gaze. "Someday, maybe. It's not going to be today or tomorrow, or anytime soon. You couldn't even take this fortress, and with every passing moment, your ability to do so is further compromised."

The Matron glared at Torbjorn from behind her mask and shrank as Torbjorn grew. "Just like you can sense *Izze* in there, she can sense all of you," Torbjorn declared, a grin creeping across his face. "We backed it up with reports from lookouts and scouting parties, but she told us that the other wights, your children, are leaving you.

"I'm sure some will stay, your most faithful children, but as the siege wears on, your hold on them weakens since they realize that whatever restoration you promised them isn't worth risking the immortal life they already have by fighting *tozel*-whatsits who have somehow found a way to kill you."

Impossibly, it now looked as though the dwarf and the wights' queen stood eye to eye.

"You claim to be eternal, and who am I to disagree?" The ondwan shrugged. "Even you can't deny that your position has been compromised. It was in danger of being compromised when you launched your attempted infiltration. You were reckless, and it didn't just cost you a bunch of bolt fodder. It cost you another one of your children and a powerful one, from what I saw. How many more can you lose before they all abandon you?"

Torbjorn nodded at Gromic, who unhooked a horn from his belt. Filling his massive chest, he blew a resounding note that struck the walls of the mountain and then rose into the sky. A heartbeat later, from the other side of the mountain at the Cliff Gate, another horn blew, and the skirling of war pipes came right on its heels.

A heartbeat after, a bear roared in the distance.

"Your granddaughter proved very helpful in picking out the camps and patrol patterns of your children in the forest below," Torbjorn continued with an icy smile the Matron's glare could not melt. "Right now, two very skilled rangers are ensuring that my wight-eating bear makes eternity very short for some unlucky children."

The Matron took a step forward, and her golden fingers lengthened until each digit was a slender blade. "I could kill every one of you right now. I could tear through you, then walk over to your meager fortress and pluck my granddaughter out with ease."

Moving to Torbjorn's side, Mabon drew out his family sword, pitting the white gleam against the rippling aura of deep gold.

"Maybe to the first," Torbjorn nodded. "You might find it a little harder than you think, though. And if you could have done the second thing, you would already have done it. Even if you could eventually hack your way through, Gromic's performance has ensured this private meeting of ours is about to get crowded."

Torbjorn nodded at the surface of Heimlagu, which was bubbling and frothy. Sinuous forms speckled like the starry sky looked like trapped constellations beneath the surface.

"Do you want to lay a one-wight siege while also fighting a school of hungry sumplings? You know that the more you fight, the more you'll draw."

The Matron's gaze swept over those arrayed against her and heard the sounds that indicated violence was growing below the face of Greyshelf. Inch by inch, the blade-like fingers receded, and the angry aura resumed its honey hue.

"You spoke of negotiation? What are your terms?"

Torbjorn squared his shoulders and looked at the Matron levelly. "Well, negotiation just rations discontent between two parties," Torbjorn mused, not in any rush though the Heimlagu continued to seethe. "I want you all back in your tombs and asleep forever while you want to bring about the old order, with your kind as undisputed tyrants over the world.

"To strike a balance between our mutually exclusive goals, how about you all go back to the Waellafens—so sorry about Cer'Ren—and don't come back until you're ready for Round Two. I know you'll eventually try again, but I imagine it's going to take you quite a bit of time to gather the necessary support. I think we could all use a rest."

The Matron's mask was inscrutable, but when she spoke, her voice was firm without being harsh or lofty.

"Yes, but only if you grant us Cer'Ren, excluding the citadel. The border shall be the Mereseep."

Torbjorn considered the counteroffer. He wondered what was so important about Cer'Ren that she was willing to stake everything on that point, but he could feel the multitude of eyes peeking hungrily from the surface of the lake.

"Deal." Torbjorn nodded. "Now, let's have Gromic give us another note to celebrate, then get out of here before this dock gets crowded."

CHAPTER TWENTY-TWO

"I think you'll like it here."

Torbjorn sank down in the snow next to the mound of stones he'd spent the last few hours raising. That had come after he'd spent a handful of hours working on the frigid patch of earth to hollow out an appropriate space. It had been hard, sweaty work in mountain air so high that it was thin in the lungs and burned nose, throat, and chest. The dwarf had barely felt it as he labored, not bothering to stop for more than a moment to wipe sweat from his brow.

He'd finished the first of his two tasks for this little trip, so he'd allowed himself to take a real rest. He was now regretting it. Every ache and pain he'd been able to ignore until then returned with a vengeance as he sat next to the cairn he'd just raised over the remains of his friend.

"The view's fantastic."

It certainly was. The little shelf overlooked the Heimlagu, and from that position, an observer could track the passing of the stars as their reflections crossed the glassy surface of the lake. When the sun rose, the icy crown of one of the highest peaks in the central Wyrmspines shone with brilliant hues of pink and orange, and when the sun set, such as it was now, that frosty slope became a study in shades of reds and purples.

Torbjorn sat for a time beside his friend's grave and watched the red hues grow richer, darkening until the peak blushed at the attention it was receiving. "Oh, I almost forgot," the dwarf said, straightening as he reached inside his coat and produced a folded square of parchment. "Got it in writing today."

Torbjorn unfolded the parchment and scanned its contents. He didn't suppose Klaus needed to know the details, though he admitted that if the dwarf was there, he'd have pored over it. Torbjorn thought that he might tuck the parchment between two stones in honor of that before he left. It was just a formality to confirm what had taken place.

"I'm not the ondwan anymore." He sighed in relief. "Not sure I was cut out for it. When I was the tweldwan, I was always driving schildwans to reassignment or retirement with my utter lack of logistical appreciation. Even if I'd gotten around to choosing a vindwan, I'm not sure I would've listened to 'im."

The wind set the parchment aflutter, and Torbjorn tightened his grip while pointing with the other hand at a very relevant portion of the document.

"However, in recognition of my 'extraordinary efforts in the Ysgand Vale campaign,'" he quoted, trying to sound as dry and stuffy as Klaus had when reading such things, "Emperor Hral Dromson of Clan Cyniburg, my dear old dad, is going to remove the censure and judgments leveled against me. However, due to reports of my unorthodox methods, including 'unvetted battlefield prosthetics,' I won't be inducted back into the Sufstan Holt'Dwan, or any Holt'Dwan, due to risks to 'morale and group cohesion.'"

Torbjorn chuckled as he climbed back to his feet, moving slowly to counter his stiffness.

"It gets a little dodgy after that." He groaned and planted a hand on the cairn to keep him upright as he stretched. "Seems like Stendwan Assface, as our favorite myrkling so aptly named him, has moved a fair number of pieces behind the scenes. In retaliation for me stealing his attempt to be the one who solved the Ysgand Vale situation, he's had a special auxiliary military attachment formed."

He used his wooden hand to pry loose a stone that would have shredded fleshy fingers, then slid the parchment into place. The stone sank back down with a soft click, and Torbjorn shook his head.

"It seems I'm a Bad Badger again without quite being a shabr'dwan." Torbjorn sighed. "Gave the others an out, but like fools, they all ignored me and signed right up. We even picked up another one. Name's Clahdi. She's a ranger and the only one I've ever thought could give Waelon a run for his money when it comes to stubbornness. I'm sure she'll fit right in."

Torbjorn glanced at the worcsvine he'd "requisitioned" since it sounded better than "had Haeda steal" for this task. One of the bundles it had carried was beneath the stone now, marked with Klaus' runes. The other lay across the back of the pig. He'd almost felt bad for putting them on the same beast, but time was of the essence.

"We're headed to Heimgrud soon to report in," Torbjorn muttered, breath flaring out in feathery white trails. "I don't imagine Assface is going to have our interests at heart like you did, but with the Emperor's mark next to my name, he has to at least make it look like he's not trying to get me killed."

Torbjorn had to do the other thing, but there was a gravity to his friend's cairn that he hadn't felt until he tried to step away from it. It was like stepping away would mean the labor was done, which would mean that Klaus was truly gone. The presence that had been with him, watching, protecting, serving since he was a child, with nothing but love and devotion binding them together, was gone.

The dwarf struggled, his throat refusing to comply. "I'm going to miss you. I already do."

The formerly crimson peak now bore bruised shades, and Torbjorn watched it and wondered if that would eventually happen to the wound in his heart, the red giving way to the congealing, darkening shades that still showed pain but settled deeper and clung on.

He shook his head, then looked at the thing he had left to do. "I'm not a poet, Klaus," he confessed, one hand still on the cairn's stones. "I'm not a sculptor or a smith or anything else that could give you something worthy of you and what you've done. I'm just a dwan, a soldier, a fighter."

The stones were silent as the tears rolled down his cheeks, but having his hand there made it feel like the words weren't in vain. "I guess I'll keep fighting. I'll endure, I won't give up, and I'll keep making the hard calls to do the hard thing. The right thing you would have wanted and admired. That'll have to be my tribute, my memorial to you. Not a statue, not a song, but a choice, a life."

Torbjorn stood for a moment longer, then, so quickly he almost lost his balance, he lifted his hand off the cairn and stepped away. "Someday," he promised. "Someday, I'll come back, and we'll catch up. Count on it."

Then he reached for the large bundle still atop the worcsvine's sturdy back.

"At least this will be quicker," he muttered as he untied the cords that fastened the bundle to the swine, then held onto one end as it slid to the ground.

"I suppose I should say something for you too," he grumbled as he squatted and hefted the bundle onto his shoulder. He nearly toppled over from the ungainly weight, but his feet found purchase. Then he put one foot in front of the other.

"You were resourceful," he puffed as his taxed body informed him that it was quite unhappy with him. "In some ways, you were braver than most could understand."

He was halfway in, and he thought about just plopping the bundle on the snow and rolling or pushing it along. He felt a cramp in his lower back as he took another step and thought that in a few minutes, he might not have a choice. That made him more determined to keep going.

Torbjorn's next words came between heavy breaths. "Whatever else, I think you did love me in your way. Or maybe just the idea of me. I don't know."

He blinked away sweat and realized that he had reached a clear patch of rock at the edge of the shelf with an uninterrupted path straight down.

He set the bundle down. "I guess that whatever you loved about me or in me, you loved it too much. You lost sight, lost perspective, and in the end, you put yourself in a place where you weren't just your own worst enemy, but you became mine."

He'd thought he'd run out of tears and had none for this moment, but they came all the same.

"I wish things had been different," he murmured. "I wish *you'd* been different."

He stared down at the bundle, wondering if it would have mattered. If any of the what-ifs would have changed anything. He could see a different life lived by different dwarves, creating a different family.

"Wishes are all you left me with."

He pressed his foot against the bundle and shoved it over the edge, then inched closer and watched it plummet into the water far below with a loud smack that echoed up to where he stood.

The bundle bobbed for a time, and he wondered if it would sink before he confirmed that his payment had been accepted. Luckily, he didn't have to wait long. The water bubbled around the sodden bundle.

"Compensation for last time," he shouted to the seething waters as the bundle was yanked under the surface. "Hopefully, she tastes better than she lived."

AUTHOR'S NOTES - AARON D. SCHNEIDER

WRITTEN JUNE 15 2023

Dear Reader,

Okay, so is that a little better then?

I know many of you were more than a little disgruntled with me for ending book 3 at the beginning of the siege at Greyshelf, but at least now I hope that you feel your patience has been rewarded. The Bad Badgers, with grit and pluck, have managed to do the impossible, and though it's cost them something in more than one way, they are standing on the other side bloodied but unbowed. In that way you could say their journey is not unlike your own my Dear Reader, and I hope there is some comfort and joy in that.

And if not, would you at least accept a shrug and a sorry from a craftsman doing his best?

Well, love me or hate me, the wheel keeps turning and Torbjorn and company are going to see the world turned even more on its head before our time with them is through. The wheezers may be beaten back, and the fiercest fighting in the Vale may be over for now, but there are still so many loose threads, each one being long enough that a good sharp tug could set all sorts of things to unraveling.

Exactly what though, you'll just have to wait and see?

As for me and mine, we are doing well enough I suppose, even though life continues to carry on at a frenetic pace. Growing children, new branches sprouting along my career, and even some relocation going on. All good things, all things for which I am thankful, but all things which sap my energy and gobble up my time leaving me to wonder some days what happened and how I got here. I often have to sit there and reflect, sifting the passed hours, days, months, and years, in my mind parsing out the glints of gold and jewels from the grit and grind of so much else.

If I may get philosophical (and you know me there is little chance of stopping me) it seems so much of life is something which is only understood after the fact and even then dimly. I set courses, chart goals, and stride off into the unknown, but its only once I come to some plateau, some level ground just before another mountain or valley that I can even begin to appreciate where I've been and take stock of where I'm headed. The bits in between, these perpetual moments are things hardly remembered, hardly glimpsed as one petty struggle flows from some small anxiety born of some lesser compromise until like a bullet from a gun you realize even the smallest variances can put you far and away from where you were aiming.

Sometimes it is bad, sometimes it is good, but the one thing it is is inevitable.

If we try to insist we will seize every moment, whether to savor or to strive, what we find eventually is that we've only set ourself up for more of the same except perhaps with a bit more vigor and fanfare. You try to grip the sand hard and it just slips between your fingers faster, *"Erschaffen und sogleich zerstört"* (Created and destroyed at once) as some German poets have said.

We may or may not be the captains of our soul as William Earnest Henley says, but a captain for all his maps and all his commands is but one small creature on a vast ocean, one that can just as easily swallow him as it can bear him to new horizons and wonders undreamed. We may be skipper of the ship, but what good is that if the ship can be driven off course despite all our efforts and even sunk no matter our straining intentions?

The short answer is that it is no good, if that is all there is. Burning motes in the darkness profit nothing and fireflies in dark jars are tragedies without meaning, without purpose. It all only means something if there is something beyond the fireflies and the jar, beyond the captain and the sea, something which doesn't exist in retrospect. Something beyond the tyranny of time that can give definition and meaning.

If you've read anything of mine I hope you know what I'm referring to, and if not I'd invite you to head over to my website and you can hear me say a little more about it (https://www.aarondschneider.com/about-author-aaron-d-schneider/). I'm not trying to be coy, there's just things I can and can't say in certain spaces, but there's nothing I want to keep from you, Dear Reader.

But onward we roll to the next book, the next passage, the next sentence. I hope you'll join me there and once we come to another one of these plateau's I hope we can sit beside the fire for a moment and remember together. Remember where we've been, where we've been brought, and where we never thought we'd be.

Until then, my sincerest regards,
Aaron D. Schneider
06/15/2023

AUTHOR NOTES - MICHAEL ANDERLE

WRITTEN JUNE 13, 2023

First, thank you for not only reading this story, but these author notes in the back as well!

Team Elf or Team Dwarf?

As an author, I constantly find myself evolving and adapting, not just in terms of my craft but in my personal tastes as well. It could be age, could be maturity...could be boredom, and wanting to try something new. Not sure, really.

One such change has been my shift of loyalty in the age-old debate of fantasy races: Elves or Dwarves?

When I was younger – think teens and twenties - elves held a place in my heart. The ethereal, magical beings, tall and slender (yes, I know, hard to believe I was tall and skinny), kind and gentle, elves captivated my imagination.

The elegance and grace elves symbolize in fantasy literature, and their timeless wisdom were all very appealing to me a while back.

However, as time passed, my body shape morphed into something a bit more 'dwarvish,' without drinking beer, mind you. I've found myself increasingly drawn to the dwarven way of life. This shift isn't just a matter of physical similarities; it goes much deeper than that.

The Dwarves, with their grit, boisterous attitudes, sheer joy for life, and ability to work hard, play harder and not take life too seriously, all strike a chord within me. Their camaraderie and jovial spirits are infectious, their craftsmanship admirable, and their resilience in the face of adversity is downright inspirational.

Today, given the choice, I would gladly clink mugs with a dwarf over sharing a serene forest walk with an elf.

So, the question I ask you now, dear reader, is this: If you had the chance to spend a weekend in the company of either an elf or a dwarf, which would you choose? Would you find solace in the enchanting tranquility of the elf, or would you choose the hearty, earthy charm of the dwarf?

I look forward to hearing your choice and diving back into the stories with you in our next story!

Ad Aeternitatem,

Michael Anderle

I have a couple of short stories you can read that I am sharing from my STORIES with Michael Anderle newsletter here:
https://michael.beehiiv.com/

OTHER BOOKS BY AARON D. SCHNEIDER

World's First Wizard

(with Michael Anderle)

Witchmarked (Book 1)

Sorcerybound (Book 2)

Wizardborn (Book 3)

The Outcast Royal Series

(with Michael Anderle)

Circle In The Deep (Book 1)

Voice On The Wind (Book 2)

Doom Under The Shadow (Book 3)

Incidental Inquisitors

(with Michael Anderle)

Last Gasp (Book 1)

Dire Song (Book 2)

Silk Webs (Book 3)

Hard Hand (Book 4)

Shot Dead (Book 5)

Dark Deed (Book 6)

The Warring Realm Series

War-Born

War-Torn

War-Sworn

Rings of the Inconquo

(with A.L. Knorr)

Born of Metal (Book 1)

Metal Guardian (Book 2)

Metal Angel (Book 3)

Join Aaron's Email List

https://www.aarondschneider.com/free-short-story-download-the-tops-tails-of-dreams/

CONNECT WITH THE AUTHORS

Connect with Aaron Schneider

Website:
https://www.aarondschneider.com/

Email List:
https://www.aarondschneider.com/free-short-story-download-the-tops-tails-of-dreams/

Facebook:
https://www.facebook.com/authoraarondschneider/

Instagram:
https://www.instagram.com/aarond.schneider/

TikTok
https://www.tiktok.com/@aarondschneiderauthor?lang=en

Amazon:
https://www.amazon.com/Aaron-D-Schneider/e/B07H8WZ2HT/

Connect with Michael Anderle and sign up for his email list here:

Website: http://lmbpn.com

Email List: https://michael.beehiiv.com/

https://www.facebook.com/LMBPNPublishing

https://twitter.com/MichaelAnderle

https://www.instagram.com/lmbpn_publishing/

https://www.bookbub.com/authors/michael-anderle

BOOKS BY MICHAEL ANDERLE

Sign up for the LMBPN email list to be notified of new releases and special deals!

https://lmbpn.com/email/

For a complete list of books by Michael Anderle, please visit:

www.lmbpn.com/ma-books/

www.ingramcontent.com/pod-product-compliance
Lightning Source LLC
LaVergne TN
LVHW041917070526
838199LV00051BA/2653